A FLIGHT OF FANCY

THE RAEK RIDERS SERIES

A FLIGHT OF FANCY

THE RAEK RIDERS SERIES
BOOK 4

MELANIE K. MOSCHELLA

ISBN: 979-8-9891986-6-5 (paperback)
IBSN: 979-8-9891986-7-2 (e-book)

www.melaniekmoschella.com

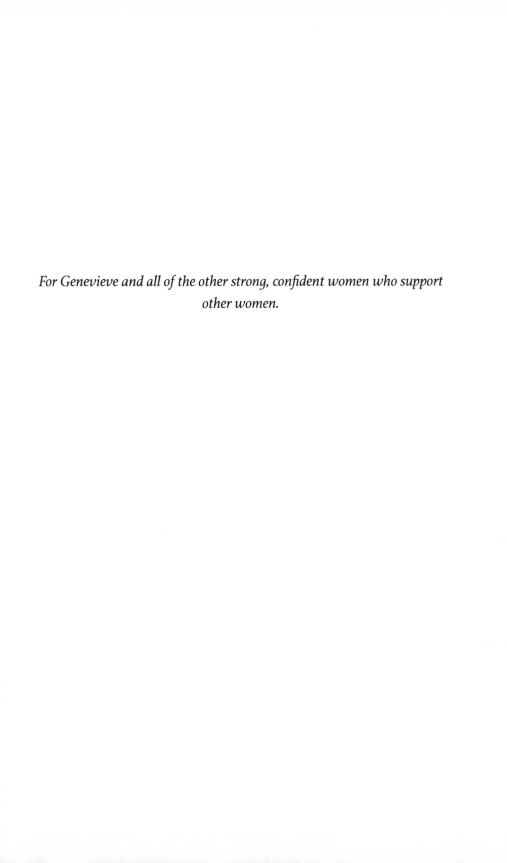

For Genevieve and all of the other strong, confident women who support other women.

NOTE TO READER

Dear Reader,

This series addresses serious, potentially upsetting topics. For a full list of sensitive subject matter, please visit my website: melaniekmoschella.com and select the Content Warnings page. I hope you will join my characters in finding the strength they need to overcome their struggles. However, if you feel any of these topics might be detrimental to your well-being, I encourage you to pass on my books and find your reading bliss elsewhere.

With love,
Melanie

A FLIGHT OF FANCY

1

MEERA

Every nerve in Meera's body sparked with tension on her way back to the peninsula from Kennick's family home. Being on edge made the relatively short flight feel eternally long, but eventually, Shaya landed on the grassy slope, crushing flowers beneath her massive, clawed feet. Meera leapt from her back, charged and ready to fight an enemy that was not there. As she released the shape-shield she was using to block out the wind, a warm summer's breeze buffeted her face half-heartedly, and white lace flowers beat ineffectually at her shins. She was otherwise unaccosted.

Taking a deep breath, she tried to calm herself after the council's attack. Meera had no idea what to expect now that the majority of the Queen's Council had declared her a threat to Levisade and had sought to detain or kill her, but she refused to run and hide; the Riders' Holt was her home—whether she was an official rider or not—and she wouldn't abandon it so easily.

Hadjal and Sodhu emerged from their ancient wooden house and waved to her. They appeared mildly intrigued by Shaya's arrival, considering Meera had not seen or heard from her raek in weeks. Shaya, of course, was not at all remorseful for her long absence. Rather, she seemed quite pleased with herself for showing up right when she had been needed. Meera ignored the smugness emanating from the raek as Shaya began to lick and preen her already spotlessly glossy feathers. Then she took another steadying breath and loped easily through the thick grass to tell her family her news.

"Well?" Hadjal asked, wondering whether Darreal's council had accepted Meera as the newest Raek Rider of Levisade.

Meera hadn't actually told the others—except for Kennick— that she'd had no intention of swearing an oath to the riders or to Levisade. She had already pledged herself to helping Shaya end the war; her loyalties were spoken for. Beyond that, she felt compelled to maintain her autonomy and the ability to act on her own conscience. She had been a traitor once to free Shael and didn't relish the idea of being one again. "They tried to kill me!" she announced without preamble. Then she sat at the table and helped herself to some fruit, having barely eaten anything that day.

Neither Hadjal nor Sodhu moved for several seconds; they stood staring at Meera and processing what she had said. Sodhu, who flinched from conflict of any sort, looked like she wanted to wrap her two long braids around her face and hide from the world, but Hadjal's golden-hued eyes were calculating. Finally, she sighed. "Before you explain, let me get the others," she replied, walking away to drag her fellow riders from their training. It was mid-afternoon, and they wouldn't normally gather for dinner for several more hours.

Meera squished a palmful of grapes between her teeth all at once and regarded Sodhu. "It's alright," she told the older knell woman. "You can tell Darreal I'm here." She knew Sodhu regularly reported to the queen. It seemed to be how she fulfilled her role as a council member even though she never attended meetings. Sodhu nodded and went into the house, presumably to write a letter and send it with her carrier bird.

Meera dug her fingernails into the vibrant peel of an orange, but after several attempts at removing the fruit from its waxy armor, she grew frustrated and ignited the orange in pale flames, burning away the peel and leaving the inner fruit intact. When Isbaen approached the table, she handed him a slice, which he took with a friendly smile. He didn't ask her what was going on; he knew she would explain soon enough. Isbaen, as usual, had the calm patience of a heron waiting for fish.

"Where's Gendryl?" Meera asked, inquiring after his new partner. Gendryl had been spending a lot of time on the peninsula lately. Meera was still trying to get to know the shy knell man, but she enjoyed seeing him with Isbaen—their joy in one another radiated off of them, often lightening her mood.

"He returned to his farm to make sure everything was running smoothly in his absence and to visit the animals," Isbaen replied. At Meera's confused look, he explained, "Gendryl has a dairy farm. Cheesemaking is his passion."

Meera nodded and wondered how she had not known that. She loved cheese, so this bit of information only made her like Gendryl even more.

After several minutes, Katrea and Florean arrived at the table together looking wary. Then Shael appeared, sweaty from whatever he had been doing. He broke a slice off of Meera's orange and crammed it into his mouth before sitting in his usual seat next to her, and the casual interaction eased some of Meera's tension; she felt like she and Shael were truly on their way to being friends again after their short-lived, misbegotten romance.

Finally, Hadjal returned with a scowling Soleille. "This had better be good, Meera," Soleille spat, clearly disgruntled from being interrupted. Her stormy face was at odds with her sunny blonde hair.

"Define good," Meera replied tonelessly. All of the other riders were gathered except for Kennick—who she hoped wasn't having a hard time cleaning up after her hasty departure—and they all looked at her expectantly. "So ... I should maybe tell you all that I never actually wanted the council to make me a rider ..." she began awkwardly, grimacing at the looks of shock and confusion around her.

"Instead, I asked them to consider helping Shaya and I end the war. Darreal seemed receptive to the idea, but ... well, the other council members declared that I was a threat to Levisade and tried to detain me against Darreal's wishes. When they couldn't detain me, they tried to kill me, so I jumped out the window and left." Meera told her story in an undignified flurry of words before looking down at the table and drumming her fingers against the wood.

"The council acted against Darreal's orders?" Sodhu asked, sounding alarmed.

Meera nodded.

"Where is Kennick?" Shael asked.

"He's still there, I guess," she replied. Glancing up at the sky, she hoped to see Endu any moment.

"Why did you not tell us your plan, Meera? We thought you wanted to be accepted as a rider," Isbaen said.

Meera felt shame churn in her gut as she appraised the sincere expression on his handsome, angular face. "I do—I mean, I want to be one of you, I just don't want to swear any oaths that I can't keep," she explained.

Isbaen hummed in understanding, but Meera refrained from comparing him to his brother. Then she glanced at Hadjal, who looked extremely tired and didn't meet her gaze. Hadjal was the unofficial leader of the riders, and she and Meera had been struggling to coexist lately. Meera wondered if the older knell woman would now see fit to cast her out entirely—she had not been swift to accept Meera's abilities, after all.

Hadjal took a deep breath and looked up at everyone. "All we can do is wait and see what will happen next," she said. "If Darreal did not want Meera captured, then there is no reason we cannot continue to shelter her and train with her. I do not know how Darreal will regain her authority, but there is nothing we need to do unless called upon."

Everyone nodded their agreement. Meera felt relieved that she wouldn't be thrown out of her cabin, but she didn't much like the idea of waiting around for news. Just then, Shaya squawked as Endu descended from the clouds above and landed on the slope. Standing from the bench, Meera ran for Kennick, surging with relief. He leapt gracefully from his raek and caught her as she pummeled into him. She didn't hug him, exactly, but she grabbed his waist and held him steady to inspect him for damage. "Are you okay?" she asked. "The council didn't turn on you, did they?"

"No," he replied.

Realizing, she was still clutching him, she dropped her hands to her sides. Kennick was gazing down at her without any of his usual humor; his dark eyes looked troubled. "I was worried you would be far away. I did not know if you would come back here," he admitted.

Meera shrugged. "This is my home," she said. Looking up at him, she wanted to tell him that he was her family, but she didn't. The night before had left things unsettled between them.

"You did not need to run. I would have fought with you," he said. Meera gazed at him; she had never actually seen Kennick upset before and thought that this might be it—subtle as it was.

His arms were crossed instead of loose, and a very slight crease showed between his eyebrows.

"You did fight with me," she replied. Then, quieter, she added, "I'm sorry I left you there—I shouldn't have."

With a shake of his head, Kennick's momentary anger subsided just like that, and his arms uncrossed. "You needed to leave," he said with a loose shrug. Then he turned and started untying two bags from Endu's straps.

"What happened after I left?" Meera asked.

"There was a lot of confusion, which was made worse when my mother's temper flared, and she set the walls on fire. Everyone ran out of the room. The last I saw of Darreal, she was striding down the hallway, alone. I summoned Endu, packed our bags, and left. I had hoped to catch you in the air, but you were much too fast," he replied with his back turned to her.

Meera nodded dully even though he couldn't see her. She was feeling worse and worse for leaving him there. He turned and handed her her bag, which looked fuller than she remembered. Peering inside, she found her dress and shoes from the ball. The ball felt like it had been weeks ago. "Thank you. Your mother probably would have burned my stuff if you hadn't gotten it," she said.

For a moment, they both stood with their bags slung over their shoulders and regarded each other awkwardly. Meera felt like there was something she still needed to say, but she wasn't sure what it was. She wanted the usual gleam to return to Kennick's eyes and for his pointy canine tooth to make an appearance when he smirked.

Shaya was still in the clearing, and she shifted her weight to observe Kennick and Endu. Endu shifted in return and some sort of raek show-down ensued. Meera hoped they wouldn't start fighting. "Is this your new mate?" Shaya asked her.

"No!" Meera replied mentally, feeling blood rush to her face even though she knew Kennick couldn't hear them.

"He has better plumage than the last one," Shaya commented.

Meera felt laughter bubble in her stomach, but she pushed it down. "Not too gaudy for you?" she asked her raek.

Shaya puffed a bit of smoke. "No, but maybe it is the summer air talking," she replied.

Meera did laugh then, realizing her raek was feeling lustful. She wondered whether Shaya was appraising Kennick's plumage or Endu's.

Kennick had been looking between the two raeken with caution, but his attention moved to Meera in curiosity. "What?" he asked.

She was still laughing and wiped a stray tear from her eye. "Shaya likes your plumage," she said, which made Kennick grin. "Also, we might want to leave these two alone," she added, gesturing to their raeken with a pointed look.

Kennick's eyes widened, and his eyebrows rose in understanding. He laughed with her, and they walked to Hadjal's table. Everyone greeted him, relieved that he had returned safely. Then Hadjal, Isbaen, and Florean questioned Kennick about what had happened even though he didn't have anything new to add to Meera's story. After a while, the questions ran dry, and the riders all sat for several moments in silence together, each individually digesting the current situation.

"So, since no one is in imminent danger ... Meera, how was the ball?" Soleille asked, leaning forward excitedly. Her earlier irritation at being interrupted was obviously forgotten. "I want to know everything!" she continued before Meera could even answer. "In fact, I want to see the dress! You have the dress, right?" Soleille rose from her bench and went around the table to grab Meera, hauling her to her feet and dragging her toward the cabin.

"Seriously?" Meera asked. "Right now?"

"Right now!" Soleille chirped.

"I want to see it!" Katrea said, getting up and following them.

"You do?" Meera asked, baffled.

"No, but I do not want to miss anything," Katrea said honestly, making Meera laugh.

Wrenching her arm free of Soleille's surprisingly strong grip, she walked toward her cabin with the other two female riders— the young-ish ones, anyway. Once they were all stuffed into the small space together, Soleille continued her stream of enthusiasm: "I want to know everything! Who was there, what they were wearing, who they danced with—did you dance? What happened with Kennick? Oh! Start there!"

Meera had started pulling out her dress and shoes, but at that, she stopped and gaped at Soleille. "With Kennick?" she asked in mock confusion. "Nothing happened ..."

"Meera, you are a terrible liar," Katrea intoned. The large, muscular woman was sitting on what had been Meera's father's bed and making it look doll-sized.

"What happened?" Soleille gasped, leaning so close to Meera that she flinched away.

Meera wanted to bond with these women, but she also didn't quite feel comfortable discussing Kennick with them. He was her friend, too, and she didn't want to betray his trust. Soleille was like a prying older sister who, Meera suspected, might blab her secrets to anyone who would listen the second she walked away. "Nothing —really," she lied.

Soleille looked annoyed, but she let the matter drop. "Well, let us see the dress!" she chirped.

Meera pulled out the dress, which was carefully folded, and as she unfolded the shimmering bluish white fabric, the necklace Kennick had made her fell out onto her bed. She smiled at it, unsurprised that he had tried once more to make her keep the extravagant piece of jewelry. Picking it up, she saw that he had fixed the damage she had caused, made it more pliable with little hinges, and added clasps to the back.

"Oooh, what is that?" Katrea asked, eyes drawn to the sparkling diamonds.

"Turn around, and I'll show you!" Meera said forcefully.

Both Katrea and Soleille turned their backs to her impatiently. Meera hadn't actually needed privacy to change; she just didn't want them staring at her while she sorted through the emotions her outfit from the night before caused her. Now that it was the light of day and she had survived her meeting with the council, she wondered whether she had made the right decision. She couldn't exactly lie to herself about the fluttering feelings Kennick caused in her stomach.

Changing into her dress, she put on her shoes and necklace, leaving her hair half-back as it was. She didn't have a large mirror in the tiny cabin, but she didn't need one; the feel of the dress on her body and the swirling necklace overlaying her silvery scars brought back how beautiful she had felt the previous evening. Meera tried not to also think about the feeling of Kennick's lips on hers, but she was unsuccessful. "Okay," she said.

Soleille and Katrea both turned in unison and gasped. Soleille, for once, seemed speechless—at first, anyway. "Kennick gave you that dress and that necklace, and he did not try to take you to bed with him?" she finally asked, sounding incredulous.

Meera rolled her eyes.

Katrea whistled low. "I have never seen so many diamonds," she said, staring at the necklace. Meera had had the same thought the night before, and she sighed; she really shouldn't keep it, but she really wanted to.

"Come on! Hadjal and Sodhu have to see this," Soleille said

before once more grabbing Meera's arm and hauling her away. "No! Soleille, stop," Meera argued as they rounded Hadjal's house. She felt like she had already made enough of a spectacle of herself that day—and every other day—and didn't need to be paraded around in her new finery.

Soleille was deaf to her pleas, however; she dragged Meera up to the table, where the other riders still loitered. Katrea followed behind them. "Tada!" Soleille cried, as if she had something to do with making Meera look so good.

Meera rolled her eyes again. Unfortunately, she then looked straight into Shael's pained face and quickly averted her gaze. Hadjal and Sodhu both fussed over how pretty she looked, and even Florean gave her a compliment. "This is some fine work you did," Soleille said to Kennick, who already looked pleased enough with himself. "I expect you to do the same for me next summer," she added threateningly.

He laughed. "I could not possibly dress you better than you dress yourself, Soleille," he said flatteringly.

Soleille practically purred, and Meera found herself wondering whether the two of them had ever slept together. But she pushed the thought aside. Feeling like the show was over, she unclasped the necklace from her neck and held it out for Kennick. He put his hands obstinately behind his back. Undeterred, she stepped forward, wrenched one of his hands from behind his back with her knell strength, and dropped the necklace into it.

At first, Meera worried he would be offended, but Kennick merely laughed like they were playing his favorite game. "You know, you did that with a lot more pizazz last time," he said, referring to her impromptu metal shaping. He slipped the necklace into one of his human-style pockets, but Meera had a feeling she would see it again. The feeling tickled her stomach and made her smile.

"Funny story about that," she said. "Shaya came back because she thought someone was strangling me," she told him.

He laughed with her, and everyone else looked confused— except Shael, who was staring down at the table like he might die if he looked anywhere else. At the sight of him, Meera gave everyone a mock curtsy and hurried away to change. She had thought she and Shael were ready to be friends, but the look on his face told her otherwise; he was clearly not over his feelings for her. The thought was extremely confusing because all Meera had wanted weeks ago was to have proof of Shael's love for her. Now, it was written all over his face, and she wished that it wasn't. Was she flighty? Had she flitted from Shael to Kennick too easily?

She felt tempted to judge her feelings, but she didn't actually think she was being unreasonable. She couldn't help how she felt. Besides, she had returned from her training ready to be with Shael, and he had pushed her away—not for the first time, either. Shael had hurt her, and Kennick never had—not yet anyway. Kennick made her feel seen and heard and understood and beautiful. He made her laugh.

Meera sighed. Then there was the fact that Kennick had confessed his feelings for her, and she had turned him down. Why had she done that? She remembered her reasons, but at that moment, she couldn't remember why she had thought they outweighed the possibility of love. What if she could be with Kennick and not have it end in disaster? If she never tried, wouldn't she always wonder? She probably would.

2

MEERA

The next few days passed restlessly while everyone waited for news. Meera struggled to sleep at night and found herself constantly on edge. It gave her some comfort that Shaya stayed nearby, but she suspected her raek's behavior had more to do with her infatuation with Endu than concern for her. The bizarre, pseudo flirtatious behavior of their raeken only added an extra layer of discomfort to her interactions with Kennick—although, they spent time together and sparred like nothing had ever happened. Neither one of them ever mentioned the night of the ball. Meera oscillated between fretting about her relationship with Kennick and worrying about her future in Levisade.

Finally, a letter came for her from Darreal. Sodhu and Hadjal both received letters as well, and everyone gathered around the table to hear what news they bore. Meera unrolled hers quickly and stood to read it; her body coursed with too many sparking nerves for her to sit down.

The note read:

Meera Hailship,

I hereby appoint you and Shaya as Levisade's first Ambas-sadors to the Wild Raeken. In this role, you are both welcome to remain within Levisade so long as you follow our laws. Failure to follow our laws will result in your immediate expulsion. For your role, you will be granted a stipend (details below).

Furthermore, I am hosting a summit meeting in two months that I expect you both to attend. In my role as queen, I will be conducting this meeting with my newly appointed council and Aegorn's human heads of state to discuss the war, the details of which are as follows ...

Meera's eyes briefly skimmed the rest of the note, which detailed the plans for Darreal's summit as well as the sum of her monthly stipend. She was pleased to be welcome in Levisade and relieved to have a source of income, but her heart also pounded at the thought of standing in front of people and giving yet another speech about why knell should help end the war. Her last speech hadn't been planned and hadn't exactly ended well.

Somehow, when Meera had agreed to help Shaya end the war, she had not imagined her role being so formal. She wasn't sure exactly what she had pictured—considering she also wasn't keen on flying into battle and killing people—but violence was at least something she knew how to train for ... With a sigh, she thought she was at least safe and could remain at the peninsula—for now.

"Well?" Hadjal asked. Everyone was staring at Meera expec-tantly. Rather than explain, she read the note aloud, which elicited a lot of relieved exclamations.

"Newly appointed council?" Florean asked.

Sodhu unrolled her own note. "Darreal says that for the first forty years of her reign, she changed little set in place by her predecessor—her uncle—but that she now finds it is time for her to set a new path for Levisade and for Aegorn," she summarized. "She says she is appointing new council members and ejecting some of the previous ones. She asks that I remain on the council."

"Good for her!" Meera cried. She approved of Darreal taking action and hoped that the queen's goals for Aegorn would align with her own.

"What is in yours?" Florean asked Hadjal, who was reading her letter to herself.

"She asks me to be on the council as a representative of the riders. She says I am now the official leader of the riders and will, therefore, be the bridge between us and the council," Hadjal said, sounding emotional. She was clearly touched by the appointment.

"That is long overdue!" Florean said, patting Hadjal on the shoulder.

"Here! Here!" Soleille cried, holding up her fist in lieu of a glass.

"Someone get the wine!" Katrea called.

Sodhu bustled into the house to do so, and everyone devolved into excited conversation about the prospects of these changes. Shael turned to Meera with a tentative smile playing on his lips. "Congratulations," he said.

"Thanks," she replied, still processing the implications of her newly appointed role.

Then, shocking her, Shael said, "Meera I say this as your friend—I hope you will use your stipend to buy some new clothes."

Meera laughed, looking down at herself. She owned three outfits and trained heavily in them every day. Her current blue outfit was probably in the best condition, and two days ago, she had grown hot and unceremoniously torn the sleeves from her shirt.

"I second that," Kennick said, grinning at her. "I know a good designer."

"I don't think I can afford your designer," Meera replied. She would just go into town again and buy whatever the shop there sold.

"You will need something for the summit," Kennick reminded her.

Meera didn't want to think about the summit. "I'll borrow something from you," she replied jokingly. "Your clothes are a little much for my tastes, but they'll do." She looked pointedly down at the sleeveless green shirt Kennick was wearing, which was crisscrossed with hanging silver chains. His ear cuffs also had dangling hoops of chains to match. Meera actually thought he looked really good, as usual, even if his style was a little outlandish, but that didn't stop her from staring at his shirt like he was smeared in horse dung.

Kennick proceeded to challenge her to a hand-to-hand fight with his shirt as the stakes, which she agreed to on the pretense of wanting to burn it. Shael laughed and said he would take on the champion, and the three of them wandered out into the field to resume their training. Kennick won both matches, but Meera and Shael teamed up against him in a third and managed to win his shirt off of him. Then they passed it back and forth and wore it around their necks like a medallion for the rest of the day, and Meera had to try really hard not to stare at Kennick when he was shirtless through dinner.

THE NEXT FEW weeks were relatively uneventful. Meera experienced a lull; she was relieved, knowing she was not going to be hunted down by the members of the Queen's Council, and the summit was far enough in the future that she wasn't overly concerned about it yet. She trained every day but focused more on her shaping than sword fighting and hand-to-hand. She still sparred with the other riders—mostly Kennick and occasionally Isbaen, Katrea, or Shael—but she wanted to hone her magical abilities. The council members' attack on her had made her realize how important her shaping would be in a similar situation —more so than any other form of combat.

Meera felt her raek fire and wind abilities always came to her naturally, but she had work to do on her rock shaping and had barely scratched the surface of her water and metal abilities. Her rock shaping progressed steadily with practice—practice Shaya had to fly her away for, lest she churn up the whole peninsula. However, after weeks of effort, she could only make ripples in water and still hadn't managed to shape metal after her first time. Meera tried every meal to bend her silverware but without any success.

"Maybe you need to trigger your metal shaping with the same kind of panic that you felt the first time you did it," Kennick suggested one evening.

Meera dropped the unbent fork in her hand and stared at him, wondering for a heart-stopping moment whether he was suggesting they recreate their kiss in the garden. The look on her face clearly amused Kennick—making his pointy tooth appear on his lower lip—but he didn't say anything about it. "Here," he said, taking off one of his rings and slipping it onto her pointer finger across the table.

Meera wasn't sure what he was doing until she felt the ring get uncomfortably tight, making her flesh bulge and skin turn color. "Um ... ow," she said.

"Take it off, or I will make it tighter," Kennick threatened, tightening the ring a tiny bit more.

Meera stared hard at the band of metal and tried to sense it, but she couldn't. She didn't feel any panic, either—just moderate discomfort. She tried and tried to shape the ring, but her finger went lifeless from lack of blood.

"You should not leave it much longer," Kennick warned.

"See?" she asked. "How am I supposed to panic when I know you won't let my finger fall off?" She felt the ring loosen, and she played with it between her fingers for a bit instead of handing it back.

"I might have, but Soleille is not here," Kennick joked.

Right on cue, Soleille came rushing up to the table and grabbed a plate. "Sorry I am late, but I have news!" she sang. Everyone gave her their full attention even though she proceeded to spend several minutes loading her plate with food and ignoring them all. Meera rolled her eyes at Kennick and Isbaen, and they both smiled back. Soleille loved attention.

"Anyway," she finally said, putting her plate down, "I have been assigned two apprentices through the Healer's Guild! They will be my first ones. They are twin girls, who can both shape living things, and they will be arriving here in a couple days!"

Soleille was so excited, Meera wondered whether she realized that teaching two girls how to shape was going to be a lot of work. "I didn't know there was a Healer's Guild," she said. Soleille gave her a look like she was clueless, so she refrained from asking any questions about the guild.

"Congratulations!" Sodhu said warmly. "They will, of course, be welcome here with all of us. Will they be staying in your house?"

"I guess so," Soleille replied around the food in her mouth. "It will prevent me from having much privacy, but they are eighteen-years-old ... They are not children, so I suppose I can still have company over."

"I am not sure that is the education they are hoping for," Isbaen said.

"You never know," Soleille replied with a coy smile, and Meera could only imagine what the two knell girls would learn living with Soleille for an extended time.

―――――――――

THE GIRLS ARRIVED two days later, although Meera thought it was more fair to call them women; they were hardly younger than her and didn't look anything like children. Both young women were beautiful with high cheekbones and thick eyelashes. They were remarkably similar looking in the face—almost identical—except the one, Theora, had palest blonde hair, and the other, Misteal, had dark brown hair.

The biggest difference in the twin's appearance, strangely, wasn't their hair but their bearings; Theora was as unassuming as her hair was fair, and Misteal projected a bold confidence that belied her age. Meera liked Theora, although she was hard to hear at times even with Meera's knell ears. However, she wasn't as fond of Misteal, who had made the wrong first impression on her—immediately batting her eyelashes at Kennick, saying, "You can call me Misty."

Kennick had given Misty his usual charming smile, and Meera had found the young woman difficult to tolerate after that. Otherwise, the twins blended fairly seamlessly into life on the peninsula. They trailed after Soleille all day, while she tried in vain to get them to shape plants in any way. Soleille's teaching tactics seemed to consist of showing-off then walking away to let the twins try on their own.

Meera often found herself laughing at how little progress they were making, but if she was being honest, she hadn't been making much progress herself. Try as she might, she couldn't seem to walk onto the lake. On one particularly hot day, she joined Soleille and the twins on the beach and tried to step onto the lake's surface repeatedly while they attempted to sense and shape apples Soleille had given them. Soleille had long since eaten her own apple and tossed away the core.

Hadjal had tried to help Meera sense the lake water for a while, but she had left ten failed attempts in. After splashing into the shallows for what felt like the hundredth time, Meera splashed back out and made a sound of frustration. She didn't get it; she couldn't seem to walk on the water whether she tried really hard to focus on it or tried to distract herself and do it instinctively.

"Maybe you need to dance," suggested Soleille, bored of watching her proteges stare at their apples.

"Maybe," Meera said, but she felt foolish trying to dance onto the lake.

"Here," Soleille said, kicking off her shoes and taking Meera's waist.

Meera laughed as Soleille danced her around the beach before heading for the water. They both crashed into the shallows. Unperturbed, they tried again and again until Florean showed up to play his string instrument for them.

Suddenly, Meera's training became a party, and Katrea, Shael, and Kennick also appeared to help. Meera wasn't learning anything, but she was having a lot of fun splashing in and out of the water with her friends. The twins stopped what they were doing to watch, and Misteal got up to dance.

Meera motioned for Shael to dance with her. For the most part, they had been doing well as friends. It didn't even feel awkward when he took her hand and waist and led her through a waltz. If anything, it was fun—Shael was a good dancer. Regardless, they splashed into the water several times.

When Katrea stepped forward to do what she insisted was a traditional jig, Meera and Shael stood aside to give her space, not wanting one of her powerful legs to kick out and hit them. Then they laughed with everyone else even though whatever Katrea was doing was actually very impressive.

Meera's eyes landed on Theora, who was sitting at the edge of the beach smiling tentatively at everyone but not joining in, and she nudged Shael's arm. "Shael, what do you think of Theora?" she asked, curiously. Theora was quiet and kind, if a little meek. She wasn't that much younger than Shael, and she was very pretty.

"What do you mean?" he asked, his previously smiling face going slightly stony.

"Why don't you ask her to dance?" she suggested.

Shael's entire body stilled, and his green eyes darkened. Meera immediately wished she could take it back—reel her words back into her mouth and swallow them down—but it was too late.

"Just because you've moved on, doesn't mean I'm ready yet!" Shael said furiously, resorting to his human style of speech.

Before Meera could answer, he stormed away, and she watched him go. When she turned back to the beach, Kennick caught her eye from next to Florean. He gave her a questioning rise of his brows, and she shook her head. Looking away, Meera considered what Shael had said and supposed he was right; she had moved on—her heart had anyway. She was growing more and more aware of her feelings for Kennick, which frustrated her because she seemed to have missed her chance with him.

Kennick had treated her as nothing more than a friend since they had returned from his parent's house, and Meera couldn't help but assume that his infatuation had been as short-lived as she had feared it would be. She wondered if her feelings were incredibly obvious or if Shael was just making assumptions about what had happened between her and Kennick at the ball. Then, as she remembered that night, she realized something: at the ball, she had been focused on Kennick when she had stepped onto the pond. She had also been with him the first time she had walked on water—though she still didn't remember the night of the Spring Equinox.

Thinking about Kennick, Meera edged toward the water. When she didn't think anyone was looking, she reached out a toe and tapped it on the surface of the lake as if it was solid ground. She quickly pulled her foot back onto the beach. Her water shaping seemed to be inexplicably mixed up in her feelings for Kennick, which was not something she felt up for exploring at the moment. Her training was over for the day.

3

MEERA

S everal days later, Meera approached the lake once more. She was ready to delve into her emotions and test her theory about her water shaping. Soleille had the twins sitting on the beach again and was showing them how she could shape fish up to the lake's surface. Theora looked intrigued, but Misty was clearly bored and stared off into the distance.

"Misty, pay attention!" Soleille snapped, giving Meera a tortured sideways look.

"But I do not even want to lure fish!" Misty whined.

"You think I do?" Soleille asked. Meera had to turn away to hide her smile as she forced down laughter. Soleille really was a terrible teacher.

"Ugh!" Soleille exclaimed like the twins were already more than she could handle that day. "Just pay attention, okay? You will be free to do whatever you want after lunch, since I will be getting ready for my Genway date, anyway."

Misty perked up at that. Meera shut her eyes and tried to focus, but it was difficult for her not to keep listening. "I forgot that tonight is Genway!" Misty cried. "Is your date very handsome?"

Meera didn't hear Soleille respond, but she must have gestured something because both girls erupted in fits of giggles. "What's Genway?" she asked, caving and turning to join the conversation.

"The Eve of the Battle of Genway is a knell holiday, but everyone just calls it Genway," Soleille told her.

"What is it for?" Meera asked.

"The legend goes that two warring groups of knell were poised to battle in Genway. The night before the battle was to take place, a brave but weak warrior snuck into the enemy's camp to seduce their best warrior and tire her out before the battle—" Soleille started to say.

"Seriously?" Meera interrupted.

"Yes. Anyway, the story is that he seduced the warrior and went to her bed, but the two of them fell so deeply in love that they rose the next day and brought their warring people together in peace," Soleille finished.

Meera laughed. "So how is Genway celebrated?" she asked, pretty sure she could guess the answer to that question.

"Genway is celebrated in pairs. It is tradition to invite someone you are interested in for an evening picnic, except you are not really there to eat," Soleille explained with a wink.

"Are all knell holidays sexual?" Meera asked.

"Almost!" Misty answered, sounding excited. "Genway is the best, though."

"Have you celebrated Genway?" Soleille asked her, sounding skeptical.

"Not yet, but I will," Misty replied defensively.

"We should get back to work," Soleille said, rubbing her temples like the thought of training the twins anymore was painful for her. "You two try to sense the fish under the water. I am going to get a cup of tea."

Meera rolled her eyes as Soleille ascended the slope to Hadjal's house. Then she turned back to the lake and tried to focus once more.

"I am going to ask Kennick to celebrate Genway with me!" Misty whispered excitedly to her sister.

Meera's attention immediately shot back to the twins, though she didn't turn or look.

"Is he not ... a little too old?" Theora asked quietly.

Meera agreed with the shy sister, but Misty made a sound of deep exasperation. "What is nine years between knell?" she asked. "I mean, do you even know of any men closer to our age? There are maybe one or two but not many ..."

Meera supposed between the long lives of knell and their low birth-rate, nine years might not seem like such a great age difference. She wondered what Kennick would think of that. The thought of him celebrating Genway with Misty upset her deeply but not because of her age.

Meera sighed; she supposed she was there to sort through her feelings and how they related to her water shaping, so she shut her eyes once more and let herself feel. She thought of Kennick and Misty and swirled with jealousy. Then she thought of the women who had approached her at the ball, warning her of Kennick's short attention span, and she felt her fear and insecurity. Under those two thin layers, however, she harbored a deep pool of love and respect for Kennick. She was attracted to him, and she trusted him even if her attraction was also tangled up in her fear.

Letting herself experience all of her thoughts and emotions without judgment helped her lighten her consciousness, but she still didn't understand how her feelings related to her water shaping. Opening her eyes, she pictured Kennick and stepped out onto the lake's surface, shaping the water under her with ease. She heard the twins gasp, but she ignored them and kept walking. Staring out over the sparkling blue lake, she tried to feel her connection to her water shaping and sense the water itself without relying on whatever emotion attached her to it.

Gliding out over the lake, she swept her toes in arcs across the surface and watched the ripples she made extend out in front of her. Then she crouched down and touched the water with her fingertips, playing with solidifying it and letting her hand breach the surface. Meera slowly got a feel for how she connected with the water, but her mind was still on Kennick. Meandering over to the rock that protruded from the water, she climbed onto it, and as she stood on the rock, she couldn't help but think of Shael sitting there and waiting for her to wake up for three weeks.

Focusing on Shael broke Meera's connection with her shaping. She tried to step out onto the lake once more, but her toes kept splashing into the water. It seemed she hadn't attuned herself to her water abilities enough to do use them at will yet. Crouching down, she poked at the water instead, but her fingers continued to submerge.

"Are you stuck?" called a voice from above on the cliff.

Meera looked up to see Kennick grinning down at her. At the sight of him, she stepped out onto the lake's surface without hesitation and walked to the rock wall leading up to the cliff. She climbed the wall easily—much more easily than she had in her human body—and when she reached the lip, she popped herself over it and plopped down next to where Kennick was sitting. Both of their legs dangled over the water below.

"My mistake. You had everything under control," Kennick said, leaning back onto his hands. He was shirtless and must have been doing something rigorous—he glistened with sweat, and his hair was dark with it.

"Were you going to swim?" she asked.

"I was, but I did not want to disturb you. You seem to have had a break-through," he replied.

Meera shrugged. She was not about to explain her methods to him. Then she lay back and blocked the sun from her eyes with her hands, realizing she was sweating too; it was a hot day. "I'd swim," she said, peering at Kennick from under her hands.

He casually drew his feet up onto the cliff, leaned forward, and sprung into the water in a graceful dive. Meera watched him disappear under the surface. Rising, she stepped off the cliff, but instead of letting herself fall into the water, she caught herself first with her wind shaping, then with her water shaping. She landed on the lake's surface a little way away from where Kennick's head emerged, bobbing, with his hair slicked back and his ear cuffs looking oddly out of place.

He gave her a mischievous grin before disappearing under the water. Meera knew what he was thinking and smiled, looking under her feet for him. When she saw him approach, she ran. They made a game of him trying to catch her until Meera got so hot from the sun beating down on her and reflecting off the lake's surface that she sat down and let Kennick win. He broke through the surface, breathing heavily from the exertion of swimming hard. "I give!" she told him.

With a grin, he reached up and tugged her into the water. She let herself finally break through the surface and felt the relief of the cold water on her baking skin. Then she stayed under for a long while, holding her breath and letting the lake cool her throbbing head. Her long hair extended out around her like creeping seaweed. Opening her eyes, she found Kennick looking at her underwater, and she was surprised by how well she could see and realized she hadn't been swimming since she had changed. They both broke the surface at the same time.

"I need to eat," Kennick announced. "You practically doubled my workout."

"I like food," Meera replied before splashing water at him and diving back under the surface to swim to the beach.

When she stepped out of the water, her hair and clothes clung to her greedily. It took her a while to find the knot that had been holding her hair back and detangle it. Meanwhile, Kennick stood next to her, also dripping. Meera had been practicing using her wind shaping to dry her hair after her baths since it had grown so long and took an eternity to dry, and she implemented her technique now, circling airflow over her hair in a way that would dry it without blowing it all over the place. Then she did the same on her clothes. When she was done, she gave Kennick a smug look, directing her eyes at his still dripping pants since she was now perfectly dry.

"Am I going to have to beg?" he asked.

With a laugh, she dried him too, trying not to stare at the rippling muscles of his torso while she did so. Then they both walked up to Hadjal's table where Kennick had left his shirt. The others were already gathering to eat.

MEERA WAS ENJOYING her lunch and had completely forgotten about Genway when she heard Misty whisper to her sister, "I am going to do it!" from the other side of Shael.

Florean and Katrea were having a loud argument about music at the far end of the table, so no one else was talking. Meera's heart started to thump in her chest, and she couldn't help but hone in on Misty, anticipating and dreading her question to

Kennick. Shael gave her a look—clearly noticing that something was going on—but she smiled at him as if to say everything was fine.

However, when Katrea finally ceded to Florean in their argument, and the two quieted down, Meera tensed—she could no longer eat, she was so nervous. Was Misty really going to ask Kennick to Genway at lunch in front of everyone? Hunching on the bench—bowels churning with anxiety—Meera feared she would actually break into tears right in her seat if he said yes, but what could she do?

Leaning forward to peer at Misty around Shael, she saw the beautiful young woman staring at Kennick while she chewed her food. When she swallowed her last bite, she opened her mouth to speak—still fixating on Kennick. Her sister, Theora looked about as anxious as Meera felt, making Meera think that Misty actually meant to do it.

Misty started to form his name: "Ken—"

But in a rush of panic, Meera opened her mouth and talked over her. "Kennick, will you celebrate Genway with me?" she asked, whipping her eyes from Misty to look at Kennick across from her.

Everyone at the table went unnaturally still and quiet—except Shael, who choked a little on his lunch. Misty's mouth gaped in outrage, but Meera didn't look at anyone but Kennick, whose dark eyes widened in surprise. She felt like there was food lodged in her throat, and she gripped the fabric of her pants under the table. Blood flooded her entire face. Regardless of how he responded, she was already extremely mortified and regretting her hasty decision. The food in her stomach tossed in agitation, trying to leave Meera behind with her own mess. Vaguely, she wondered whether vomiting on the table would make the situation better or worse.

"Do you know what Genway is, Meera?" Kennick asked very slowly like he was talking to a moron.

She was a moron, she thought uncharitably. "Yes," she managed to say through her tight throat. She could see Soleille's wide eyes fixed on her in her peripheral vision and all but sensed the woman's excitement. Kennick was sitting very still and looking at Meera with an unusually serious expression. She almost wished he would laugh at her. Maybe she should laugh, she thought, and try to play it off as a joke. But she was a terrible liar, and anyone who could see her face right now would know it was not a joke ...

"Yes," Kennick said simply, and Meera's insides burst. She hadn't really known what she had hoped for. Kennick saying *no* might have even been a relief, but he had said *yes*! Meera tingled all over, struggling to stay upright on her bench. She wasn't sure if she wanted to run or grin. Giving him a jerky little nod, she looked down at her food.

"Speaking of," Soleille said loudly, breaking the tension and drawing everyone's attention to herself. "I better go and get ready for my Genway plans." She made a show of rising slowly, clearly hoping someone would ask her about her plans, but either everyone was still chewing on Meera's inadvertent display, or they simply did not care; no one asked. Soleille stomped away, and Meera watched her go, wishing she had been able to ask her more questions about Genway traditions.

It slowly dawned on Meera that the most mortifying part of her day might not even be behind her. Now she had to actually go on some sort of sex picnic with Kennick. Was she ready for that? She didn't know. She felt slightly giddy knowing he had agreed to it, but she wasn't sure she could actually show up. She could feel Kennick's attention on her, but she refused to look back up at him.

And it didn't help her nerves that she seemed to have put Shael into a state of comatose shock next to her.

What had she done? She just kept mentally screaming at herself in her head for being stupid. This was worse than when she had volunteered to feed Cerun behind the palace and thought she would die ... She tried to tell herself that her current situation wasn't actually worse because she almost definitely wouldn't die of embarrassment, but her meager consolations did little to sway her own mind.

Just then, a messenger bird flew down in front of her. Meera stared at it for a moment, wondering who would have already heard of her idiocy at lunch to have written to her about it—but of course, the letter wouldn't be about her asking Kennick to celebrate Genway. She fumbled the paper free from the bird's leg. The bird's sharp beak and wary yellow eyes added to her anxiety, but once she had the letter, it flew away.

Meera used her letter as an excuse to leave the table, not looking at anyone as she fled, and she walked it all the way down to the beach before sitting and opening it. It was from her father:

Meera,

Ned just arrived to start his apprenticeship. He seems a keen boy with a willingness to learn and work. I still have much to do here.

Love,
Your Father

Was that all? Meera read the note three times before crumpling it up and burning it with her raek fire. She hadn't heard from her father since he had left except for Darreal's message that he was doing well. While she was glad that Ned—the boy she had saved from a fall at Kennick's family home—had reached him safely, she wished her father had had more to say to her. In that moment, especially, she could have used more unconditional love and encouragement. Tears pricked her eyes, and she lay back in the sand and covered her face with her hands.

Footsteps sounded near her head, and Meera peeked through her fingers, expecting to see Kennick wanting to have a conversation she was not ready for. Instead, Shael stood looking down at her. "Everything okay?" he asked, peering around for her letter.

She probably looked like she had just received terrible news, she realized. Sitting upright, she dusted the sand from her hair as best she could. "Fine," she said.

"Can we talk?" he asked.

She nodded, wondering if she was about to get rightly told off for making a display of her feelings for Kennick in front of him and everyone else. Shael sat down, but he didn't look angry. "I'm sorry," she said preemptively. "I'm sorry, and I'm embarrassed," she modified, grimacing at him.

Shael gave her a commiseratory smile, which she thought was exceedingly generous of him. "Meera, I know I freaked out the other day, but I just wanted to say that if you are ready to move on —which, clearly, you are—then you should, and I wish you every happiness," he said kindly.

"I just want you to be happy too," she replied, nudging his knee with her own.

"I will be," he said with a confidence that surprised her. He really did seem to be making progress. They smiled at each other tentatively before Shael gave her a brief hug and left the beach. Meera half-wanted to ask him for advice on what she should do in her current predicament, but she knew that their reestablished friendship was still far too new for that. She was on her own.

After another minute, she scrambled to her feet and headed

into town, skirting into the woods so as not to pass Hadjal's house. She supposed if she was taking Kennick on a picnic, she should get some food. She bought pastries and cheese; it was her ideal picnic even if it wasn't exactly a complete dinner. She didn't think the food necessarily mattered on Genway, anyway. She considered buying something new to wear but would feel embarrassed showing up in clothes that Kennick would know were new.

Instead, she went back to her cabin, where she packed the food, some water, and two blankets into her bag. Then she paced the small space. Meera still wasn't sure if she actually wanted to sleep with Kennick let alone what she might want to bring for the occasion. For a while, she fretted with her hair—taking it out and twisting it back several times, finally stopping because it looked the same each time. She considered changing her clothes, but again, didn't want to look like she was trying too hard to look good when she was still half-considering trying to play her invitation off as a joke.

Her stomach hurt from her anxiety, and she wondered if she should just tell Kennick she was sick. Then she wondered where she was even supposed to meet him and at what time. Throwing herself down on her bed, she buried her face in her lavender-smelling pillow. She was glad her father wasn't there to watch her go on a sex picnic, but she wished Shaya were at least around to keep her mental company. Shaya had disappeared again a week before, and Meera hadn't heard from her since.

Eventually, a knock sounded at the cabin's door, startling her off the bed. She swung the door open and stared at Kennick, who stood before her in clean clothes with his hands in his pockets and a mellow smile on his face. The fresh air that hit Meera when she opened the door was a relief from her stuffy cabin, but it was not enough to make up for the nausea and lightheadedness she felt when faced with the imminent prospect of her picnic. She tried to look composed.

"Ready?" Kennick asked.

No, she thought; she was absolutely not ready. But she nodded and turned to get her bag. It was earlier than everyone usually gathered for dinner, and Meera was glad because when they passed Hadjal's table, there was no one to gawp at them. She hadn't actually considered where they would have their picnic, but Kennick seemed to be going somewhere, so she followed him. He led her down to the beach then to the left. They walked between the lake and the edge of the trees for a while, both silent.

"I thought we could sit here," he said finally, stopping in a seemingly random place along the bank.

"Why?" Meera asked curiously, wondering if she was missing something.

"It was the first place you walked on water," he replied. "Do you still not remember that night?"

Meera knew he was referring to the night of the Spring Equinox when he had walked her home, and she shook her head; she remembered bits of their walk home but not that. Kennick continued to stand and look at her, and she had to look away; he was just too perfect and beautiful in his nice, light-blue shirt, and she was a hot mess who didn't know what to do with her hands. If she sweated any more, she was going to have to invent a reason to swim other than "I'm embarrassed by my pit stains."

"Did you bring a blanket?" he asked.

Nodding, she pulled out the blankets she had brought, handing him one. They spread them out to overlap on the sandy dirt and both sat down, simultaneously on the edge of the lake and tucked into the forest. It was extremely bright out, so Meera was glad to be in the shade. She started pulling food out of her bag even though she was far too nervous and uncomfortable to eat. It was early, and she doubted Kennick was hungry yet either. Still, it gave her a place to look and something to do with her hands.

Kennick took one of her hands, forcing her to look up at his face. His dark eyes were serious. "Meera, you do not have to be embarrassed if this is what you want," he said.

Meera stared at him and swallowed. He had said the night of the ball that he knew she was attracted to him—which she was—but she still wasn't sure what she was doing with him on a Genway picnic. Gazing into his eyes, she tried to decide what she was doing there—what to say.

4

KENNICK

Kennick was seriously confused by Meera's behavior that day. Her question at lunch had shocked him in a way he had not thought she was capable of; he had been sure he knew Meera well enough to understand her actions, but her invitation to celebrate Genway had thrown him. He had been waiting for her to admit her attraction to him since the ball. He found it difficult every time they trained or talked not to try to kiss her again, but he felt determined to give her the time she needed. Weeks had gone by, and she had not made any move in the slightest to advance their relationship. Then, Genway?

Kennick could not understand why Meera had not asked him on the lake when they swam. Why ask him at lunch in front of everyone when she was clearly embarrassed? He had agreed, of course, and he had gone home and washed and changed on the off-chance she actually knew what she had invited him to do and did not change her mind. Now, he sat on a blanket in the spot where he had realized he had feelings for her and watched while she struggled to explain herself.

"Kennick, I—I don't know what I'm doing here," she admitted, putting her free hand over her face. He squeezed the hand he held in reassurance. "I—I asked you here for … not the right reason, I guess. I mean, I do … you know, but I don't. I don't know about Genway, anyway. I—I'm not making any sense, am I?" she asked with a grimace.

"Meera, what do you want? What do you want tonight to be?" he asked.

She shook her head and looked down. Then she squeezed his hand. "I'm sorry, Kennick. I knew Misty was going to ask you to celebrate Genway with her, so I asked you first," she admitted.

If Misty had asked Kennick to celebrate Genway, he would have politely refused, and he felt that should be so obvious that he did not say so. "You do not wish to celebrate Genway?" he asked, his meaning clear.

She shook her head. Kennick was not overly disappointed by her admission, but he was surprised that Meera would ask him there for such a petty reason and—he acknowledged—a little hurt. He let go of her hand. "So, you do not wish to be here?" he asked.

Meera's eyes widened, and she grabbed for his hand, which he let her have—though in his confusion, he did not hold it in return. "I always want to spend time with you!" she said sincerely, large brown eyes fixed on him.

Kennick nodded, but he assumed she meant as friends and was feeling slightly foolish—something he did not often feel. He had admitted his love for Meera weeks ago and felt that she was either being unusually cruel or extremely obtuse for inviting him there. Looking out over the lake, he felt unsure of what to say or do next. She was gripping his hand rather hard and also gazing at the water.

Kennick thought he should probably say something; he did

not want Meera to think he was angry with her for not wanting to have sex with him. He was hurt, but that was hard for him to admit; he did not usually let himself feel hurt. He rarely let people's opinions and actions affect him at all. Meera was different; what she said and did affect him.

"Kennick, I have figured out why I can sometimes walk on water and sometimes can't," she said.

He looked at her—assuming she was trying to change the subject—and struggled to convey polite interest.

"It's you," she said. Then she took a deep breath like she was struggling with what she was telling him. "When I'm focused on you, I can walk on water. Otherwise, I fall through. It's you. It's something about how I feel about you or how you make me feel."

Kennick gazed at her intently. Her words tightened something in his chest, and he felt shaken. Meera was not just admitting her attraction to him, she was admitting true feelings. That was more than he had even thought to hope for—far more than he could have expected from her Genway invitation.

"You ... asked me what I want," she continued tremulously. "Genway—Genway doesn't feel right, but I want you. I do." She was looking at him searchingly, and he wondered how she could not see how moved he was by everything she had said. Kennick was used to people wanting his body, but she wanted more. She didn't want his body—not that night, anyway—but she wanted *him*.

He drew her hand to his lips and kissed her knuckles. He wanted to do more, but Meera offered him feelings and connection beyond the physical, and he did not want to cross that line yet either. She was right; Genway was not the night. He would rather wait until she felt less pressure and could come to him on her own. "You have me," he told her. "I am yours whenever you are ready." He meant his heart and his body.

She smiled shyly at him, then she looked down and fiddled more with the food she had brought. "I hope you aren't too hungry because in an effort to make this picnic as disappointing for you as possible, I only packed pastries and cheese," she said, scrunching her nose in embarrassment.

"You have not disappointed me," he told her earnestly. He refrained from mentioning how much he enjoyed watching her eat pastries. "Will you take me onto the lake before we eat?"

Meera nodded, and they both stood. She kept a tight hold of his hand, and he rubbed little circles on the back of hers with his thumb. Together, they stepped out onto the vibrant blue surface of the water and walked toward the center of the lake. It was vaguely disconcerting for Kennick to be standing on the water without any control, but he enjoyed holding Meera's hand and watching the ripples they made. Then he swung her around a bit on the pretense of testing her abilities, and they both laughed, easing the tension between them.

Kennick had to keep reminding himself not to grab Meera and kiss her; he did not want to upset her and ruin their time together. He could not tell what she was thinking or whether her water shaping was really a product of his nearness, but he enjoyed the thought. Part of him wished his love for her had enlivened a new ability within him, but he was content as he was and did not begrudge Meera her impressive slew of abilities.

When they returned to their blankets, they ate some of the pastries and cheese Meera had brought. She had not thought to pack a knife, so Kennick shaped one out of one of his metal wrist cuffs. He also handed her one of his rings for her to try to shape with. Her metal shaping—unlike her water shaping—was not buoyed by his presence, however, and she quickly grew frustrated. When she put the ring on and tried to make it fit, claiming the design looked better on her, Kennick had to admit that he liked the sight of his ring on her hand. He did not, however, let her keep that one; he had something much better in mind.

As they ate and talked and laughed, it slowly grew dark. Kennick looked out at the moon and smiled at his memory of Meera dancing under it. "Are you planning to dance tonight?" he asked.

"Did you bring vapors with you?" she asked in return. Then her voice grew more serious. "I don't have any plans tonight. We can go if you want ..."

"I would like to stay," he said, wrapping an arm around her shoulders.

She snuggled against him even though the summer air was not remotely cold, and they sat like that for a long time, looking out at the moon over the water. He was not sure who started it, but eventually, they were both yawning. Kennick lay back, and Meera followed—still in the crook of his arm. He fell asleep with her head on his shoulder and the smell of her lavender hair oil in his nose.

5

MEERA

Meera lay with Kennick's arm around her and listened to his even breathing, realizing he had fallen asleep. She supposed they really were going to spend the entire night outside on their blankets. All evening, she had tried to rack up the nerve to kiss him—to claim him as hers as he had said he was—but she had never managed it. Now he was asleep, and she cursed herself for being a coward. Meera felt tired but incapable of sleep at the same time. The day had been too fraught with feeling—too momentous for her to sleep, especially with Kennick lying next to her.

Slowly, she sat up, trying not to disturb him. He moved slightly but didn't seem to wake; she watched his sleeping face to make sure. Kennick looked so peaceful despite lying on the ground still wearing all of his metal. Meera couldn't imagine sleeping in his large ear cuffs would be comfortable, but she couldn't shape them off for him.

Leaning over to study their intricate little designs in the moonlight, she traced the shapes of the summer flowers. Then her finger moved across Kennick's cheek lightly, and he didn't stir. Knell sleep was very deep sleep. Meera marveled at the seemingly flawless knell man in front of her—the one who appeared to love her and want to be with her despite the fact that she was not quite human and not quite knell and had more powers than he ever would. There was something about being with Kennick that always felt so simple and pure even when she did her best to complicate things and ruin them.

She considered, then, if that was how he connected her to her water shaping—a sense of purity, of flowing ease that connected her to the water when she was more like her passionate flames, flighty wind, and blunt-edged rocks. Kennick gave her a sense of steady and quiet; he soothed her like the water. Meera wondered whether he would be more suited to water shaping than metal, but she supposed when he handled metal, it looked like liquid in his hands.

Still leaning over his face, she glanced down at his lips, and on impulse, she bent down and gave them a fleeting kiss. There, she thought, now she could go to sleep knowing she wasn't a complete coward. She lay back down a little apart from Kennick and took his hand lightly in hers. It took her a while, but eventually she fell asleep.

MEERA WAS the first awake in the morning and quickly rose and ducked into the woods to pee. When she returned, Kennick was sitting up. He smiled at her and stood. "My turn," he said and walked past her a little way into the trees to relieve himself.

Meera shook out their blankets and folded them, putting

them back into her bag. She couldn't help but fret about what time it was and whether everyone would be at breakfast to see them exit the woods, but the sun had barely risen; it must be earlier than that when everyone usually gathered. Noticing the pastries in her bag, she pulled one out and started eating it. It was never too early for her to have breakfast. Kennick returned and laughed at her.

Meera washed her food down with some water, which she then offered to Kennick. He took the bladder, and she couldn't resist staring at him while he drank. Now what? She had only ever managed to kiss him after he was already asleep, so she wasn't sure what they were now. Were they together? She didn't know how these things worked in the knell world. Kennick's dark eyes glinted at her with amusement, and she assumed some of her confusion was written plain on her face.

"I will walk you back," he said, picking up her bag. Meera supposed he was being gentlemanly and would then return to his house before breakfast.

"Where do you live?" she asked, suddenly realizing she didn't know. She had been to Shael's and Soleille's and had a rough idea of where Katrea and Isbaen lived—though no idea of where Florean lived. She knew what direction Kennick came from, but that was all.

"Why? Should we go there instead?" he teased.

"I don't know ... It must not be very nice considering you chose to sleep on the ground with me," she replied, smiling.

"I live that way," he said, pointing vaguely behind them.

She had already known that and rolled her eyes at him. They walked alongside the lake until they got to the beach. Meera couldn't see anyone at Hadjal's house and sighed in relief before they continued up the slope toward her cabin. "You know what they will all think, right?" Kennick asked, studying her.

Meera shrugged her shoulders; she knew. When she met Kennick's gaze, however, she thought there was more of a question there. They were half-way up the slope—in full view from all directions—and she stopped and reached out a hand to stop him as well. She was a warrior at heart, she reminded herself. She took her bag from him, which he handed over, clearly thinking she wanted something from it. Then she tossed the bag on the ground.

Meeting Kennick's confused gaze, Meera stepped in toward him. She raised herself onto her tiptoes but still couldn't reach him, so she cupped his cheek and guided him down to meet her. He bent willingly and smiling for the kiss they had both been waiting for.

Meera kissed Kennick with all of the feelings she had been pushing down since she had met him. She kissed him deeply and hungrily, leaving behind no room for doubt about her attraction to him. Kennick met her fire with molten fluidity, drawing her even closer to him and melting her insides. Finally, Meera broke away to look at him, feeling like her heart was going to break down the walls of her chest. Kennick grinned down at her with such joy in his eyes that she couldn't help but grin back foolishly.

"Will you spend the day with me?" she asked—because that was all she wanted: more Kennick—kissing, walking, talking, sparring, swimming ... She didn't care.

"Every day and every night," he told her, making her heart jump.

Reaching up, she kissed him again, softly this time. When she broke away, she did so hurriedly—bending to pick up her bag before she could change her mind. Then she smiled at him as she backed up the slope a few steps before turning and walking to her cabin.

Meera washed and changed quickly. She arrived at breakfast

after most but before Kennick. Misty glared at her, but otherwise, no one commented on her first Genway. Soleille wasn't there, for which Meera felt grateful—sure she would have wanted details. When Kennick arrived in clean clothes, Meera had to work really hard not to make eyes at him all breakfast. He, of course, was the picture of cool dignity, which made it even harder for her not to grin at him and try to elicit a laugh. She felt bubbly and giddy like she had inhaled vapors.

They both made a show of joining Isbaen for some post-breakfast stretches and meditation, but Meera could not clear her mind that morning; her thoughts were abuzz with Kennick. After-ward, she suggested to him that they go for a run, and he tossed his shirt onto Hadjal's table and challenged her to a race to the cliff. Meera agreed with enthusiasm; she had plenty of extra energy to burn. Together, they ran around the right side of the lake and up the steep slope to the far cliff. Meera ran her hardest, but Kennick's legs were longer, and he beat her there.

When she reached him, she made a show of collapsing onto the rock next to him, panting. The day was already hot, and she was sweating through her clothes. She wondered vaguely why she—a woman—couldn't also run around shirtless, but she didn't say so, knowing what Kennick's response would surely be. The water below them looked tempting, but it was still early, so Meera suggested they spar.

Together, they walked around the nearby rock formations and through a patch of woods to the clearing where they often sparred. Meera became instantly aware of how alone and secluded they were. The grass was soft under her bare feet, and she had thoughts of letting Kennick pin her down. When she faced him, she saw a gleam in his dark eyes that betrayed more than a competitive spirit, and she felt a throb low in her body in answer to his look.

Her eyes roved shamelessly over his bare chest and abs, and Kennick smirked in response, flashing his pointy canine tooth over his bottom lip. Meera wanted to feel that tooth on her own lip, but she stayed where she was. Instead, she untied the ribbon on her wrap shirt, peeling it from her damp skin. She threw the shirt on the ground.

"What are you doing?" Kennick asked, but he was grinning—they both knew they weren't going to spar.

"Evening the playing field," she replied with a coy smile, sounding more confident than she felt. Her heart pounded as she removed her breast wrap and flung it aside with her shirt. Kennick was always encouraging her to be more assertive and to make moves when they sparred. Meera didn't know much about sex, but she figured nudity was a good place to start. Kennick's eyes on her breasts gave her shivers in spite of the heat.

They were both breathing heavily, but neither one of them took a step toward the other. They seemed to be having a different kind of sparring match—a stand-off. Meera shrugged and pulled off her pants, leaving herself completely exposed. She supposed Kennick was the only rider who hadn't seen her naked, anyway. Tossing her pants to the side, she raised her eyebrows at him in mock challenge. She could already see the outline of him straining at his pants, and her heart beat even faster despite her false bravado.

"Meera, I want you to say it," Kennick said, his voice lower than usual.

"Say what?" she asked, trying not to fidget with her arms.

"Before I get too excited, I want you to tell me what you want from me," he replied.

Meera crossed her arms over her bare chest uncertainly. She didn't know what to say. "I—Kennick, I love you, and I want you, but ... I've never done this before, so I can't exactly give you any details," she said in embarrassment. She wished she had started this by kissing him like a normal person. Why had she just stood there and taken off her clothes?

Something cracked in Kennick's face, which flooded suddenly with emotion. Stepping toward her, he took her face gently in his hands and kissed her softly. "Do you really love me?" he asked in a quiet whisper against her mouth, looking searchingly into her eyes.

"Of course!" Meera cried, grabbing at him in response to the vulnerability in his voice. Hadn't she said that? Hadn't it been obvious? "I love you!" she repeated, pressing her forehead against his.

"I love you, Meera," he said, and they both lost some of their urgent desire as they shook with emotion and held one another.

Kennick kissed her long and slow and some of his tears ran into their mouths. She wrapped her arms around his neck to hold him down where she could reach him, and he clutched her back, keeping his hands in neutral territory despite her nakedness. Over time, their kiss changed and deepened. "You want this?" Kennick asked again.

"Yes," Meera said, rolling her eyes at him.

He chuckled low in his throat and whispered, "Leave the details to me," before sweeping her into his arms and laying her gently on the grass. He kneeled and leaned over her, whisking his glossy hair over one shoulder.

Meera smiled up at him, reached out, and ran her fingers through his dark red hair. "Not all the details," she amended, and she tapped one of his ear cuffs and said, "Off."

Kennick grinned, and his ear cuffs both flew off. He also removed the metal from his wrists and fingers. Before he could lean back over her, Meera sat up and ran her hands over his bare, olive-toned skin. She played with his masculine hands and touched the muscles of his chest, and he smiled down at her with desire in his liquid eyes.

Touching his bare ear with a mischievous smile, she rose up on her knees to take his naked earlobe in her mouth. Then she sucked and nibbled it, trailing her hands along his neck and shoulders at the same time. Kennick emitted a low groan, and his hands skimmed her waist and hips. On a whim, Meera stuck her tongue in his ear, hoping for more sounds of pleasure, and he grabbed the undersides of her thighs and pulled her up to straddle him, making her gasp.

"If this is your first time, then I am going to be in trouble," he said into her ear.

Meera grinned delightedly and kissed him, wrapping her arms around his shoulders and pressing her breasts to his chest. His hands still on her hips, he pulled her more firmly to him, grinding his hardness into her. Meera moaned into his mouth and took up the movement herself, knowing her desire was soaking into his pants.

Kennick bucked up on his knees and flipped her onto her back, laying himself down on top of her. One of his hands traveled up and kneaded her breast. The other moved between them, fingering first her sensitive bundle of nerves then her opening. Meera clutched him behind his head and spread her knees out wider, arching her back to press into him. She was aflame with sensation.

Kennick pulled away from their kiss and looked down her body, chuckling. Meera raised her head to look and saw that she was actually aflame with pale, flickering raek fire that was harmless to them both. "That tickles," he murmured before kissing her ear as she had done to him and trailing his kiss down her neck.

Both of his hands were on her breasts. Then his mouth replaced one of them, nipping her nipple and flicking it with his tongue. Meera writhed, trying to press her lower self into him, but he was out of reach.

Kennick inched down her body until he could brace Meera's knees over his shoulders. Then he took her in his mouth and looked up at her—dark eyes flashing—while he licked and sucked in ways that made her squirm and ache for more. She reached a hand down toward him, and he interlaced his fingers with hers. The fingers of his other hand prodded her opening, stretching her, while his mouth continued to work. Meera tilted her hips, and his two fingers slid into her, pressing in and out. The tension in her body rose, but she wanted Kennick back with her and tugged at his hand.

He withdrew his hand and his mouth from her and released her legs, climbing up to rejoin her. When they kissed, she could taste herself on him. She ran her hands down his torso and tugged at his pants. He lifted off of her enough to pull his pants down and kick them off, and she saw his hard shaft swing out before he leaned back down to reclaim her mouth.

As Kennick's tongue thrust in a seductive rhythm into Meera's mouth, she felt him poise himself at her slick entrance and press into her. She gripped his hips in encouragement even as the pressure became intense. Intensity turned to pain, but as Kennick buried himself in her, Meera was suddenly in her body and his— feeling pain and pleasure. She gasped, and her eyelids flew wide open. She stared into Kennick's likewise startled face.

As they gaped at one another, Meera felt his concern and love for her—she actually felt it in her mind. Were they sharing minds? She no sooner had the thought when she heard Kennick's answering thought: "I think we are."

They stared at one another for a moment, their confusion and alarm mingling together in their heads. Then Kennick's hardness throbbed a reminder of what they were doing, and they both felt his need—Kennick in a literal sense and Meera as a phantom limb. She pulled him back down to kiss her and encouraged his movement. Even as her own flesh burned from the friction, she felt his pleasure in the squeeze of her around him.

Despite their confusion and her pain, they joined together in a wash of mutual love and joy. Meera felt Kennick's consciousness around her like an embrace. Sharing minds with Shaya had never given her such a feeling of absolute connection and togetherness. Tears fell down her face, but she didn't know if they were hers or his. Then she felt Kennick's pleasure grow with each thrust until, finally, it shattered, pulsing in Meera's mind if not her body. Kennick shuddered and went limp over her. They were both breathing hard and trembling, and it took Meera a moment to realize that their mental connection was broken.

Kennick propped himself on his elbows and touched her face, wiping at the tears still streaming from her eyes. They had been her tears. "Are you okay?" he asked, his dark eyes penetrating.

"Yes!" Meera breathed, confused.

She wanted to see Kennick smiling, not looking so serious. She pulled him back down to kiss him in reassurance. He kissed her gently, and pulled his hips back, slowly sliding himself free of her. Meera winced at the last bit of burning friction, but she smiled at Kennick, glowing with her love for him. He shifted onto his side and she hers. He stroked her face and her hair but still looked alarmed.

"We touched minds," Meera said, searching his eyes for answers.

"I know," he replied.

"Is that—does that usually happen?" she asked, wondering if it was a knell thing.

Kennick's eyes cleared somewhat of their fog as he focused on her. "That never happens," he replied, sounding dazed.

"It was amazing, though," Meera said, brushing her fingers along his angular cheek.

He turned his face into her hand and kissed it. "It was, but you were in pain," he replied, sounding anguished. Glancing down her body, he shot upright. Alarmed, Meera also sat up and looked down at herself. She had some blood on her thighs, and it was on Kennick as well. She was unconcerned, but Kennick's eyes were wide and wild. "What happened?" he asked.

"What do you mean?" she asked. Scrambling onto her knees, she took his face in her hands. "Kennick, this is normal. It's normal for women to have pain and bleed the first time. Have you never been with a virgin before?" she asked incredulously.

Understanding dawned on his face. "I have never been with a human," he replied quietly.

"Oh." She hadn't realized bleeding was a human thing. She quickly looked down and summoned her raek fire to burn the blood and seed from both of them.

Kennick winced at the sight of his spent manhood encased in fire, but he didn't protest. When she was done, he wrapped his arms around her and held her. "I am sorry. I did not know," he said.

"It's not your fault," she said. "I guess being knell really is better than being human, though." Meera had started to think of herself as more knell than human and wondered what else about her was still human.

Kennick swept an arm under her legs and stood, lifting her at the same time. He walked with her to a shady tree and sat down against its trunk, placing her in his lap. The shade felt good on Meera's hot skin, but mostly, Kennick holding her there made her happy beyond belief. "Human or knell or both, I love you, Meera," he said.

She smiled at him. "I know, I was in your head," she responded.

He grinned back because he knew she loved him, too; there was saying the words and hearing the words, then there was feeling them—experiencing them like a soft touch in someone's mind.

Meera leaned her head against his shoulder and shut her eyes, feeling suddenly exhausted from what little sleep she had gotten the night before and their exertions. Kennick lightly stroked her sweat-slicked skin until she drifted off. Sometime later, she was awoken by a sharp pinching sensation in her low abdomen. Even in her drowsy state, the strange feeling resonated with importance throughout her body, causing her eyes to fly open. Squirming, she woke Kennick from his light sleep. She put a hand to the spot on her stomach, which still ached faintly.

"Are you okay?" he asked, looking at her with concern again.

"Fine," she said. She assumed she was just feeling some after-effects from their intimacy. She worried briefly about getting pregnant, but she had not gotten her period since her change and assumed that she was more knell than human in that way. Knell almost never got pregnant, and Soleille had told her that they didn't menstruate. And yet ... concern niggled at her mind.

Kennick kissed her, and Meera kissed him back—her concerns forgotten. She thought she would never get enough of the feeling of his lips on hers. When he pulled away, he lightly touched her face, and they gazed at one another for several long moments. Kennick dropped his hand and held it palm up in front of her. She stared blankly at the hand, which was empty. Then, suddenly, a ring shot from across the clearing and landed in it.

The ring had a large oval diamond in the center and swirls of smaller diamonds set in platinum reaching out from it.

Meera gaped at it in shock. Was this an engagement ring? Kennick smiled at her, his pointy tooth showing. "Meera, you know that I love you, but you should know that I have never felt this way before and never expect to feel this way for anyone else. Will you marry me?" he asked.

Her mouth opened, but no sound came out. She had just done this, she kept thinking until finally, she said it: "I just did this." Then she bit her lip because it was not the answer she wanted to give. She loved Kennick, and she wanted to spend her life with him ... But she had wanted the same with Shael and couldn't help but question her judgment. She would be engaged for the second time in a year. It was embarrassing—ridiculous, even.

"It is what I want," Kennick said calmly. "What do you want, Meera?"

She wanted him; she had already told him that multiple times that day. But she had really loved Shael, too ... Did she love Kennick more? She felt like she did; she was certainly happier with Kennick. They had touched minds in a way that had solidified their connection like nothing else could have. Not to mention, they had just slept together. How could she say *yes* to Shael and *no* to Kennick?

"What do you want, Meera? Nothing else matters," he said, surely able to trace the trajectory of some of her thoughts.

"I want you," she replied, holding out her left hand for the ring.

Kennick slipped it onto her finger, smiling, and shaped the band to fit her perfectly. "When did you make this?" she asked, admiring the beautiful ring. It was big and shiny and looked slightly odd sitting only inches away from Linus's beaded bracelet, which was more than a little worse-for-wear.

"When I went home this morning. Do you like it? I can change it," he said, studying her.

"Don't. It's perfect. You're perfect," she said, kissing him heartily. "Except for this one tooth," she added, poking his pointy canine, "But it's my favorite." She grinned at him, and he grinned back.

6

KENNICK

Eventually, hunger drove them back to the peninsula. Kennick was loath to leave their special clearing, but Meera's stomach growled loudly enough to spur him into donning his pants and metal. He also caught the occasional look on her face that made him worry she was still in pain. Her pain had shocked and alarmed him, even though she assured him repeatedly that she was fine and that she had experienced his pleasure with him.

Kennick was still trying to wrap his mind around their consciousnesses joining. He had never heard of such a thing. He wondered if it was some sort of new magic of Meera's, but he did not suggest that to her. Whatever it was, he was glad of it—feeling her love for him had been the greatest moment in his life; he had never dreamed that someone might truly love him in that way. Kennick had seen Meera's hesitation when he had offered her his ring, but he understood it, knowing she had only just been engaged to Shael. He was not Shael, however, and he would not push her away or hurt her.

"I know I'm strong Kennick, but I'm not sure I'm strong enough to lug this thing around all the time!" Meera said, mock complaining about her diamond ring. She was standing exaggeratedly lopsided.

Laughing, he picked her up. "I will carry you both, then," he said, walking toward the cliff. Meera's curls tickled the bare skin of his chest. Running the last few steps, he leapt off the cliff with her, and they plunged into the refreshing water of the lake below. Meera grabbed his face underwater and kissed him, and Kennick could not remember ever being so at peace.

After they emerged from the water and Meera dried them both, he retrieved his shirt from Hadjal's table. It was almost time for dinner, but first, he had two things he wanted to do. "I am going to talk to Shael," he told Meera, who grimaced at him.

Now that they were back on the peninsula, she was looking rather bashful and covering her ring with her right hand. Kennick felt a small twinge and wondered if she was embarrassed by him. He would not be surprised if she was; his reputation was notorious. He wanted to kiss her before running off but did not want to cause her discomfort, so he just turned and left. He ran first to where Soleille was training with the twins on the beach and breathed something into her ear before seeking out Shael in the wooded clearing he and Isbaen often used. He caught the two walking to dinner.

"Kennick, is everything alright?" Isbaen asked, immediately sensing his heightened energy.

"I just want to detain Shael for a minute," he replied.

Isbaen nodded calmly and moved past them.

"What is it?" Shael asked, mild alarm in his eyes. He was carrying the new sword Isbaen had procured for him from the riders' vault. Kennick could tell from a quick sense that the blade did not suit his friend as well as his old one had. He wondered briefly whether he could shape it to better fit his frame, but he would not want to damage any ancient magic imbued by the blacksmith who had made it.

He blinked to dispel the thought, reminding himself why he was there. "Shael, I know you have noticed my interest in Meera. You know me too well not to have," Kennick started.

Shael's lips compressed, but he nodded. It was something they had both been leaving undiscussed. "I know she invited you to celebrate Genway," he replied stiffly. "You do not have to tell me what you two did. It is none of my business. Meera is her own person, and I already told her she should feel free to move on."

"It is not just that. Shael, I love Meera," Kennick said calmly.

Shael looked shocked. "You love her?" he spluttered. "I knew you were interested in her ..."

Kennick thought he probably should have talked to his friend about his feelings before—he would have, except that they were about Meera. "That is not all," he warned, feeling his chest constrict in both excitement and anxiety. This would be his first time announcing his engagement to the woman he loved; he only wished he could be certain of a welcome reception to his news. Though, he supposed announcing his love for Meera—a human —would never be met with certain joy and enthusiasm.

Shael's dark eyebrows rose in question, and Kennick took a deep breath. "I have asked her to marry me," he said. "She said yes."

Shael went completely still; his eyebrows fell to their usual place, and his expression grew blank. Kennick waited for him to process the information. A muscle twitched in Shael's cheek before he swallowed and released some of his stony tension. Kennick saw his friend's fist clench and wondered for a moment if Shael might actually hit him, but he did no such thing. "Wow," he finally said, his voice strained. "That was ... fast."

Kennick supposed it would seem extremely fast, considering Shael had only learned of his feelings moments before. He shrugged his shoulders loosely. "I feel certain it is the right decision," he replied.

Shael blew out a breath and nodded. "I had not felt certain," he admitted. "Hopefully you will do better than I did." Kennick smiled at his friend, taking that as Shael's blessing. "Congratulations," Shael added awkwardly, opening his arms to Kennick.

Kennick hugged him tightly and kissed his cheek, knowing it always made him uncomfortable. "I should get back. I left Meera alone with a ring on her finger," he said, grinning.

They walked through the trees together, but they did not speak; Kennick left Shael to his thoughts. He did not begrudge Shael his history with Meera. Rather, he was grateful to his friend for bringing her into his life. Meera was her own person, free to be with whomever she chose, and Kennick did not see any point in harboring jealousy for her past. He had his own past as well.

7

MEERA

Meera was walking toward Hadjal's table when Soleille sprung on her from behind and grabbed her arm. "Are you alright?" she asked, sounding concerned.

"Uh—yes! Why?" Meera asked, confused.

"Kennick said you needed me," Soleille replied. Meera took a moment to process that then rolled her eyes. "I will sense you in your cabin," Soleille announced, steering her around Hadjal's house in full healer-mode.

"I'm really fine!" Meera insisted. She was a little sore, but she didn't mind; it was a physical reminder that the day had been real —that she really had joined with Kennick in every way. She was glowing with joy, and yet, she kept her ring self-consciously down at her side. She was embarrassed to be engaged—again.

When they entered the cabin, Soleille shut the door behind them, spun, and gave Meera a look that clearly told her that the healer would not be put-off.

Meera sighed. "Kennick freaked out a little because we slept together, and he hadn't realized that human women bleed the first time," she admitted, looking at the floor. "I assume you know that."

"I have heard of that!" Soleille said in fascination. Then she grabbed Meera's arm again to sense her body, and without waiting for permission, she healed her. Meera barely felt anything—just a slight itch then nothing. "Okay," Soleille said, plopping onto Meera's unmade bed. "Now I want all the details. How was Genway? Mine sucked! I have decided not to date other healers anymore—I mean, is this a date or a lecture? Right?"

Meera stared at Soleille, who was barely looking at her in return and discreetly put her left hand behind her back. "Genway was ... it was good," she said vaguely.

"I am so glad you made that happen!" Soleille said. "You must have been so disappointed after the ball was a bust. Kennick was a good choice for your first, you know—experienced and everything. My first was just okay, but knell women do not have it as bad as human women. I think I was fifteen—not to say that you waited too long. You will live a long time now, after all. Anyway, Kennick was a good choice! I am sure he was a gentleman. I personally do not sleep where I eat, but that ship had already sailed for you, and you had not even gotten much out of your drama with Shael."

Meera just nodded. She might have corrected Soleille's misinterpretation of her relationship with Kennick, but she would have had to shout to get a word in over her. And when Soleille finally stopped blabbering, Meera had more important things she wanted to say. "Um ... Soleille ... what if I don't want to get pregnant?" she asked. She knew knell didn't use contraceptives, generally, but she hoped Soleille would still have some suggestions.

Soleille's eyes sharpened back into healer-mode. "Meera, you cannot tell anyone this, but there is a tea I use. I will give you some. You should drink it every night," she said.

"Will that prevent pregnancy from this past time?" she asked hopefully.

"No, it will take a while for the tea to start working," Soleille said," But really, you should not have anything to worry about. Knell almost never get pregnant, and you have not menstruated since your change, right? So, your reproductive organs seem to have changed as well."

Meera nodded. It was what she already knew, but she still felt reassured. "Okay, thanks. We should get to dinner," she said, inching for the door.

"Okay, but at some point, I want all the details!" Soleille exclaimed, following her.

They walked around Hadjal's house just as Shael and Kennick were approaching the table from the clearing, and Meera stared at them anxiously. She saw Shael say something to Kennick and break away toward her, so she waited. Soleille and Kennick both went to sit at the table with the others, who had already gathered. Kennick smiled at her. Meera watched him sit down then noticed Misty glaring at her and looked quickly away.

She grimaced at Shael when he reached her, but he smiled and gave her a quick hug. "Congratulations," he said quietly, so the others wouldn't hear.

"Thanks?" Meera replied, searching his face.

Shael glanced down at her left hand and blew out an impressed whistle. Meera covered her ring again bashfully. "I would expect nothing less from Kennick," he said. "Not that I ever expected this," he added with a wry laugh.

Meera grimaced again, looking down.

"You do not look happy," Shael said, sounding more concerned than accusatory.

"I am," she said. "I'm just a little embarrassed for always being such a spectacle."

He nodded in understanding.

Meera glanced at the table where everyone was starting to fill their plates, wondering how dinner would go. Soleille didn't even suspect that she and Kennick might have feelings for one another. Meera imagined everyone would be shocked and more than a little confused if they announced their engagement. And yet, she didn't want to hide it or keep it a secret ...

"Meera," Shael said, drawing her attention back to him. "You should know that public displays of affection are important in knell culture. The way Hadjal and Sodhu always touch hands and rub each other's backs, the way Isbaen and Gendryl sit close together and put their arms around one another ... Knell do not just touch publicly because they can or because they cannot help themselves—it is how they announce their relationships in social settings. Humans get married and it is permanent, but knell relationships are often changing ... Anyway, I just thought you should know."

He glanced pointedly at Kennick. "I think if you go over there, sit in your usual seat, and hide your ring, you might hurt him," he added, voice low.

Meera bit her lip; that probably was what she would have done. "Do you really want to watch me lick food off his knuckles like Darroah?" she asked.

Shael laughed. "No, but I want you and Kennick to both be happy," he said.

Meera was so touched that she was speechless. She grabbed Shael and gave him a tight, lingering hug. "Who are you and what have you done with Shael?" she whispered into his ear, and they both laughed, breaking apart.

"You're going to stand next to me at the wedding, not Kennick, right?" she asked. He looked aside, and she gasped in mock-outrage. "Fine! Then I'll ask Cerun."

"Go get him," Shael said, gesturing to the table.

Meera took a deep breath and walked toward Kennick. Even though she had spent the entire day naked with him, she felt suddenly shy and nervous to so much as touch him. But she wanted to claim him publicly, and she wanted to make him happy. Kennick sat at the end of the table—usually across from Meera—but instead of going to her seat, she approached him from behind and put her hands on his shoulders. He turned toward her and smiled. She squeezed herself onto the end of the bench, and he wrapped a loose arm around her. Meera could already sense that everyone was watching curiously, but she didn't look at them.

Gazing up at Kennick, she put her left hand on his cheek where all could see her beautiful—if large—ring, and she guided him down to kiss her. He bent to her lips willingly and smiled into their kiss. Meera had a feeling he would have kissed her with more vigor but spared her the humiliation. When they broke apart, he took her hand from his face and brought it to his lips. "I asked Meera to marry me," he announced to everyone.

The other riders struggled to hide their surprise, but they all gave their congratulations.

"Kennick is getting married?" Soleille cried. "It is a Genway miracle!"

Meera and Kennick both laughed along with everyone else. Then Meera realized how ridiculously hungry she was and started filling up her plate with food. "I think you should put in your wedding vows that you will never cause me to miss another meal," she told Kennick, shoveling in her food.

"I would not dream of it," he told her. Then he leaned to whisper in her ear: "I like watching you enjoy your food too much." The way he said it left Meera in no doubt as to his meaning, and her body trembled with reaction that she felt down to her bare toes. She was suddenly glad Soleille had healed her and anticipated getting Kennick alone again.

"Where do you live?" she asked him for the second time that day.

"Over there," he said again, pointing to the woods beyond the clearing.

Meera rolled her eyes. "I should have never agreed to marry you before seeing where you live," she said. "What was I thinking? What if your house is full of stuffed dead animals or you're a slob."

"Do I look like a slob?" he asked.

Meera looked at him and tried to picture what his house might be like. "Oh no," she said. "It's all metal, isn't it?"

He laughed guiltily. "Not all."

MEERA AND KENNICK continued to eat and talk with their friends, enjoying one another's close proximity—but Meera did not use Kennick's fingers as utensils and suck food off of them. She could get onboard with a little public affection in small touches and brief kisses, but she drew the line there. Her human upbringing still dictated her sense of propriety, and she would not stoop to Darroah's levels. Kennick seemed happy just to have her next to him, and he repeatedly stroked her back and touched her leg under the table.

Everyone appeared to accept their relationship despite their initial confusion. Soleille, thankfully, did not demand to hear details. In fact, soon after she finished eating, Soleille stood and disappeared for a time. She returned a little later and slipped Meera a large packet of tea. "For your headache," she said loudly.

Meera glared at her. Soleille might be a worse liar than she was. No one commented, but Meera felt Kennick look down at her. She met his eyes and smiled, trying to convey that she would tell him later. He clearly didn't forget the exchange, however, because after everyone had eaten, Sodhu offered to bring out some of her fruity wine for them to all celebrate their engagement, and Kennick declined, saying he was eager to spend the evening alone with his betrothed. His statement made Meera blush, and she stared adamantly at the table until they rose and left.

She walked automatically toward her cabin, thinking to pack her few belongings; Kennick hadn't explicitly invited her to move in with him, but she assumed they would live together right away. He had promised her his days and nights, after all.

"Are you alright?" he asked once they rounded the corner of Hadjal's house.

"I'm fine," she said, turning to him just outside the cabin.

"What is the tea for?" he persisted, eyeing it in her hand like it offended him.

Meera swallowed, suddenly hoping it wouldn't offend him. She had no real idea what Kennick's thoughts on contraceptives were. "It ... uh," she started unsuccessfully. Kennick only looked more concerned at her stammering, so she took his hand reassuringly. "I don't think Soleille wants me to tell anyone this," she said quietly, "But I asked her for something to prevent pregnancy. I ... hope that's okay with you—is it?"

"She gave you a tea to prevent pregnancy?" Kennick asked blankly. It clearly had not been a consideration in his mind.

Meera nodded and bit her lip, wondering if it was technically illegal in Levisade or just frowned upon. Then she had a ridiculous daydream about Darreal banishing her from Levisade—not because she endangered anyone, but because she drank a birth control tea—and she had to clamp down the nervous laughter that threatened to burst forth. "Are you mad?" she asked, eyeing Kennick's smooth face. She thought maybe she should have talked to him about it first. She definitely should have thought this through before sleeping with him ...

"I am surprised that Soleille makes such teas since they are taboo, but no, I am not mad. I am glad she is living by her own beliefs as a healer," he replied.

"No," Meera said, slightly exasperated, "Are you mad at me?"

"Why would I be mad at you?" he asked, squeezing her hand and rubbing his thumb across her ring.

"I ... don't know—because I just told you I don't want to have your babies?" she said uncertainly. "Not that I don't—I mean, I don't right now."

Kennick smirked at her obvious discomfort discussing the matter. Then he shrugged. "Pregnancy is so rare, it probably does not make any difference," he said. "You should take it if you want to. It does not especially matter to me."

Meera looked at him searchingly, but he appeared to be genuinely unconcerned either way. She marveled at how rare knell pregnancy really seemed to be. Kennick didn't even appear to think it was a possibility or anything worth worrying about. It eased her mind, somewhat, though she still planned to take her tea. She supposed this was a new risk for her but one he was used to; he had already slept with many women and never impregnated any of them. She didn't like the thought.

Meera turned to her cabin and went inside to pack and focus on her joy at moving in with the man that she loved. All of her personal items still fit into her one bag, except her sword, which she strung over her shoulder. She took extra care folding her ball gown and putting it in with her other clothes. Then she added her mother's earrings and ring. The site of the ring gave her pause, and Kennick looked at it over her shoulder. He didn't comment on it, however.

When Meera finally turned around with her possessions, he stood patiently by the door looking smug. "Going somewhere?" he asked.

"Your house," she said confidently.

"Are you?" he asked with raised brows. "Where is it?"

She laughed. "It's that way," she said, pointing vaguely. Then she hoisted her bag onto her shoulder and left the cabin, skirting Hadjal's house for the woods. Meera walked the path that led to the clearing where she and Shael used to train, and Kennick walked behind her. Grinning, she wondered how long he was going to keep up the game. "Are you at least going to tell me if I'm getting warmer or colder?" she asked, meandering through the woods past the clearing.

"No, but keep going down that path, and you'll be moving in with Isbaen," he told her.

"I bet if I had figured out how to sense metal I could find it," she said, trying unsuccessfully to tap into her metal shaping.

"You do not have a very good sense of direction, do you?" Kennick asked, laughing when they ended up back at the clearing.

Meera shrugged. "I have other talents," she said. Then she sighed dramatically and plopped onto the grass. "Oh well, I guess I'll sleep outside again. It's too bad—I thought you might have a big soft bed to roll around in."

"We made do with grass just fine earlier," he reminded her.

"Come on!" she cried, standing back up. "Is your house really embarrassing or something? I'm going to find out eventually. I mean, I can give you time to go hide the shrine you keep of me, but I'm just going to dig it out later."

"My house is not embarrassing," Kennick said. "I just never

bring women home with me." He was teasing her, but Meera still felt rankled by the statement. She both didn't want to be referred to as one of his women and didn't want to be reminded of them at all.

She crossed her arms over her chest and glowered. "Well, now I'm not going even if you beg me," she said testily.

"What if I carry you?" he asked, eyes glinting. Meera should have known that challenging Kennick could get him to do almost anything.

"You can try," she replied, a glint in her own eyes.

He stepped forward and scooped her up, bag and all. "That was easy," he said, walking into the woods with her.

Meera wanted to get to her new home, but she also wanted to win. "I haven't started yet," she said, trailing a fingernail down the sensitive skin of his neck. She pulled herself up using his shoulders and kissed him in the same spot.

He chuckled low in his throat. "That will just make me want to get there faster," he said, picking up his pace.

"If you can get us there at all," Meera teased, reaching a hand up under his shirt.

She continued to taunt him with her hands and whisper in his ear as he walked with her. They eventually made it to his house, but by the time they got there, they were both too worked up to care. Meera dropped her bag and sword on the floor unceremoniously and caught fleeting glimpses of metal furniture and big windows on their way through the main room before Kennick carried her to the bedroom and threw her down on his big, soft bed. Giggling, she pulled him down with her, delirious with joy and desire. In the end, they both won.

8

MEERA

For the next two days, Meera and Kennick stayed at home, enjoying their togetherness and time away from the communal lifestyle of the peninsula. They cooked together, ate together, and swam in the small lake behind his house. Kennick's house was not large, but it was extremely nice with massive, picturesque windows and wood beams across the ceilings. He had a closet the size of a room where he kept his clothes, in which Meera amused herself for an entire afternoon pulling out his most outlandish outfits and teasing him about them.

While Meera's life with Kennick was new and exciting, she felt as if she was finally exhaling after a long and rigorous stretch of training. She lounged more than she had in months, even attempting to read some books—although, she found Kennick's presence so distracting, they were never able to read for long. Meera's favorite room was the enormous bathroom attached to the bedroom, which housed a big, marble bathtub. They spent many hours in the tub; she kept the water just the right temperature with her raek fire and shaped a cool breeze when they grew hot.

Meera was happier than ever before, and she was trying very hard to keep it that way—blocking out thoughts of Darreal's summit and whether Shaya would return in time. The summit was in less than two weeks, and neither she nor Kennick had a raek to ride there. Endu had not acknowledged Kennick since he had asked a human to marry him. Meera felt bad that she had come between the pair, but Kennick assured her that she was only the last grain of sand in the heap that had toppled their relationship.

Meera told herself she would start to think about the summit and the rest of her life in a week's time. Until then, she intended to think of nothing but Kennick and allow herself to feel like she was constantly walking on water. That was her intention, anyway. But on her third morning in her new home, she had a rude awakening —literally.

Rolling over in their white fluffy bedding, she reached out and groped for Kennick with a hand even though she could sense he wasn't there. Sighing, she sat up and stretched before walking naked to the glass doors looking out over the lake. She peered out at the bright summer morning and realized she must have slept in fairly late. Kennick had probably arisen and gone for a run without her—or gone to buy her morning pastries, she thought with a smile.

It was then that Meera heard a knock on the front door followed by voices. She froze and listened but didn't think it sounded like any of the riders. She relaxed, however, when she heard Kennick's laughter. Turning to a mirror, she thought she ought to do something about her wild hair before getting dressed and going to see who it was. Between the summer humidity and getting playful in the bed the night before, her curls were extra voluminous that morning. Pushing her masses of hair behind her shoulders, she reached for one of Kennick's silk robes to pull on.

However, before she could grasp the robe, a voice sounded right outside the door: "Nonsense, darling! Where is she?" The door flew open, and in walked an extremely robust woman in an impeccably draped tan dress. The woman was knell, but she was much fuller-figured than any knell Meera had ever seen. She had the usual knell high cheekbones as well as dramatically arched eyebrows and glossy black hair. Behind the knell woman entered a flustered looking human woman, who seemed somehow out of place in her fine dress.

Meera stood there naked, gaping at the pair. They gaped in return, eyes roving over her expanse of swirling silvery scar and her nudity. Then—before Meera could think or speak—the human woman screamed a horrible, piercing shriek and pointed at her, crying, "Look! Look what he did to her! I knew it!" She turned and fled.

Meera grabbed Kennick's robe and pulled it on just as Kennick appeared in the doorway, looking angrier than she had ever seen him. She reached for him in her confusion, and he went to her, putting a reassuring arm around her shoulder before turning to the well-dressed knell woman. "Meera, this is Follaria —the designer and friend I told you about," he said. He sounded calm, but she could feel his heavy breathing as he reigned in his temper. "Follaria, this is my betrothed, Meera," he added.

"What's going on?" Meera asked him quietly.

"I am sorry, I should have stopped them—or I should have warned them," Kennick said, but Meera still didn't understand what was happening.

"Warned them what? What's going on?" she asked again, louder.

"This is all my fault, my dear!" Follaria said, sweeping toward them and moving her full figure in a way that almost made Meera blush. "When I got Kennick's letter saying that his fiancé needed some new clothes—Well! I just could not wait! The girls and I canceled our other appointments and came as soon as we could. I mean, I just had to see the woman who had finally captured my most handsome friend's heart!"

Meera stared at her. Follaria was talking directly to her, yet she sounded overly loud and dramatized like she was putting on a theater performance. Meera was beginning to understand why Follaria was there, but she still didn't know what the screaming and pointing was about.

"I apologize sincerely for my assistant's behavior," Follaria continued. "It was quite unacceptable—quite inappropriate! I will admit, I am also surprised, but I have known my dear Kennick for long enough that I must assume there is nothing uncouth going on here ..." She looked between Meera and Kennick like she was hoping for an explanation, but Meera still didn't know what she was talking about.

"What *is* going on here?" she demanded of Kennick, getting angry that he had allowed these strangers to barge in on her privacy.

"They are surprised that you are human," he explained quietly. Meera let that sink in. She supposed the woman had screamed and left because she thought Kennick was abusing her in some way; her scar would look inherently suspicious to someone who already assumed the worst of knell and expected them to prey upon humans.

"I am surprised you did not hear of Meera after the ball," Kennick remarked to Follaria.

"The ball?" she asked in shocked intrigue. "I heard my dress was worn by a very powerful new raek rider," she said. "Is this her?" Follaria looked at Meera with even more interest if that was possible.

Meera crossed her arms over her chest, beginning to feel like a zoo exhibit. "I think it's time for these people to leave," she said to Kennick, averting her eyes from the audacious woman. She'd had enough; she was ready to be alone in her love bubble again—not that she was feeling particularly loving toward Kennick at the moment.

Follaria put a hand to her chest like she was extremely affronted—or rather like a heroine in a drama would do if she were affronted.

Kennick turned to Meera and leaned down to talk quietly to her. "Meera, I am sorry. This is my fault. Please. Follaria is my friend, and you need new clothes for the summit," he said, fixing his dark eyes on her imploringly.

Meera didn't want the woman there anymore, but she knew Follaria was important to Kennick. "Okay," she huffed.

"Thank you," he said, bending to kiss her.

Meera pulled away quickly, uncomfortable being watched by Follaria. Then she turned to the keen-eyed woman. "The dress you made me is extraordinary, and Kennick has told me many kind things about you," she said, making an effort to be friendly.

"Well, I normally do not design looks for people I cannot see, but Kennick insisted and gave me very specific instructions. Had I known your complexion, I might have made different choices, but that is neither here nor there. Tell me dear, how did a human such as yourself become a raek rider and nab the wealthiest young bachelor in Levisade?" she asked, looking hungry for gossip.

Meera bristled at being told her dress wasn't the right color for her; she loved that dress. She also didn't like the not-so-subtle accusation that she was using Kennick for his money; she didn't even know why he would have money since his parents still lived.

Kennick put a quelling hand on hers, but she snatched it away. The movement had the unintended effect of drawing Follaria's eyes to her diamond ring.

"I think I will wear what I have," Meera said icily. "Or I'll just go naked—that seems to have an effect on people."

"Follaria, please behave. It took me weeks to seduce Meera," Kennick said with a charming smile.

Meera rolled her eyes, but the knell woman laughed. "You are so naughty, Kennick! What will your parents think?" she asked. Then she turned to Meera. "If you want to gain the respect of the knell leadership, you are going to need the clothes for it."

Meera sighed. She really did need better clothes. "Fine, but I'm paying for them," she said.

Follaria laughed again—so hard that her curves jiggled with her mirth. "Dear, you cannot afford me," she told Meera.

"I will pay," Kennick said. "Do not worry about it, Meera. We will be married soon. What difference does it make?"

"My pride will not allow it," she told him stubbornly, and she walked to the dresser drawer where she had thrown her few belongings. Pulling out her money bag, containing what was left of her stipend from Darreal—it wasn't much—she handed some to Kennick. "For my boots," she said, finally paying him back for the boots he had bought her the day they had met.

He frowned at her but took the money, probably waiting until they were alone to argue about it. Then Meera turned toward Follaria with the rest of her money in her palm. The woman shook her head, indicating it was nowhere near enough. "Fine," Meera said. "What if I pay you in gossip?"

Follaria's black eyebrows arched even higher onto her brow. "That is tempting," she said. She put a hand on one of her rolling hips and tapped a finger to her chin in deliberation.

Meera stared her down. She could sense Kennick's amusement next to her, and she ignored him.

"You know," Follaria said finally. "I will make you what you need as an engagement present. Kennick being engaged to a human is probably the juiciest gossip I will be privy to in my lifetime. Plus, I like you—you are fiery," she added.

Meera laughed and so did Kennick. Then she ignited herself in harmless pale raek fire. She was careful not to singe Kennick's robe, though she considered burning it just for the spectacle; Follaria was clearly a woman who would appreciate it. The knell woman's eyes widened in fascination and delight. "I understand the color of the dress, now," she said to Kennick, nodding in approval. "And your choice in bride."

Kennick grinned and grabbed Meera through her flames to kiss her. She let him this time. Then he helped her decide on colors and styles for her summit attire while Follaria took her measurements. Meera wasn't particular, but she did insist on pants for every outfit—she was a raek rider, after all.

―――――――――――

ORDERING her garments made the approaching summit feel that much more real, and Meera could no longer stay at home with Kennick and pretend the world outside didn't exist. They returned to their training at the peninsula, and she focused on her shaping. She also began contemplating what she would say to the new Queen's Council and the human leaders of Aegorn. The trouble was, she had no idea what was expected of her.

Meera tried each day to contact Shaya, growing increasingly anxious that she wouldn't return in time to fly her to the Levisade Estate. If Shaya was there, maybe she could just show the council some of the history she had shown Meera or frighten them into ending the war—Meera was not keen on giving any more speeches. She didn't hear from her raek, however, until two days before they were meant to leave.

Shaya descended from the sky like a falling cloud, landing in the middle of the grassy slope next to Hadjal's house, and Meera ran up from where she had been training on the beach. "There you are!" she cried. She wondered why she had not felt Shaya coming, but she still struggled to understand her connection with her raek. Shaya seemed to be in control of their shared mental space. Her raek didn't answer; she just gave her a look like Meera was stating the obvious with unnecessary human dialogue.

"You smell different," Shaya announced finally, sniffing at Meera, whose stomach flipped over at the words. She had been drinking Soleille's tea each night but continued to have odd sensations in her abdomen and the sneaking suspicion that she could be pregnant. She had not told Kennick about her suspicion—too afraid to even admit it to herself. But Shaya was probably just smelling Kennick on her.

"I moved in with Kennick—you know, the one with the red plumage," Meera replied. "We're going to get married—like permanent mates."

Shaya huffed a puff of smoke at her. "Raeken do not mate for life unless they find their true mate," she said. "My mother and sire were true mates, and even after my sire died, she did not mate again. Of course, by then she had already lain many eggs. True mates are always the most fruitful."

"How do raeken know if they're true mates?" Meera asked curiously. She had never heard of such a thing before.

"They touch minds as raeken and their riders do. Raeken communicate mentally, but we only share the images we project out to one another. We cannot share our thoughts and feelings," Shaya explained.

Meera's stomach practically fell out of her body. She and Kennick had only touched minds once more since that first time —also during intimacy—but neither of them had found any answers about the phenomenon. Could they be true mates?

Shaya, made curious by Meera's strong emotions, listened in on her racing thoughts. "It would seem that the red-feathered warrior is your true mate," she said approvingly. "You are lucky to have found him so young."

"But what does that mean?" Meera asked.

"It means you will be very fertile together," Shaya replied, sounding pleased.

Meera was not pleased. "But—but why would you want me to be fertile?" she asked in exasperation. "Don't you want me to be a warrior and help you end the war?"

Shaya narrowed her eyes at Meera. "Mothers are the fiercest warriors," she replied like it was obvious.

Meera thought she might be sick. She had more than enough going on in her life and did not want to add a baby to the list. The thought of her riding Shaya into war with a baby on her breast made her want to lie down. She didn't really know that she was pregnant, she reassured herself; it had only been a couple weeks, and she had been paranoid since her first time—she couldn't have possibly known that early.

Taking a deep breath, she allowed herself a moment to appreciate that Kennick was her true mate. It was a comforting thought even if she hadn't been having any doubts about their relationship. She was excited to share the knowledge with him, but then it occurred to her to wonder why she would have a true mate like a raek if it was not something knell usually experienced. What was she? Was she part raek as well as part human and knell? She did have raek fire ... The thought was disconcerting, but she pushed it aside for the moment. She was what she was.

MEERA WAITED until she and Kennick were walking home to tell him the news. "I learned something today," she said simply.

"Oh?" he inquired.

She took a deep breath. "Shaya said something—" she started to say.

"I saw her! You must be glad she is back to take you to the summit," Kennick interjected. "I would not have been able to drop you off with Endu ignoring me. One of the others would have taken you, but you will make a better impression on your own raek."

Meera was about to continue her earlier train of thought when she realized what he had said. "Drop me off?" she asked. "You're not going with me?"

Kennick looked sideways at her with furrowed brows. The golden light of the setting sun dappled on his hair through the trees, making it look more red and orange than usual. "I was not invited by the queen, and you did not ask me to go with you—not that I blame you. I actually think it would be better for you and the war efforts to go without me," he replied. His posture was loose with his usual easy elegance, but Meera thought she detected a little strain in his voice.

"I just assumed ..." she started to say, trailing off. Even before they had declared their love for one another, Meera had always pictured Kennick being with her when she went to the summit. She knew he would not be able to actually join the official meetings, but there were social gatherings on the itinerary as well. "Why would it be better if you didn't come?" she asked in confusion.

"I know these people, Meera—I could tell you their names and where they live and what they are like. I have known them my whole life ... But they also know me, and they do not respect me. You know what my reputation is like," he said.

"But everyone seemed friendly toward you at the ball ... Why would this be any different?" she asked.

Kennick laughed, but she didn't see what was funny. "My mother's ball, you mean? Her friends were on their best behavior because they knew Andreena might burn their clothes off otherwise," he said with humor. Then he noticed her troubled expression and took her hand. "It is okay, Meera. You need to gain the respect of the knell leadership, and it is better you do that without them knowing about our engagement."

"Won't they already know? Follaria knows ..." she said.

"The knell population is not large, but knell keep very strict inner circles. Follaria does not interact with the most elite families —not anymore, anyway. When she took me in, my mother saw to it that her friends stopped commissioning her designs," he explained. Meera supposed Follaria really had been a good friend to Kennick. Did he think that she would not stand by him as well?

"Kennick, I want you to come to the summit with me," she said, squeezing his hand. "You are my true mate, and I don't care who knows it."

"Your what?" he asked, grinning at her.

"Shaya says we sometimes touch minds because we are true mates. It's apparently a raek thing, and I am apparently part-raek," she said, shrugging her shoulders.

"And what are true mates?" he asked.

"I'm not really sure, but it is the only time raeken mate for life," she explained, leaving out the part about them being extra fertile. Meera still wasn't ready to broach her fear with Kennick and didn't want to see him get excited about the prospect of their fertility—she assumed he would be, considering how much the knell valued pregnancy. Still, she smiled shyly at him, hoping he was pleased by the news.

He was pleased. Kennick bent down and lifted Meera up from under her butt, holding her where he could kiss her without bending. She wrapped her arms around his neck and kissed him back. However, they were both smiling too much and broke apart laughing when their teeth clanked together. Still, he held her there and gazed at her. "Will you come with me to the summit?" she asked, peering into his dark eyes with all of the love she felt for him.

"I would go with you anywhere," he told her huskily.

Suddenly, they weren't smiling anymore, and it was some time before they finally made it home.

9

MEERA

The morning of their departure, Meera stood in one of her new outfits, assessing herself in the mirror. Her shirt and pant set was a light greenish blue and form-fitted. Rather than tying at her side, the shirt cinched in a straight line down her front, accentuating her slim waist and fitting her perfectly. The shirt's collar was wide at the top to display her scars, and the pants skimmed her legs lightly before tapering at her ankle boots. Follaria had even thought to make her a few new breast wraps.

Meera felt like a new person—a stylish, powerful person. She even walked a little straighter and more confidently. With her hair twisted up on the top of her head and her sword strapped to her back, she thought she truly looked the part of a warrior. Kennick came up behind her and wrapped his arms around her. He wore a light beige color in materials as fine as her own, and his muscle-corded arms in no way detracted from her image in the mirror. "What do you think?" she asked.

"You are perfect," he told her. He tried to hold her closer but was impeded by their swords. He wore his on his waist, and its hilt bumped against Meera's sheathed blade.

She laughed. "Two swords are a little too unwieldy," she remarked.

"I have found that to be true," he agreed with a smirk. She didn't want to know what he was talking about.

Their bags were packed, and they were ready to walk to the peninsula to see everyone before flying to the Levisade Estate. Meera looked around at their bedroom sadly; she would miss her new home. "We'll be back in a few days," Kennick told her, seeing the look on her face. He was beginning to talk more and more like a human as they spent more time together, Meera noticed, though he still spoke with a knell lilt to his words that she enjoyed.

When they reached the peninsula, their fellow riders wished them well and gave Meera words of encouragement. Hadjal and Sodhu had left the day before on two of Darreal's horses since they were both expected at the queen's events, but Meera wished they could all be going; she would have liked to have more of her family around her.

As she tied her bag onto Shaya with long leather straps, Kennick debated with Endu about whether or not the raek would fly him to the estate. From what Meera understood, Endu had been torn all week between not wanting to associate with a human and not wanting his rider to appear in front of important knell riding another's raek. Eventually, it seemed he decided to take Kennick because Kennick also tied his bag to his raek before walking over to her.

"I'm a little disappointed," she told him. "I had plans for you." She gave him a coy smile.

"In the sky?" Kennick asked, sounding incredulous.

Meera gave him a look—he wasn't normally fazed by any of her ideas for them. She supposed she had finally found something he had never done before—not that he appeared keen to try it. "Oh well," she said. "Maybe on the way home."

He smiled, but she saw him swallow nervously as well. She laughed at the look on his face, then she patted Kennick's shoulder roughly in what she thought seemed like a hearty warrior's goodbye before leaping onto Shaya and shouting, "To battle!"

THE FIRST EVENT on the itinerary was an outdoor lunch for the knell leadership to reacquaint themselves with one another. It was something of a knell-only welcome party. Darreal had requested that Meera arrive on her raek after the party had started in order to make a strong first-impression. Meera wasn't sure about making speeches, but she knew how to make an entrance.

She and Shaya arrived over the Levisade Estate before Endu and Kennick. Meera had begged Shaya to wait for them, but her raek had insisted that flying so slowly was too tedious. Meera didn't believe her—she suspected Shaya was bitter about Endu's apparent rejection—but her raek did as she pleased, as usual. The party was being held in the estate's back gardens, and Shaya positioned herself over the gardens while remaining hidden in the clouds.

"Ready when you are!" Meera told her. They had already decided on a plan. Shaya was not normally willing to do as Meera wished, but the raek apparently had no objections to making a show of herself. Shaya dove down from the cloud cover high above, shooting through the blue summer sky for the ground below. Then she opened her massive mouth and emitted a sphere of pale raek fire, which Meera shaped into a spiral around her plummeting body.

Shaya pulled up suddenly from her dive to soar above the onlookers, blocking out the sun with her enormous wingspan, and Meera leapt from her back, shooting headfirst for the party below. Keeping the air around her still to avoid ripping out her twisted bun, she exalted in her free fall. She waited and waited until the last possible moment. Then she flipped forward to put her feet under her and shaped a swirl of wind under her body to slow and stop her progress just before she touched the ground.

Meera's feet fell lightly to the grass right on the edge of the garden gathering, and Shaya swooped down and landed behind her. The gusts of wind they created buffeted the assembled knell and blew their annoyingly shiny hair around their heads. Meera had to resist laughing. Instead, she fixed her eyes on Darreal, who wore a dress of green and had her usual gold circlet on her brow. She strode toward the queen with confident steps.

Meera hoped her entrance had been satisfactorily impressive for Darreal. Rather than curtsy to the queen, she grasped her shoulders briefly and kissed her cheek as she had seen knell friends greet one another. Meera felt she had an ally in Darreal and hoped they could be friends as well.

"Welcome, Meera," Darreal said. Then the queen proceeded to introduce her to the group of knell gathered in her immediate vicinity. Meera tried to remember their names but immediately forgot most of them—she was too busy concentrating on trying to look competent. To her surprise, Andreena and Destin—Kennick's parents—were among the group. Meera ignored them, irritated to see them there. She supposed Darreal could not afford to make powerful enemies among the knell elite.

Meera had no sooner greeted those around her and declined refreshments when Endu landed in the wildflower field behind the estate gardens. Looking toward him, she noticed two knell approaching Shaya—presumably to retrieve her bag from the raek's side—and her eyes widened in alarm. "Don't touch them!" she commanded Shaya mentally even as she made her excuses to Darreal's group. She rushed to untie her bag before the obviously frightened knell got too close, and Shaya decided to impale them. Meera handed her bag to one of the knell, and Kennick approached and gave his to the other. They both looked extremely relieved to get away from Shaya, who was swishing her tail menacingly and exhaling smoke through her nostrils.

"Sorry we left you behind," Meera said to Kennick, rolling her eyes toward Shaya.

He shrugged his shoulders loosely.

"Your parents are here," she warned.

"I'm not surprised," he said, looking unconcerned. Meera couldn't help but wonder how and when Kennick would break the news to them of their engagement, assuming they had not already heard.

"I want to smell the queen," Shaya announced, following them toward the party. Meera didn't bother arguing with her; she wouldn't be able to stop Shaya from doing whatever Shaya wanted to do. Her raek remained a distance away, however, observing through her large, eerie eyes as well as Meera's.

"Try not to offend or hurt anyone. We're supposed to be getting people to like us," Meera called back to her aloud.

"Funny, I was going to say the same to you," Kennick said with a laugh.

Meera nudged him with her elbow, then she composed herself before reentering Darreal's circle.

"Rider Kennick, I was not expecting you. A room will need to be found for you," Darreal said. Meera could never quite tell by the queen's airy tone whether she was being friendly or not.

"No need—" she started to say, but Andreena cut her off.

"Kennick can stay in our suite of rooms, Darreal. Not to

worry," she asserted, clearly not wanting anyone to know her son would be sharing a room with a human.

"Kennick never fails to find a bed to fall into," a woman near Meera whispered loudly to her companion, who sniggered.

Meera glowered at the pair and supposed this was what Kennick had warned her about. They had all obviously heard with their knell ears, but Kennick appeared unfazed. Meera, on the other hand, fumed inwardly, and he must have sensed it because he put a quelling arm around her, his hand landing casually on her hip. If a look could burn, Andreena's was singeing holes in her son's face.

"Meera, a word?" Darreal said, stepping out of the circle.

Kennick removed his hand from Meera's hip, and she followed the queen to a part of the patio clear of people. With knell hearing, it was difficult to get privacy. When Darreal turned to her, her golden-brown eyes were filled with an intensity Meera had never seen in them before; the queen was usually so vague and airy that the look startled her. "What is it?" she asked quietly.

"Meera, if you and I are to accomplish our goal at this summit, then you must appear both respectable and powerful. We need the knell to accept you. I thought you understood that, yet here you are with Kennick, of all people. I told you before, Meera: Kennick is a joke. Plenty have lain with him in private—that is not an issue—but staking a public claim to him makes you a joke. You will give everyone the notion that you are a foolish, naive human girl being easily led astray by a pretty knell face, and they will not respect you.

"You are here to earn people's respect, seeing as you have already made yourself the face of interference in the war—a goal I have been slowly working toward for years, I might add. This war has been waging for almost the entirety of my seventy-three-year life, and I would like to put an end to it once and for all. Knell, however, do not change easily or quickly. They do not like humans, and they do not like newcomers," she said, giving Meera a pointed look for being both. "Your only job at this summit is to not embarrass yourself or me. Do you understand?"

Darreal's entire speech had been barely more audible than a breath, but Meera had heard and sensed the queen's passion and was shocked—shocked and outraged. For all she could tell, the queen had not done anything these many years to end the war. Now she was acting as if Meera were standing in the way of peace when she had joined with Shaya and trained these past months to fight for it. Not to mention, she did not like the way Darreal had spoken about Kennick.

"I like this queen," Shaya remarked in her mind. "She has sharp teeth."

Meera ignored her; her focus remained on Darreal. "Kennick is my true mate, and we are getting married. I will gladly suck the air from anyone's lungs, should they dare laugh at us. Is that respectable and powerful enough for you?" she asked in a deadly low voice. She could feel the flames yearning to escape her skin.

Darreal looked vaguely surprised by her response, but before she could say anything, a blonde man with a sword stepped between them. Meera's posture must have looked threatening, she thought, eyeing the warrior. Shaya tensed in her mind, but she assured the raek that everything was fine.

"Meera, this is my champion, Lethian," Darreal said in a neutral tone.

Meera nodded curtly at the man.

"You look different than last I saw you," Lethian remarked.

"Have we met?" Meera asked in confusion. She thought she would remember someone as large and well-muscled as Lethian.

"Not exactly. You were encased in fire," he replied.

Meera scowled at the man, daring him to say something about

seeing her naked. The party was already putting her in a foul mood, and she wouldn't mind shouting at someone.

"That is a large sword for such a slight woman. Can you use it?" he asked.

She narrowed her eyes at him; she couldn't quite tell if he was insulting her or just stating the obvious. "You're welcome to find out," she replied testily.

Lethian smiled a genuine smile. "Rider Meera, I challenge you to a Champion's Challenge three days from now!" he said in a booming voice that carried over the patio. Everyone looked over in interest.

Meera stared at him blankly. "Is that a fight?" she asked.

"A fight with weapons and shaping before all those who wish to attend. The winner is considered the greatest warrior in Levisade and has the honor of protecting our queen. We fight until one of us forfeits or cannot go on," he replied, eyes flashing with excitement.

Meera glanced at Darreal, who didn't look displeased by the challenge. Meera wasn't sure she wanted be the Queen's Champion, but she supposed a fight would be a good way for her to earn respect. She shrugged her shoulders. "Sounds like fun," she said.

Discussions broke out all around, and knell in fine clothes stared at Meera like a mildly intriguing mole on someone's face or a new racehorse. Lethian grinned. Then he looked at Darreal, who nodded, and he stepped away to return their privacy to them.

Meera and Darreal eyed one another for a long moment. "Tread wisely, Meera. Respect and fear are not the same thing," Darreal said opaquely before walking away.

Meera watched her go, thinking she and the queen might not be friends after all. Then she turned to find Kennick waiting for her by a food table. He was standing alone, looking serious. Meera considered all the queen had said—really considered it without her anger clouding her judgment. She supposed she should do whatever was best for their cause, and yet, she could not turn Kennick away after inviting him there.

"I thought this might happen," he said when she approached him. "Should I go?" He didn't sound upset or unwilling, which only made Meera want to fight for him even more.

Glancing down at the table next to him, she picked up a small jelly tart and bit into it. Then, in a poor attempt at a stage voice, she said, "These are very good, Kennick. We should have them at our wedding!" She nearly choked on her own bad performance; she was many things, but she was not an actress.

Kennick grinned and bent to kiss her—no doubt tasting the tart she had yet to swallow. "We should have these in our bedroom," he whispered in her ear. Louder, he said, "Whatever you want, my love." His acting was much better than hers.

They moved across the patio together and were met with many congratulations, though Meera doubted any of them were sincere. Kennick kept her hand in his to prevent her from lashing out at anyone who made backhanded comments within hearing distance. A particularly tall woman whispered loudly to her companion: "I suppose that Kennick might as well marry her—no respectable knell woman would go to bed with him after he has been sullied by a human." And Kennick's hand tightened on Meera's like a vice when she tried to turn toward the woman.

"Ignore them," he told her. "Hearing everything and pretending you do not is just part of knell life."

Meera settled for heating the liquid in the woman's glass with unseen raek fire until the woman dropped the fine glass on the patio with a loud smash. She heard several titters of laughter and felt slightly better, but then she reprimanded herself internally; she knew shouldn't use her shaping in underhanded ways. If

Kennick had noticed what she'd done, he didn't comment on it. He was looking toward his parents, who were standing on the edge of the party with the bitter expressions of toads. "I should go and talk to them," he said with a frown.

Meera wasn't sure they deserved his consideration, but they were his parents, so she didn't argue. "Do you want me to come?" she offered.

"Will you behave without me?" he asked.

"Do I ever behave?" she replied with raised brows.

He squeezed her hand before walking away, and Meera sighed; between the two of them, they didn't have much in the way of actual family. She supposed her father was close by in the estate, and she should tell him her news … But she really didn't think he would care. He seemed to want to bury himself away in his work and forget about everything else in the world—his daughter included.

Suddenly, Meera felt a little nauseous and lightheaded. Putting a hand to her stomach, she wondered if the tart had upset her or if she hadn't eaten enough that day. Then she quickly removed the hand when she remembered where she was and another possible cause for nausea.

"Everything alright, Meera?" She turned to find Hadjal and Sodhu looking at her with mingled concern and kindness. She had forgotten they would be there, and her heart lightened. She and Kennick had the riders, after all, and they were the best family she could have hoped for.

10

MEERA

The next day consisted of multiple long and extremely tedious meetings led by Darreal. First, the new Queen's Council met—which Meera was pleased to see Andreena and the rock-shaping woman who had attacked her were no longer a part of. Odon was, however, and he was as loud and odorous as ever. Then they met with the largest landowners of Levisade, including Andreena and Destin. Kennick's parents avoided looking at Meera entirely, which probably wasn't difficult considering she was never called on to speak.

In fact, Meera sat in silence the entire day, attempting to look alert and respectable while Darreal fielded a seemingly endless stream of concerns about ending the war from Levisade's most powerful knell. She began to realize that Darreal had been serious when she had explained her purpose at the summit: she was not there to give speeches or rouse anyone to action—she was only there out of necessity and to show the knell that their queen was not being manipulated or controlled by a human with mysterious abilities.

By the end of the day, Meera felt extremely weary even though she hadn't done much of anything. Her butt was sore from endless sitting, and she craved the outdoors and open skies. Resisting the urge to stretch when she stood from her seat, she filed toward the door with the prominent knell business owners who had been present in the final meeting of the day. She smoothed her shirt—still trying to look respectable—and thought how silly it was that Follaria had designed her warrior attire for this political nonsense.

As she approached the door, she noticed that Darreal was showing small signs of weariness as well. The queen's light, airy tone and patience had persisted through each meeting when Meera would have long since resorted to shouting at people and slamming her hands on the table. Meera now understood what the queen had meant about having worked toward change very slowly from the start of her rule; it was clear Darreal had needed to first build trust with the knell who—even after forty years—treated her like a new and young queen.

The queen's strain showed subtly under her eyes and in the set of her girlish pink lips. Meera hung back and waited for the other knell to leave the room. Darreal saw her waiting and regarded her with patience, though Meera suspected she dreaded yet another question after such a long day of questions. Meera waited until only the two of them and Lethian remained. She had often glanced at the Queen's Champion throughout the day—partly because she anticipated their fight—but also because she was beginning to suspect Lethian's devotion to his queen went beyond that of a warrior. When she approached Darreal, Lethian honed his focus on her but did not object.

"You know, we should be friends," Meera said to Darreal bluntly. "Who else can a queen befriend other than another powerful woman bearing exceptional responsibilities?"

The statement was clearly not what Darreal had been expecting, and her delicately arched eyebrows rose as her only response. Meera thought she caught a hint of a smile on Lethian's face and supposed she was probably right in thinking that Darreal didn't have any friends to turn to at the end of her long days as queen.

"I fancy a flight. Care to join me?" Meera asked. She knew Shaya was out back basking in the sun. She also knew her raek liked the knell queen and had been curious to get closer to her.

Darreal continued to look shocked, and Lethian appeared less than pleased by the suggestion.

"She would be perfectly safe with me," Meera assured the blonde warrior. "Have you ever flown before?" she asked Darreal.

"No," she replied quietly, sounding thoughtful.

Meera wondered what the queen's life must be like living in the estate surrounded by people who could always hear her and judged her every word. She leaned toward her conspiratorially. "You know, in the sky there's no one to hear you shout or inspect your posture. Do you own pants?" she asked, looking down at Darreal's long dress.

A slow smile spread across the queen's face.

NOT LONG AFTER, Meera was helping Darreal onto Shaya's back. The queen had changed into pants and a shirt and was doing her best not to appear nervous. Shaya stood very still—much more so than she ever did for Meera—and held her scaly head proudly in the air. Some knell looked on from the estate's patio, and Lethian watched sourly from the ground below them.

"Lethian, do you know Kennick?" Meera asked him.

"Of course," the warrior replied.

"He's always up for sparring. He wouldn't balk from a match

with the Queen's Champion," she told him. Lethian's face brightened.

Meera settled herself behind Darreal and told her to grip Shaya's feathers before they lunged into the air. At first, Darreal tensed, probably regretting her decision, but as they evened out high above, her posture relaxed. Shaya flew them away from the estate and over the forests that made up most of Levisade. Meera kept the air around their heads still, as it was her preferred way of flying. She and Darreal could have easily talked, but instead, Meera leaned back and let the queen forget about her; she could sense the woman craved space and solitude, and she was more than happy to lounge and look up at the endless expanse of sky above. It was not long before the day's meetings felt far away, and all of Meera's troubles seemed small.

In front of her, Darreal's shoulders relaxed, and her head tilted back for the sun to hit her face. Meera smiled to see her enjoying herself and encouraged Shaya to do a mild dive. Her raek listened to her—for once—leaning forward to give Meera and Darreal the heady, stomach-lifting feeling of falling. Darreal laughed loudly— a sound Meera had never heard from her before—and they continued to fly for over an hour, not going anywhere in particular.

As Meera lay back, however, she began to feel the burden of her worries once more. She was tired—too tired; she was far more exhausted than was warranted and had had two more bouts of nausea since the day before. Her breasts felt tender as well, although she acknowledged that that could be from all the attention they had received the night before. Still, her pregnancy paranoia was quickly growing.

"Raeken know right away when they have conceived," Shaya remarked suddenly in her mind.

Meera jumped. Somehow, she still couldn't tell when her raek was monitoring her thoughts. Then Shaya's words hit her. "What?" she shouted mentally. "Why didn't you tell me that before?" She thought back to the strange pinch and sense of gravitas she had felt soon after joining with Kennick for the first time. Now that she knew their mind-touching was a raek thing, she could easily believe that she had sensed her pregnancy as early as a raek would have.

"You did not ask," Shaya replied lazily.

Meera didn't bother berating her; she was too busy spiraling into panic. She didn't want to be pregnant—not yet, anyway. Her body had only just changed and then changed some more. Her relationship with Kennick was still new. She was pledged to a task that was probably already larger than she could handle. Suddenly lurching upright, she asked Shaya to take them back to the estate. She thought she might be sick.

When they returned, Darreal thanked her with genuine warmth, and Meera excused herself to go lie down in her room.

Kennick returned sometime later, sweaty and content. "Long day?" he asked.

"Yes," she replied. She wasn't ready to mention her suspicions yet; she still hoped she was wrong. Meera wondered if Soleille might be able to tell, but Soleille wasn't there. As she watched Kennick change his clothes and splash water on his face, the love for him that twisted in her belly was so strong, she thought maybe it wouldn't be so bad if his child also grew within her. But the thought of her body altering once again and her life growing even more complex and burdensome still left her reeling.

———

THE NEXT DAY was just as long and tedious as the one before. Meera sat straight and silent as Darreal and her council met with the human leaders of Aegorn to discuss the war and the general state of the land. The meeting might have been informative, except that the human leaders were entirely too terrified to say much of anything. They were clearly uncomfortable being in Levisade at all, and Meera's presence did not put them at ease; rather, she got the impression they thought she had been abducted and changed by the knell somehow.

Overall, by the end of the summit, Meera didn't feel like anything had been accomplished—she certainly hadn't achieved anything. She was beginning to think endeavoring to end the war would take her a lifetime of dull, pointless meetings. Her head throbbed from the thought, and she longed to fly again. But she was missing Kennick and sought him out first.

She found him on the back patio with his parents. She considered pretending she hadn't seen them and skirting around their table to find Shaya, but she supposed since she was marrying Kennick, she ought to make some effort with his parents. Kennick had agreed to have dinner with her father that night, after all. Meera still hadn't actually seen her father since arriving at the estate. Ned had run messages between them. Meera had been glad to see the boy looking well-fed and happy, but she wished her father would have taken the time to find her himself. She felt like an afterthought in his life—an inconvenience even.

"Hello," she said tentatively, walking up behind Kennick and putting her hand on his shoulder.

He promptly reached up and pulled her down to sit on his lap. His parents glowered at her. "Mother, father, you remember Meera," he said, feigning obliviousness to their obvious hatred of her.

"Of course," Andreena said through thin lips. "Meera, that is quite a ring my son gave you. You should know that the diamond was purchased by our ancestors with the wealth they amassed from exploiting humans." She made the statement in a sticky-sweet voice of mock-concern.

Meera looked down at her ring and wondered how true that was. "Your ancestors *were* humans," she reminded Andreena.

The woman gave her a look of solid ice. It was chilling for the mere fact that she resembled Kennick so strongly, and it was a look Meera would never expect to see from the man she loved.

Since Andreena appeared to be done talking to her, Meera turned toward Destin. She hadn't quite figured out Kennick's father yet, though she could hardly view him favorably considering who he was married to. Destin sat staring to the side at a flowering bush. He looked like he might be communing with the bush in some way, so Meera left him to it. Instead, she turned around to face Kennick, who gave her a warm smile that was the complete antithesis of his mother's expression. "I'm going to fly. Do you want to come?" she asked. She hoped he did.

"If you and Shaya will have me," he replied.

Meera shrugged; she could never speak for Shaya. When they approached the enormous raek where she sprawled in the fields crushing wildflowers, however, they found her amenable to a flight. From what Meera could tell, she had been spending her time at the estate flexing her wings and enjoying the admiration of the knell who passed by to look at her. Meera rolled her eyes as Shaya rose and stretched languidly. Then she climbed onto the raek's shoulders, and Kennick jumped up to settle himself behind her.

"Where to?" he asked in her ear, making her shiver.

"Nowhere," she sighed.

As they flew, Meera leaned back into Kennick and enjoyed the feeling of his solid chest behind her head and his arms wrapped around her. The freedom of flying and Kennick's loving touch were her two favorite things—sweet foods were next in line, she thought, feeling her stomach rumble. She ignored her hunger, however, and as she sat against Kennick in the warm sunshine, she became ravenous for something other than food. Unconcerned by their position so high up, Meera flipped herself around to face him and wrapped her legs around his waist. Then she gave him a mischievous look and raised her eyebrows in question.

He laughed. "Why don't we land?"

"Why?" she asked, pulling him down to kiss her. She saw no reason why they should land. They were perfectly alone in the sky —Shaya didn't count; she was like a big rock, she thought. If Shaya heard the thought, she didn't seem to care.

Meera pressed herself into Kennick, and the gentle rise and fall of Shaya's wings quickly seduced them both. Kennick undid the front lacing of her shirt and exposed her breasts to the open air. Then he balanced himself with the strength of his legs and used his hands to cup them and toy with her nipples while he kissed her. It didn't take Meera long to want more, but there was a question of how.

Laughing and fumbling, she reached around Kennick to pull off one of her boots. Then she held the boot while she lay back and freed her one leg from her pants. Kennick held on to her other leg nervously, but Meera had no fear of falling. Once her necessary body parts were bared, she returned her boot to her foot and remounted Kennick, tugging at the waist of his pants.

His hardness sprung free of its confines as ready for her as she was for him. The sunlight glinted off his reddish nest of hair as she eyed him greedily, and her insides oozed with longing and anticipation. Grasping him firmly, she hovered over him, bringing his tip to her slippery opening. Kennick groaned as she slowly lowered herself onto him. Then he gripped her hips as she rose and fell with the slow, steady beat of Shaya's wings.

Without warning, Shaya turned, and Meera and Kennick both slid to the side and had to brace themselves on each other and the raek's slick feathers. Meera laughed, but her laughter quickly broke off when she caught sight of the raw fear in Kennick's dark eyes. He tried to hide it and look away even as she felt his erection go limp within her. Every other part of him was taut with tension, and she could feel his heart thudding wildly in his chest.

Meera looked searchingly at Kennick, then she cupped his face in her hands. "Are you afraid of heights?" she asked, thinking back to how he had gripped her ankle on their last flight together and refused to jump with her.

He met her gaze with one that was open and vulnerable, and in that instant, they joined minds. Meera felt Kennick's innate fear of falling through their connection, and she clutched him to her and surrounded him with her understanding and love. She started to pull up and off of him, but he held her where she was. "No," he said. "I do not want the connection to break."

She knew what he meant because their consciousnesses only ever meshed when they were physically joined. She didn't bother asking him if he was sure because she could feel through their bond that he was. Instead, she kissed him deeply, and she pushed him back to recline, taking his hands from her body and putting them on Shaya's feathers so that he could hold on and feel safe. Leaning forward, she brushed his eyelids closed with her fingertips to help him block out their surroundings.

Willing as he may have been, Kennick's body was still recovering from his shock. Meera reached behind herself into his open pants and cupped his soft testicles, kneading them in her hand. She also stroked his thighs and stomach and teased his nipples with her other hand until he came back to life inside her. Meera exalted in the feeling of him filling her once more, and she threw back her head and let the wind whip her face, keeping Kennick shielded by her air shaping.

At first, she moved on him slowly. Then, when her need grew, she replaced her slow, full movements with shorter, faster ones. Kennick met her with each thrust, and their minds remained as synchronized as their movements. When Meera's tension rose, she put one hand on her breast to pinch her nipple and the other to her sensitive folds, helping her pleasure crest and climax.

She gasped in a breath of sky, and as she pulsed around Kennick, he spilled into her with release. Meera collapsed over his body, and he freed one of his hands to grasp her to him. They were both panting and trembling, and Meera noticed—to her surprise—they were still mentally connected to one another. She grinned at him, and he smiled back.

Even though she was loath to jar their mysterious connection loose, she lifted herself off of him to clean and dress them both. She knew Kennick would feel more secure if they returned to their usual riding posture. To their continued amazement, their mental link persisted. Kennick held Meera tightly against his chest and kissed her ear once she settled in front of him. She smiled into the blue expanse stretching out before them, and they both sighed into one another's love.

When they reached the estate, Kennick suggested mentally that they jump.

"What?" Meera asked. "No—we don't have to do that! I don't care if you're afraid of heights, Kennick. You don't have anything to prove to me." She knew he could feel the truth of her words, but he insisted.

"I want to," he said against her neck. She could also feel the truth of his words.

When Shaya swooped over the fields behind the estate, they

both stood together. They didn't have to speak; Kennick could sense Meera's thoughts and actions and followed her lead. She took his hand in a tight grip and smiled at him before tipping forward. Together they fell from Shaya's back with their arms and legs spread wide, facing the colorful swath of wildflower fields far beneath them. For a moment, Meera's senses were overwhelmed by Kennick's panic; his fear surged in her mind, and she worried he might crush the bones of her hand, he held it so tightly. Then she focused on the fall and her own joy and freedom as she plummeted through the air, and her thrill overcame Kennick's fear, filling them both.

Meera didn't wait until the last moment to catch them; she pooled wind beneath them, gradually ramping up its power. They slowed as they reached the ground, almost stopping before they leaned to bring their feet beneath them. Meera had no trouble calibrating her shaping to catch Kennick as well as herself because she could feel his body in space as well as sense it. The second their feet touched down in the grass, however, their connection broke.

Kennick was breathing hard, but he was grinning. Meera leapt into his arms and kissed him before realizing there was a large group of knell observing them from the patio. Then she broke away with some embarrassment. He didn't seem to mind. "You are amazing, Meera. It was a little overwhelming to feel you use your power," he admitted.

"Yes, I know—I'm amazing. I'm still not any good at metal shaping, though, so I guess I'll keep you around for a bit," she teased. She didn't bother reminding Kennick that he was still better at sword fighting and hand-to-hand combat and a faster runner; she knew he wasn't insecure. His confidence had once annoyed her, but she now realized it was part of why they worked together—she didn't have to worry that her strength would challenge his own.

As they walked toward the patio and their onlookers, Kennick mused, "You know, they all think I am a joke, but they do not realize the real joke is that I am a raek rider who is afraid of flying."

"That doesn't make you a joke. That makes you brave for doing it anyway. I would be afraid of flying too if I couldn't catch myself," Meera replied, giving him a heartfelt look. Then she thought for a moment. "You know, I bet you could catch yourself if you wore enough metal."

Kennick looked at her thoughtfully, then he laughed. "You want me to wear more metal?" he asked with a wry grin. She was always teasing him about his jewelry.

"I wouldn't recommend catching yourself by your ears," she replied grimacing.

"It is not a bad idea. We'll have to figure it out one day," he said.

Meera grinned and took his hand. She liked being included in all of Kennick's future plans and looked forward to a day of jumping off the cliff over the lake with him. Together they collected a tray of dinner for three from the estate kitchen and went to their room to await her father. Their room was large enough to have a full-sized table, but Meera kept glancing at the bed and fretting that her father would be picturing her and Kennick in it together during their meal. Her worries turned out to be unfounded.

Orson Hailship arrived at their door as scheduled. He hugged Meera and shook Kennick's hand in the human style, congratulating them on their engagement and exclaiming at Meera's large ring. Meera was glad to see her father looking well; he was less thin and had life in his eyes. Her joy at his hearty appearance quickly dissipated, however, when he spent the entirety of their short dinner talking about his research while shoveling his food quickly into his mouth so that he could get back to it. He showed very little interest in Meera's life and none whatsoever in Kennick.

Finally, he said he would try to go to her fight the next day but didn't seem to want to, and he scurried out the door. Meera was left staring after her father with a full plate of food in front of her and an empty feeling in her chest. Kennick rubbed her shoulder consolingly. "At least your parents care enough to hate me," Meera said. "My father's downright indifferent. I think he'd be happy if I was marrying Odon as long as it didn't interfere with his research." She said it with humor, but it hurt.

"Maybe he is not indifferent," Kennick replied. "Maybe he just trusts you to manage your own life."

Meera shrugged and pushed her plate away. He could trust her and show interest at the same time, she thought. "How was your sparring with Lethian yesterday? Do you think I can beat him?" she asked, changing the subject. She was beginning to feel nervous for her challenge the next day.

"I think you can beat anyone in a match with shaping," Kennick said with certainty.

Meera supposed that was true, though she had never actually fought anyone with shaping before—other than the Queen's Council, but that had not been a true fight. She was used to suppressing her magic when she sparred. "How is his swordsman-ship? Did you win?" she asked curiously.

"I won one out of three times," Kennick said.

"That's not great odds for me since I can never beat you," she replied.

"You never try," he teased; he was always pestering Meera to attack more and defend less.

She sighed dramatically. "I guess I can try to win this one," she said.

"In that case, I think it is time for you to go to bed," he told her. Standing rapidly, he snatched her up and threw her over his shoulder.

Meera shrieked with delight, not caring that all the knell in the vicinity would hear her.

11

MEERA

The next morning, Meera dressed for battle in a lightweight pant and shirt set in deep plum purple. Her clothes were simple but exceedingly elegant, considering Follaria had made them. After spending extra time pulling up her hair and pinning it in place, she swung her sword over her shoulder. As she stood and appraised herself in the mirror, she thought that she looked prepared—more prepared than she felt, at least.

"Ready?" Kennick asked, startling her and making her heart race. "For breakfast," he clarified with a smile, seeing her alarmed expression.

"Can we eat in here?" she asked.

"I made plans for us to eat on the patio," he told her.

Meera sighed, but she nodded. She wasn't sure she was up for making conversation with anyone who might be out there—especially not Kennick's parents. Regardless, she took the hand he offered her and followed him out of their room and through the winding halls of the estate to the back doors. She started to walk toward an empty table, but Kennick stopped her and gestured to a crowded one. There—seated on the patio—were the other riders. They had all come to see her fight and support her. Meera felt tears prick her eyes when she saw them waving and smiling at her. "You're here!" she exclaimed, approaching her beloved makeshift family.

"Of course, we are!" Florean replied gruffly. "I have only ever missed one Champion's Challenge in my lifetime, and I regretted choosing that funeral over the fight. Never again."

Meera laughed; she was too happy to see everyone to be offended by Florean. Walking around the table, she hugged each of them, including Sodhu and Hadjal even though they had already been at the estate. She even embraced Theora and Misty briefly. Theora returned her gesture, but Misty snubbed her, probably still angry about Genway. Meera didn't care.

Isbaen had Gendryl with him, and she hugged him as well. "Did you fly here?" she asked the shy knell man.

Everyone laughed; apparently getting Gendryl onto Hillgari had been an event. Meera laughed along with them but squeezed Gendryl's shoulder in reassurance. She thought he was brave and acclimating well to their little group. She remembered how hard it had been for her to live among the riders at first.

"Sit and eat, Meera!" Katrea bid her.

Meera did as she was told, though her stomach fluttered too much for her to reap much enjoyment from her food.

"Have you been preparing?" Shael asked her.

She shook her head dolefully. "I have been sitting in meetings for two days. Don't ask me what was said—I've blocked it all out already," she replied.

Hadjal gave her an exasperated look. "Those meetings were extremely important," she told her.

"Were they?" Meera asked rhetorically. She hoped Darreal was pleased by her poise and restraint in the meetings, but now it was time for her to show the knell that humans could be as fierce as they were.

"You look ready," Soleille said, eyeing her face.

"Of course, she is ready!" Katrea cried, slapping Meera on the back and nearly knocking her out of her chair.

"Do not cripple her before the fight!" Soleille told Katrea.

"I'm fine!" Meera said quickly, hoping Soleille wouldn't scan her body. She wasn't ready to know whether her recent suspicions were true.

Kennick saw her expression and must have assumed she was feeling anxious about the fight because he took her hand and gave her a bolstering smile. Meera took a deep breath and exhaled it shakily.

ALL TOO SOON, she was standing at the edge of the Champion's Stadium located on the far western side of the estate. Removing her sword from her back, she unsheathed it. Kennick held out his hand to sharpen the blade, and Meera grimaced; she had never actually cut into anyone with her sword and never wanted to. Her heart was thumping in her chest in anticipation. The air rang with near deafening noise from the large crowd in the stand despite how quiet and reserved knell tended to be. She thought there must be a huge gathering to see the fight, but she couldn't yet see the spectators from her position.

"You better go take your seat," she told Kennick. Lethian stood nearby and looked ready. Meera assumed they would be called out soon. Kennick bent to give her a kiss before leaving, but she barely kissed him back—she was too distracted.

As he turned to go, she grabbed his arm. "Take this," she said, pulling off her ring and handing it to him. He looked a little surprised, so she explained, "I don't want to worry about it while I'm fighting."

He nodded and pocketed the ring. He had no sooner left to climb the stadium when Darreal's voice rang out over the crowd. She was not exceedingly loud, but everyone immediately quieted. "I welcome current champion, Lethian, and competitor, Meera Hailship!" she cried.

Meera and Lethian looked at one another before walking out onto the bare expanse of dirt. The stadium was well-used, and Meera assumed many knell trained there. Seats rose up behind her as she strode toward the center of the large area, but they only spanned in a half circle. The other side of the stadium was open to wildflower fields beyond where Shaya and the other riders' raeken were gathered to watch the fight. Meera stared at them; as accustomed as she was to having raeken around her, it was very strange and awe-provoking to see them all standing in a line with one another. Their multi-colored feathers and scales dazzled in the light of the sun—beautiful distractions from their deadliness.

Turning to face the queen, she felt suddenly exposed by the amount of faces staring back at her. She almost wished they would all blur together, but her knell eyes could make out every detail of their expressions as they appraised her and her competitor. Lethian seemed unconcerned, stretching his legs and swinging his sword to loosen his arms. Meera stood still as a startled rabbit. Then she caught sight of Kennick and the others in the stadium, and she smiled up at them. Kennick winked at her, and she blew him a kiss, causing a lot of whispering in the crowd.

"Your Kennick is a fine warrior," Lethian remarked.

Meera turned to him and smiled. She liked Lethian—he was both straight-forward and understated.

"Do you think you can win?" he asked her earnestly.

She shrugged. "I'm not sure if I want to," she said honestly. "I have seen the way you look at Darreal, and I think she already has the best champion for the job. My focus lies elsewhere."

Lethian looked down somewhat bashfully. "Let us at least put on a good show," he replied.

Meera nodded and grinned. Then they stepped apart from one another and waited for Darreal's signal. Meera gripped her sword loosely in her right hand and rolled her shoulders back, channeling Aegwren. She hoped he was with her in spirit, and when she carried his sword, she often felt that he was.

"Begin!" Darreal called from her seat in the front center of the stadium. The crowd stilled and tensed.

Meera shut her eyes, conjuring a view of her surroundings by sensing the air and the ground beneath her. She paid special attention to the rocks and dirt in the stadium because she knew Lethian had rock shaping abilities. She could see him clearly in her mind's eye and waited for him to move, sword still loose by her side. The warrior seemed to hesitate, surprised by her stance, but she did not take advantage of his surprise; her natural tendency was always toward defense.

Her heart beat rapidly in anticipation, and her stomach churned, but she cleared her mind, bringing herself only to the present and to the movements in her surroundings. When Lethian finally acted, he did so quickly—coming at her with his sword. Meera let him, waiting until the last moment to spin easily out of the way, keeping her knees bent and preparing herself for his next move. It came almost immediately.

For a while, Lethian attacked with his blade, and Meera evaded and parried the attacks. She began to feel that Lethian moved in a rhythm and fought the urge to be lulled by his repetition. She remembered Fendwren warning Aegwren to never fight in rhythm and suspected Lethian knew better and was trying to trick her. Remaining on edge, she wasn't surprised when, during Lethian's next assault, the ground shifted beneath her—she felt the slightest tremor in the dirt and jumped into the air to avoid the hole Lethian created.

No sooner had Meera leapt, than hard-packed pellets of dirt flew at her from all directions. She shaped a gust of wind to blow them off-course while midair and parried the blow Lethian tried to deal her from below with his sword. Unable to touch back down, she shaped a chunk of ground from below to soar up under her, and she pushed off of it to leap clear of Lethian, landing unconcernedly with her back to her opponent.

Lethian's attack persisted with both sword and shaping, and Meera began to enjoy herself. She had never fought like this before—using both her sword and her abilities—and it felt freeing. A smile appeared on her face, and pale flames licked down her skin and blade. She knew she could end the fight at any moment—she could burn Lethian to nothingness in a second if she wanted to—but that was not the point of the challenge. She was there to impress the spectators. Besides, she was having too much fun to want the match to end.

Meera started getting fancy with her shaping; she distracted Lethian with harmless bursts of raek fire to change her position and flung endless dirt pellets toward him, but she never truly attacked. He, however, continued to attack her, and she had fun coming up with new and creative ways of evading him—blowing clouds of dirt in his face and disappearing into large holes in the ground.

When it came to rock shaping, Lethian could overpower her in a struggle over the same patch of ground, so Meera relied mostly on her wind with some extraneous raek fire just for show.

There wasn't any water around for her to manipulate, and she hadn't yet learned how to pull moisture from the environment. They were putting on a spectacular show from what she could tell from the crowd's reactions, but she supposed at some point she would have to forfeit or attack. Still, she was in no hurry; she and Lethian were far from exhausted.

After a while, however, Meera began breathing hard and registered her thirst. She swallowed quickly to relieve her throat, and it was then—in that briefest moment—that Lethian took her by surprise: she had just averted a wave of dirt and dodged a two-part sword attack and had thought Lethian was turning to his left to face her again, but he turned jaggedly to his right, swinging for her backhanded with an awkward jerk of his elbow. His blade moved so quickly, she could not build up wind or rock in time to thwart it, nor parry with her blade.

Meera yanked her body back only a breath before Lethian's sword swiped across where her abdomen had been. He left a hairline cut on the fabric of her shirt. Air caressed the sweat-slick skin of her stomach just above her waist band, and hot terror throbbed in her gut. She felt a sudden rush of fierce protectiveness that went beyond the fear of injury, and in that fleeting whisper of time, Meera realized two things: she was pregnant, and it was time to end the fight.

Scorching raek fire emanated from her body in torrents, circling Lethian. A swipe of clawed wind sent his sword careening into the air and rent gashes in his clothes but left his skin unmarred. The ground trembled and shifted with Meera's emotion, and the next thing she knew, water gushed from below them and swirled with her raek fire as it enclosed her opponent, spitting bursts of lethal steam where they touched. Meera had never released her power so fully and opened her eyes to stare in awe at the devastation that escaped like a sigh from within her.

Her darting gaze snagged on Lethian, who stood gaping at her with pale flames reflected in his eyes. The sight of his fear grounded her. With a thought, she extinguished her fire, stilled the air and ground, and let the water soak back into the dirt. The stadium went completely motionless—leaving her and Lethian staring at one another across an expanse of empty air. For a moment, the world seemed to exhale, then the stadium crowd suddenly erupted in shouts and movement. Still clutching her sword in both hands, Meera turned and faced the onlookers.

The faces of the many spectators overwhelmed her; she was bombarded by expressions of fear—fear and revulsion. There was so much noise she wanted to clap her hands over her ears, but she held her sword raised, sensing the crowd's unease and volatility. Would they attack her as one? Try to wipe out the anomaly that she was? She reached mentally for Shaya, who had already spread her wings in readiness and bared her teeth.

The match hadn't truly ended; she and Lethian were both still able to fight. However, neither one of them moved to attack the other, nor did either of them think to forfeit. The crowd held their attention like a riled beast—jittering and swaying in agitation. Meera began to process what she had done—what she had been capable of—and her chest heaved with ragged breaths. She couldn't blame them for their fear; she was a lethal weapon. Her mind flashed to the duke, Linus, and Shael. She had hurt before, and with these abilities, she would inevitably hurt again.

Shaking, she stumbled back a step and continued to stare at the individual faces of the crowd, digesting their terror and their hate and letting it corrode her. Her gaze landed on Kennick—her Kennick—and in his dark eyes was the same fear. Meera's insides crumbled. She couldn't be there. She pleaded to Shaya in a stran-gled mix of words, images, and emotions to get her out of there.

Shaya obeyed. She leapt into the air, frightening the crowd

further. Knell began to scream and run, but the raek merely swooped down over Meera and snatched her gently in her claws. Meera held Aegwren's sword out away from her body to avoid accidentally wounding Shaya with its lethal blade. Then she screwed her eyes shut against the world and let herself be carried away.

12

MEERA

Meera didn't flee to the peninsula this time; climbing onto Shaya's back, she sent her raek an image of Aegwren's cave. She was shaking and shaken; she wanted to retreat and be as alone as she felt. She craved the comfort of her solitary dwelling in the mountains, and when they arrived, she slumped onto the bed and didn't move or even think for a long time.

Eventually, her insistent hunger roused her, and she peeled herself away from the blankets to take inventory of her food stores. She had meant to return to the cave and replenish its stocks of food, but she had forgotten. She was intimately familiar with the dwindling sacks of grain that remained and reluctantly made herself a bowl of mush to eat.

That day, she let herself wallow. She felt the pain of seeing so many people direct their fear and hatred toward her. She drew an image of Kennick's face to her mind's eye over and over again and puzzled over what he might have felt, assuming the worst. She called herself an abomination for the things she could do and cursed herself as a fool for getting pregnant. That day, she could see no glimmering light of hope and could figure no way out of the mess she had made of her life. That day, she wept and lay in bed and ignored Shaya.

WHEN MEERA FINALLY FELL ASLEEP, she fell unexpectedly into Aegwren's body. She didn't know if she was dreaming or if she had somehow found the memory in Shaya's mind. Either way, it was a relief to be with her friend once more. They were not in the training clearing this time. Rather, they were in a village or town. Aegwren walked down a dirt road with an armful of supplies from a market. He saw an older, grizzled man approaching, and Meera felt his inward dread and resignation.

"Aegwren, get that home to your mother, then ready yourself. It is well past time for your first hunt," the grey-haired, grey-bearded man told him.

Meera felt Aegwren's unease, but he merely nodded and stepped away from the man, avoiding horse dung in the road. Then he entered a small wooden house and unburdened his purchases on a table. A middle-aged woman—his mother, she presumed—came around the corner with a tired smile on her face. She wore a simple dress, and her hair was pulled back under a cap of sorts. When she looked into Aegwren's eyes, her smile faded. "What is it, my son? What is amiss?" she asked.

"Coltran says it is time for me to hunt," Aegwren replied. Meera was getting the impression it was not game they were to hunt, but raeken.

Fear and panic filled his mother's lined face, and she gripped his arm with an unexpected strength considering her thin frame. "No! Please! Damn him! Damn Coltran and his hunts! He has taken my husband from me, and now he will take my son!" The woman was so overcome, she struggled for breath, and Aegwren gripped her arms and helped her to sit. More quietly she said, "Fendwren has been keeping him away from you—fending him off—but now that he ... Oh, I fear I am doomed to lose you all." She put her hands to her face and sobbed.

At the mention of Fendwren, Meera felt Aegwren's still raw grief at the loss of his uncle. She felt her own, too, for the ghost of a man she had never really met.

"I will tell him 'no,' Mother," he said quietly.

"But then you would have to leave," his mother gasped between sobs. "The town would label you a coward and cast you out! I will lose you either way."

"If I am to be a man now, I would rather be a man who walks his own path than a man who follows others into a war he does not understand. There is something I must do, anyway. Can you bide without me, Mother? Will you manage?" he asked.

The woman sniffed in her tears and sat up straight in her chair, clasping her strong hands around her son's. "I am your mother. I will do whatever you need me to do," she told him.

Aegwren nodded gravely, kissed his mother, and left the house, walking back down the road in the direction from which he had come. Meera wondered where he meant to go and what he meant to do. She wondered if he would be as alone and outcast as she now felt.

In what looked like the town center, men were gathering with weapons—mostly spears. Aegwren scratched his cheek, and Meera could feel that it bore the beginnings of a new beard but nothing like the long ones on the faces of the men he approached. Aegwren was still young; this was only shortly after she had last lived in his memories. The grey, grizzled man—Coltran—greeted him as he approached, but his face turned wary when he saw that

Aegwren carried no weapon. "Where is your sword?" he asked in a low, accusatory voice that garnered the attention of the other men.

"I am not going with you," Aegwren replied simply. "There is something else I must do—something my uncle asked me to do for him."

"Your uncle?" Coltran boomed. "Your uncle was also a coward! I had hoped you would have your father's grit. Tell me, Aegwren, what chore does your uncle require of you from beyond the grave?" He asked in a way that provoked the other men to laugh and jeer, and Meera winced inwardly, not wanting to face the harsh judgment of another crowd of people even if it was not her they judged.

"He asked me to scatter his ashes with my father's. I will depart for the mountains in the morning. I may not return, and I ask that you all remember my father's sacrifice and look after my mother in my absence," Aegwren replied calmly, though Meera could feel his anger and resentment toward the men churning in his gut. Then he turned to walk away, but someone grabbed his arm, and he spun, ready to defend himself.

It was Coltran, but the man looked calmer than before. He reached out to Aegwren beseechingly. "Aegwren, forgive me for speaking ill of your dead. I know how much you loved your uncle —but think! That is why you must join us! These beasts rain hell-fire upon our lives and plague us with illnesses. It is not until they are all dead and gone that our village will blossom in peace and prosperity. Come! Come with us!" the man implored.

What nonsense, Meera thought. It reminded her of the dung she had heard criers fling about raeken in the streets of Altus. They were words full of emotion but free from logic.

"Fendwren's illness was not caused by raeken," Aegwren replied incredulously. "They are but animals, Coltran. They are large and deadly and dumb, but they are animals—they do not cause all of our suffering."

Coltran scoffed at Aegwren's words and shoved him away, shouting insults at him as he strode back to his mother's house. His mother no longer sat at the table crying; she was packing food and supplies into a sturdy canvas bag. Aegwren felt both joy and trepidation at the sight. To have his mother's support meant everything to him, and yet, to leave was to leave her. He went into his room to pack his clothes, but instead, he picked up the sealed clay jar containing some of Fendwren's remains and stared at it for a long time.

His uncle had requested he make this long and arduous journey. Aegwren would do it for that reason alone, but he suspected Fendwren had had another reason for the request; he suspected his uncle had foreseen Coltran's pressure and sought to get Aegwren out of the village. He suspected the journey was for him, and he thanked his Uncle Fendi for the final gift and the final lesson. For it was a lesson: he told Aegwren to stand on his own, and so he would.

Aegwren unwrapped the other gift his uncle had left for him to admire it. It was a sword—a beautiful carved sword with a large opal set into the hilt. Fendwren had meant the sword to be an eighteenth birthday gift for Aegwren, but he had given it to him when he lay sick instead, knowing he would not recover. Many did not recover from that sickness. He had said that opals were not the strongest or most precious of gems, but they stood for love and hope. He had bid Aegwren to choose both over hate.

Suddenly, Meera awoke with a gasp and sat up in her bed, disoriented. It took her several blinks to remember where she was. She stared around at Aegwren's cave, which was only just visible in the light of dawn filtering through its entrance. Then she looked down at herself to become reacquainted with being in her own body. Noticing the slice in her shirt, she remembered the fight the day before, and with a sigh, she fell back against her pillow.

Fleeing the fight felt cowardly after living through Aegwren's memory. She wished she had stood her ground and stood up for herself. She had not hurt Lethian, after all. Kennick and the riders had been there to support her, and she had left them behind. She hadn't even given Kennick the chance to overcome his shock and fear. Meera fingered her bare ring finger, missing her ring. Then, on a whim, she got up and opened the trunk where she had found Aegwren's sword. She remembered it had contained armor and other treasures.

Rifling through the odd bits of jewels, she pulled out a platinum ring. She thought maybe she could shape it to bring back to Kennick; she hated that she had left him and didn't want to return empty-handed. Staring hard at the ring, she tried to sense it—to shape it in any way at all. Nothing happened. She channeled all of her love for Kennick and desire to give him something precious, and yet, nothing happened.

Getting up, she decided to eat something. Shaping Kennick a ring might take a while, and she was hungry. While she cooked some grain, Meera pondered the memory she had experienced. She knew it was not a dream; she had never dreamt anything like Aegwren's memories before. "Shaya, did you show me that memory?" she asked mentally. Her raek was outside eating the mountain goat she had already hunted for her breakfast.

"No," Shaya replied. "I thought you dreamed powerful dreams."

Meera wondered whether she had found the memory in Shaya's mind with her subconscious. The other, stranger, possibility was that Aegwren had somehow showed it to her. She didn't know whether that could be possible, but she wouldn't have thought anything that she had experienced since meeting Shaya would have been possible. Regardless of how she had come to experience the memory, Meera was left wanting to know more. She had missed Aegwren and yearned to know his story. She wondered whether she might dream again if she stayed in the cave that night. The thought shamed her since she already felt bad for leaving Kennick, but it tempted her all the same.

She spent the entire day trying to shape the platinum ring without any success. She didn't manage to alter it at all. By the time she gave up in frustration, it was already nearing dark, and she decided to return to the peninsula in the morning. She opened the trunk to throw the platinum ring back inside, livid with herself that she would now be returning both later and empty-handed. The ring clanked onto the pile of miscellaneous treasures, but before she could close the lid, something caught her eye.

Stooping, she picked up a large, rough-cut black rock. She supposed it was a gem, really, because it shone in the firelight like one. She liked the dark stone—it reminded her of Kennick's dark, gleaming eyes. Meera pondered what it might be and whether she could shape it like she could the common rocks and dirt found in Levisade. She had managed to shape the marble floor in Andreena's dining room, though it had been difficult for her.

She thought she might be able to shape a ring from the stone, but she didn't want to try until she figured out what it was and whether it would break easily once it was whittled down. Rifling through the chest once more, she pulled out various gems and held them in her left hand while she held the black one in her right. She sensed each gem and compared them.

The black stone didn't feel quite like the rubies in a pair of earrings, nor the cabochon sapphire set into a gold goblet. Tired and frustrated, Meera kept digging, testing the rock against other gems even if she didn't recognize what they were anyway. Finally, she pulled out a ring with a diamond set into it. She sensed the diamond and found, to her surprise, that it felt almost identical to the black stone. Did diamonds come in black? She supposed so since she seemed to be holding one.

The next question was whether she could shape diamonds. Meera figured if she could sense it, she could shape it, but she could tell it wouldn't be easy. Stretching and rubbing her eyes, she shut the trunk and put the black stone on top to look at the next day. Then she extinguished the lamps on the walls and plopped onto the bed.

The second she shut her eyes to sleep, she was once more in Aegwren's body. Memories flashed by quickly as she experienced his long journey with him. He walked from his mother's house across a large stretch of land and through a seemingly endless forest to reach the base of a mountain range that Meera immediately recognized as the one she currently inhabited.

Aegwren walked, carrying his supplies on his back and hunting with traps as he went. Overall, Meera thought he was doing a much better job on his journey than she had on hers. Even so, she felt his strain and his exhaustion. Alone without distraction, his thoughts darkened, and doubt filled him—doubt that he was doing the right thing; he worried constantly about his mother and dreaded his unknown future.

Slowly, he climbed into the mountains, searching for a high peak that had been described to him as looking like an eagle's head. His father had been incinerated by a raek at the base of the eagle's sharp beak. Aegwren missed his father and mourned him, yet he could not help but rage at him for leaving his family to hunt dangerous creatures. Could raeken be blamed for killing men who approached their nests with spears? Would a bear or a wolf or a man not do the same?

It took many weeks for Aegwren to find the right mountain peak. He thinned as his food stores dwindled and he struggled to catch much to eat on the mountainside. It was summer, but the winds often beat him down. And when they dissipated, the sun threatened to roast him. Meera could feel him weakening as his scraggly beard grew thicker and longer on his cheeks, but he did not stop and slowly approached his destination. He had found the eagle's beak in the distance and stumbled steadily toward it. He was almost there.

Aegwren sensed the storm before it came. There was little shelter so high up, but he was unwilling to turn back—he was so close. He considered breaking the urn he carried and letting the mountain winds whip his uncle to join his father, but he felt honor-bound to complete his journey to the best of his ability; he walked on even as the sky darkened and clouds approached from a distance. Meera might have warned him not to, but she was a silent observer in his mind.

In desperation, Aegwren removed the clay pot containing his uncle's ashes from his bag and left the bag wedged between two rocks. He would be faster without the weight and resolved to retrieve his supplies on his way back down the slope. Despite his exhaustion and the raw, bleeding skin under his now too-small boots, he ran for the eagle's beak, his uncle clasped in his hand. The clearest path up was along the edge of a rock wall, perched over a valley below.

Aegwren meant to outrun the coming storm, but it was too fast for him; he heaved in ragged breaths and pumped his arms, but his slow, unwieldy progress up the craggy slope was no match for the smooth advance of nature's fury. First came the rain—pelting and blinding him in his ascent. Then came the winds. Nothing Aegwren had experienced thus far had prepared him for the brutal thrusts of wind that bore down on him. Crouching, he tried to grab ahold of something—anything—but his efforts were futile; there was nothing but him and the raging air.

He threw himself down toward the ground, but a gust caught him in his fall and forced him out over the edge of the sloping cliff. He plummeted even as wind continued to batter his hopelessly flailing form. Meera felt his terror as his stomach flew into his throat, and his mouth gaped in a helpless, strangled cry. He smacked against one protruding rock, then another, then another, slowing his descent even as he was bludgeoned near senseless. His uncle's clay urn flew from his hand, smashing on the hard stone below—inaudible over the shrieking wind. Aegwren hit the valley floor a moment later and lay still, beaten and broken. His pain and shock mingled with Meera's fear. Rain soaked into his clothes and ran in rivulets off his skin, but he did not move.

Meera awoke shouting for Aegwren and twisting in her bedding. She was soaked but with sweat not rain, and it took her several minutes to slow her breathing and calm her mind. He survived—she knew he survived. It was a memory that had happened thousands of years ago, she reminded herself. Still, she trembled and choked back sobs for her friend, wishing she could rejoin him. There was no way she could sleep now, however, so there was nothing she could do but rise from her bed and live her own life, forgetting for the moment about Aegwren's.

13

MEERA

Meera rose, ate some leftover grain mush, and picked up the large, rough cut black diamond she had found the night before. She took it out into the valley with her to appraise it in the light of morning. Shaya was not there, and Meera assumed she was hunting. She could only hope the raek would not get distracted and leave her in the mountains alone indefinitely.

Staring at the dark, liquid surface of the gem in her hand, she debated whether she should return to Kennick right away or wait until she had made him a ring. However, since Shaya was not there to fly her, Meera supposed she might as well start trying to shape the diamond and sat down by the creek to do so. The valley was silent except for the soft trickle of water before her.

First, she picked up a more ordinary grey rock from the edge of the creek and took the time to shape it as she imagined shaping the diamond. She had to guess at the size; she had put Kennick's many rings on her own fingers enough times to have an idea of how large to make it but no way of knowing exactly what size would fit him. Shaping off straight cuts of rock that would accentuate the reflective surface of the diamond was very different from her usual rock shaping which tended to be more freeform. She was usually clumping rocks and dirt and moving them without caring what they looked like. Getting the straight edges she desired took much more concentration and effort—and that was just on the common rock.

Eventually, she created a shape she liked with the grey rock and put it in front of her to use as a model for the diamond. Then she picked up the glistening black stone and got to work trying to shape it. Her progress was extremely slow. Each cut took her full concentration, and she shaved the diamond away in slivers to avoid potentially cutting off too much and not having enough for a solid ring. Meera was so engrossed in her efforts, she didn't even notice when Shaya returned to the valley, let alone consider flying home.

She worked for the majority of the day on her ring, making steady progress but not finishing. Eventually, her hunger forced her to put away her task and scrounge something to eat. Shaya had brought her some goat meat, which she cooked quickly with her raek fire and devoured. She did not speak to her raek, nor her raek to her; they simply coexisted in the valley in companionable silence. Meera supposed it was better than their usual arguments and random attacks—it was progress of a sort.

That night, she was so anxious to fall asleep and be reunited with Aegwren that it took her a long time to relax. When she finally drifted off, the first thing she registered from Aegwren's consciousness was pain; she felt the all-too familiar stabbing ache of broken ribs as well as pain in his head and his left arm. His legs, at least, felt relatively unharmed considering how far he had fallen.

For a time, Aegwren's eyes were closed, and Meera couldn't see anything. When he blinked them open, the rain had stopped, and he stared uncomprehendingly at grey rock. He tried to move, but the pain in his left arm—which was pinned under him—jarred him, and he froze, trembling. Then, very slowly, he used his right hand to push himself off the ground and onto his knees. The movement flooded his left arm with even more searing pain as blood rushed back into the numb limb.

Aegwren looked down, saw his forearm bent at the wrong angle, and quickly looked away, swaying. He managed to get his feet under him and pushed, teetering, to stand. Then he blinked dizzily. When his vision cleared, he was staring into an enormous pair of green raek eyes not ten feet in front of him. His heart stopped then skittered to life again, beating rapidly against his aching ribs. The dark grey raek blended into the stone wall she was crouched against, but her eyes were a bright, startling green that shone clearly against her surroundings. Isabael, Meera realized with excitement.

Meera looked around in Aegwren's peripheral vision even as he stood staring at the raek in frozen horror. She recognized the valley they were in as the one she now inhabited. Then, with a jolt, she realized that Aegwren and Isabael had met in much the same way she and Shaya had met—brought together by a storm under the overhang of a rock wall. She tingled with the strangeness of it, but she struggled to think clearly through the haze of Aegwren's overwhelming pain.

"That is odd," Shaya said, a distant voice in her mind.

Meera's attention was quickly drawn back to Aegwren when he spoke—well, first he laughed breathily. "Did you send me here to have the same resting place as you and my father, Uncle?" he asked in a rasping, disused voice, glancing at the shattered remnants of the clay urn nearby. "Are we to be reunited so soon?"

He continued to laugh in a choked, delirious kind of way. Then he looked back at the raek that he had inadvertently cornered where Meera knew the cave entrance was. "I wonder if you are the very beast that killed my father," he said ponderously. "I am ready to meet him. I ask only that you make it quick."

Isabael was thrumming with a low warning hum, her green eye fixed unblinkingly on Aegwren's swaying figure. But she looked more frightened than murderous, Meera thought.

"Well?" Aegwren asked impatiently. Meera could feel his hopelessness and resignation. He was hurt with inadequate supplies and no home to return to regardless. She could relate to his feelings; when she had journeyed to find her father, she had felt much the same way, but she had maintained the hope that the riders would find her. With another jolt, Meera realized that she and Aegwren had both been seeking their fathers, in a sense. What did all of this mean?

Losing her patience, Isabael opened her mouth threateningly and crept from her corner. Her warning hum grew in intensity, and she lunged toward Aegwren, stopping short of him and retreating. He winced but did not fall back or cry out; he stood and waited, resigned to his death and hoping to meet it with bravery rather than sobbing, begging, cowardice. His only regret was that his mother would wait for him and wonder for the rest of her life whether he would return. He consoled himself with the thought that he would explain his death to her when they met in the afterlife.

Isabael shifted forward one step and opened her mouth wider, forming a swirling sphere of green raek fire within. It grew as she approached and unhinged her jaw. Aegwren's heart clenched in his chest, but he did not back away. He shed a single tear for his mother and hoped that his uncle would have swords with which to spar wherever they were to meet again. Then—when the raek fire was only a step away from Aegwren's body and sweat trickled down his face—Isabael suddenly clamped her jaws shut. Raising her great head, she cocked it to the side and appraised him through one bulging green eye.

"She sees in him what I saw in you," Shaya said approvingly. "The heart of a warrior."

Meera was beginning to feel uncomfortable in this memory. She couldn't understand all of the similarities between her story and Aegwren's and struggled to process them through his over-whelming pain. Was she living through some sort of destiny? Was she in control of her life? She didn't like the thought that her life was possibly not her own—that she was living out a preordained path that Aegwren had lived as well. Was she being controlled?

The memory flickered and blackened as she woke herself up. It was still dark outside, but she sensed that the sun would rise soon. Lying in bed, staring at the blackness around her, she continued to trouble over the patterns connecting her life with Aegwren's. What did it all mean?

"It means the world is more complex than we will ever understand," Shaya said simply.

"Doesn't that bother you?" Meera asked mentally. "What if we are pawns and aren't really making our own decisions?"

"I make my own decisions," Shaya said with certainty.

Meera huffed a laugh because she knew that was true.

"You do as well," the raek added. "The world has patterns like the phases of the moon and the leaves falling. It is always moving in circles, and we move with it. Perhaps the phases of war and peace between races are cyclical and seasonal, perhaps not. Would you not still fight for your race as I fight for mine? Would you not have still sought your father across these mountains?"

Meera pondered Shaya's words and found that she was right; whether or not Meera was living some sort of recurring pattern, she would still choose to fight for the people she loved and the peace she believed in. Then she recalled something Kennick had told her she had said on their walk together after the Spring Equinox bonfire—something she had said about the moon not caring whether she was called the moon and shining down on them regardless—and she supposed what Shaya said was similar in a way; Meera was who she was no matter what she was called or what made her that way.

"Thank you," she said to Shaya. She felt a lot better and thought Shaya's reassuring words were perhaps the kindest her raek had ever been to her. She found them immensely comforting. She sensed some embarrassment in Shaya's mental energy before the raek abruptly announced that she was going hunting and broke their connection.

Meera got up and spent some time meditating and clearing her thoughts before working on Kennick's ring. She was in it now, she decided; she would finish the ring as quickly as she could, then she would return home and hope that Kennick could still love her after her display at the challenge and her absence. While she felt wary of seeing any more of Aegwren's memories, she supposed whether she experienced them or not, they had already happened; knowing about them did not need to alter her life. Then Meera suppressed a thought about the child growing in her stomach that would, undoubtedly, alter her life.

By the end of the day, she was almost done shaping the black diamond ring. Slipping it onto her finger, she spun it around in the light of her oil lamps to admire how it glinted in the firelight. In anticipation of finishing the next day, she washed her body, clothes, and hair, drying them all with her wind shaping. She went to bed with the black diamond on her ring finger in place of her own ring, which she missed, knowing it would likely fall off as she slept. Then she shut her eyes, resolutely ready to continue Aegwren's journey with him.

———————

MEERA OPENED her eyes and blinked, disoriented. She wasn't in Aegwren's body—she knew that immediately because he always felt familiar and comfortable. From her vantage point looking down on the valley and the odd, unworded thoughts flitting through her mind, she figured she was in Isabael's body, sitting on the wall and looking down at Aegwren. Meera thought it was the same day, but Aegwren appeared to have gone and gotten his supplies.

Isabael watched him with curiosity; she had never seen a human in the mountains before. Meera could feel the raek's fascination with Aegwren, having found him braver than she would have expected one of the strange, wingless creatures that hunted her kind with pointy non-claws to be. Isabael realized Aegwren was injured by the way he held his broken arm and walked haltingly, and she seemed to want to observe him and learn how such a defenseless creature would survive in the mountains.

Meera gaped in horror, watching through Isabael's pitiless eyes as Aegwren tried to set the bones in his own arm. The raek did not react to his strangled cries as he tugged at his left hand with his right to realign his forearm, but Meera had to look away from the scene, gorge rising in her distant throat. Finally, Aegwren gave his arm a mighty heave to straighten it. His scream rose with his effort but quickly cut off when he passed out and fell on his side.

Isabael leapt down from her perch above and sniffed at his body to see if he was dead. Meera knew he was not and wished that she could tend to him—wipe his bloody head and bring water to his cracked lips—but she could not; she could only watch from inside the raek's body in frustration. She had never felt quite so restrained in Aegwren's body. He usually acted in a way she could approve of. Isabael, however, was a creature very different from herself.

That memory flickered and was replaced by another, in which Isabael flew overhead and observed Aegwren cooking a rabbit over a fire, his left arm in a sling. He was thin and dirty and haggard, but he had meat to eat and the cave to crawl into at night. Meera learned from Isabael's flashing thoughts that she had recently fledged a young one, and she could tell that the grey raek felt somewhat listless without her child to care for and teach. Meera supposed Isabael's interest in Aegwren was related, and she tried not to think of her own imminent child.

Aegwren often watched Isabael fly by or stared at her when she perched on the lip of the valley, but he never attempted to approach nor commune with the raek. It was Isabael who made the first tentative gesture of friendship; she had noticed Aegwren cooking food less and less often as he diminished the valley's small population of animals, and on a day when she found great success in her hunting with two mountain goats and a large boar, she thought to take Aegwren a piece of the boar rather than leave it for scavengers.

After waiting for him to enter his cave, she dropped the meat in the center of the valley and flew away. The raek did not seem to entirely understand her interest in the human man or her desire to see him fed, but she acted on her impulse regardless. When Aegwren next saw her, he waved a hand at her in thanks, and Isabael stared at the gesture and tried to decipher the strange communication. After a minute, she raised a wing in reply. Aegwren grinned at her, and Meera felt the raek studying him, learning his expression as a response to her action.

So began Isabael's fascination with Aegwren, and Aegwren, in turn, started to view Isabael as a friend and talk to her as such. Meera could imagine how lonely he was without anyone to talk to for so very long, and she was not surprised when Aegwren started to shout up at Isabael and tell her all sorts of things. It was the raek's attempts to understand what he said that surprised her. She supposed curiosity was not one of Shaya's strongest traits, but all raeken had their own personalities. She felt Shaya's mental snort in response to the thought.

Eventually, Aegwren healed enough and preserved enough dried meat to travel back down the mountainside. The end of summer was near, and he could not survive in the valley forever. Isabael followed his descent, curious to see where he would go and what he would do next. Meera could tell that the raek knew of the many feuds that had been waged between raeken and humans in the area, but she had rarely left the mountains and had remained untouched by the violence. She was not very old and had only just fledged her first hatchling. She thought to follow Aegwren and see how other humans lived without claws and feathers and strong jaws.

However, when Aegwren finally made it to the base of the mountain, he waved Isabael away. Meera could understand his words as he told her to go back to the safety of the high peaks, but the raek could not; she flew away, but she returned later. Again, Aegwren tried to shoo her—he pantomimed fighting and hunting and death, but the human's strange performance only heightened Isabael's fascination with his kind. Meera studied Aegwren with the raek. To her, he finally looked like a man—his beard was full and his body fully-grown. His eyes bore the weight of long solitude, but his kind spirit remained.

Meera opened her eyes to the light of a new day and sighed, wondering whether she would ever know how Aegwren finally came to ride Isabael and join their races. But when she lifted her hands to her face to rub her eyes, she found Kennick's ring still on her finger, and she felt a sudden urgent desire to see the man she loved. She didn't want to leave him wondering where she was or whether she would return any longer. She told Shaya they would leave that day, but first, she set out to finish the ring.

14

KENNICK

This time when Meera fled, Kennick did not stay back to retrieve their possessions; he immediately ran down from the stadium to follow her. She was safe, he knew, but he did not want her to run; he wanted her to stay and defend her right to be there. She had not done anything wrong, after all —she had not even left a scratch on Lethian during the challenge, even though she clearly could have done much worse.

Kennick had never seen her unleash herself like that, but he was not surprised by what Meera was capable of. He had, however, been surprised and frightened by the crowd's reaction. Knell did not normally get so riled; his race was usually calm and slow to act. Kennick did not wait to see how Darreal would handle the situation. He raced for Endu, who stood with the other raeken on the far side of the stadium. When he reached his raek, however, Endu refused to fly after Meera. "It is better that the human goes, Kennick, and it is better that you remain here with your kind," he insisted.

"Meera is my true mate, and I belong with her! How can you —a raek—argue with that?" Kennick asked in irritation.

"Kennick!" Before Endu could answer, Shael called to Kennick from Cerun's back and extended his hand in invitation.

Kennick did not hesitate to leap onto Cerun's back behind his friend and leave his own raek behind. They flew as fast as they could but could not catch up to Meera; Shaya was simply too large and too fast. When they did not find her at Kennick's house or at the peninsula, they knew she would have gone to Aegwren's cave in the mountains, but Meera had never given them details about where it was.

She was gone—he was too late to prevent her from running —so Kennick returned to his house, thanking Shael and Cerun for their efforts and friendship. All he could do was wait for Meera to return. He was not angry with her for fleeing even if she had fled him as well. He knew she had acted on instinct. What hurt was that she did not return that day or the next ... or the next.

On the fourth day after the challenge, Kennick finally went to the peninsula to rejoin the other riders. He could no longer sit at home and wait for her. He could not imagine why she would choose to be gone for so long, and his hurt turned to concern. He did not have the utmost faith in Shaya and feared the raek may have left Meera somewhere. He was beginning to contemplate searching for her in the mountains, but he had not seen Endu since the challenge either.

While Kennick usually managed not to let the thoughts and actions of others affect his opinion of himself, by day four of not hearing from Meera or Endu he was beginning to wonder why those he loved left him behind so easily. He supposed it was not a surprising thought considering his parents had thrown him out at fifteen, but Kennick had far more faith in Meera and his raek than he had ever had in his parents ... And yet, they were nowhere to be seen.

When he and the others sat down for dinner, Isbaen gave him a reassuring smile and pat on the back. "Meera left before and returned to us healthy. We have no reason to believe she will not do the same again," he said sagely.

Kennick nodded his head, but he could not help but glance at Shael who had been left waiting for Meera the last time she had disappeared. His friend gave him an understanding look. Kennick had seen Meera return with her arms open to Shael, and he had seen his friend's hurt feelings get in the way of their love for one another, so he decided right then that no matter how long Meera made him wait, he would greet her return with love and joy; he would open his arms to her in welcome. As it turned out, he did not have long to wait.

"Meera!" Katrea cried.

Kennick looked at her, thinking she meant to say more, but Katrea was gazing past him across the clearing. His heart leapt into his throat as he turned and saw Meera approaching from the path that led to their house. She had gone home for him and had come to find him here. He dropped his fork and ran for her.

Meera did not run to meet him, but she smiled as he reached her and squeezed him back when he threw his arms around her. "Kennick, I'm sorry," she said, sniffing back her tears against his shirt. "I shouldn't have left. Then—well, I got distracted, I guess."

She laughed as he gripped her face and covered it in kisses, ending on her mouth. When they broke apart, he wiped the tears from her cheeks. He stared into her brown eyes, and everything he needed to know in that moment was shining back at him from their depths. He did not have anything to say—not yet anyway. He kissed her again, more deeply this time, and she kissed him back with the same love and enthusiasm as always.

"That tastes good. What is it?" she asked when they broke apart. He laughed, wiping the tears from his own eyes. "There wasn't any food at home," she added. Hearing Meera refer to his house as home still felt surreal to Kennick.

"Come on," he said, leading her toward the table.

Gendryl was sitting next to Isbaen, so Meera would not fit on the end with him and instead sat in her old seat next to Shael. Kennick had to content himself with pressing his ankles against hers under the table, and she rubbed her feet against his claves in return. Everyone greeted her and gave her a chance to eat before they peppered her with questions and information. Kennick watched Meera eat, his own appetite forgotten, and she devoured everything on her plate like she had not seen food in the four days since the challenge.

"Slow down, Meera! It is not going anywhere," Sodhu told her.

Meera smiled ruefully and slowed herself down. When she finished her own food, she reached over and ate what was left on Kennick's plate as well. She could have it, he thought; she could have everything that was his, he only wished she would stop running away from him. "Meera, I need you to start running toward me—not away," he told her. He only had eyes for her; he did not care who else was present.

Meera's attention snapped immediately up to him, and she put her fork down. "I will. I promise," she said.

Kennick pushed aside their plates, took her hand across the table, and slipped her ring off of his pinky and back onto her ring finger where it belonged. She smiled. Then she reached for his left hand, broke a string he had not noticed tied around her neck, and slipped a ring onto his fourth finger. It was not the only ring he wore, but it was the only one that mattered and the most spectacular by far. Kennick admired the faceted edges of the black diamond in awe. He had never seen a ring cut from a solid gem before.

"It's too big," Meera lamented.

Kennick slid the ring off, shaped platinum from one of his other rings and added a layer of it to the inside of the black diamond so that it would fit snugly.

"There. Now it is adjustable," he told her.

She squeezed his hand in both of hers and sat back in her chair, saying, "You know? I think that was a beautiful ceremony. Can we call ourselves married now?"

Everyone at the table laughed, and Kennick grinned at her. "I think we can do better," he said. "Besides, Follaria would never forgive me if I told her to stop designing your dress." Meera did not look entirely pleased, and he wondered if she was reluctant to stand in front of people after the challenge. He did not know why else she would want to forgo a wedding.

"Can I see?" Isbaen asked, reaching for Kennick's hand. Kennick gave Isbaen his hand, then Gendryl and so on until everyone had gaped and exclaimed at the ring.

He loved the ring, but he had eyes only for Meera. "Where did you get such a large diamond?" he asked her. "Have you been holding out on me?" He knew she had made the ring; who else could shape diamond?

She merely shrugged and smirked coyly.

"Is this what you meant by getting distracted?" he asked her.

"Part of it. I wasted one day trying to make one out of metal, then shaping the diamond took me almost three days," she explained.

"You could have done that here," he replied quietly.

"Yes, but I spent my nights with another man," she teased.

"Mountain man? Do tell!" Soleille chirped.

Kennick had thought Meera was just joking, but then she said,

"I visited Aegwren in my sleep. I'm not sure how exactly, but I lived through more of his memories each night, and ... well, it was hard for me to leave and not learn what happened."

The other riders perked up, asking questions about what Meera had seen and learned and offering theories on how she had done so. Kennick did not ask any questions—he merely observed her face and tried to puzzle out how Meera felt about Aegwren. She had spoken before about missing him, and she had more or less just admitted to spending several days with the first rider instead of with him. Kennick did not know what that meant.

After Meera explained her absence, Hadjal told her how Darreal had pronounced her the new Queen's Champion. Kennick had not been there to see it, but he felt grateful to Darreal for taking a stand against the gathered knell and proclaiming her acceptance of Meera so publicly.

"What?" Meera asked, looking stricken. "I don't want to be champion!"

"She did it to protect and claim you," Kennick told her. "I am sure she does not expect you to spend your life standing behind her as Lethian does."

"Also, you have relieved me of the burden of teaching, Meera," Soleille said nonchalantly, clearly not sensing Meera's mood. "The twin's parents were at the challenge and refused to let them return to the peninsula. And do you know? They did not even seem to care! After I spent so much time molding them, they just turned their backs on me! Ungrateful little wretches. I think you did me a favor scaring their parents."

Kennick glared at Sol, wishing she would be a little more sensitive. Meera did not answer her; she looked suddenly weary like a raek stood upon her shoulders. Seeing her face, Kennick rose so that they could say their goodnights and walk home.

Meera followed without hesitation, continuing to look tired and thoughtful.

They were quiet for a while as they walked, both in their own minds even though they each knew there was more to say. Kennick held Meera's hand and focused on his joy at knowing she was at least safe and had returned to him. As they neared the house, however, his confusion rose to the surface of his thoughts. "Meera, do you love Aegwren—are you in love with him?" he finally asked.

She had clearly been lost in her own thoughts and stared at him blankly for a moment. "In love with him?" she asked. "No! I think that maybe I *am* Aegwren."

Kennick had heard Meera explain the parallels in their lives and understood what she meant. "Is he that much like you?" he asked, curious and relieved.

She shrugged. "We see the world in very similar ways, but when I'm sharing his consciousness, it feels different than mine. It's hard to describe. Plus, you know—the beard and the man parts," she joked.

He smiled at her, but her mood quickly sobered. She looked troubled and stopped him just before they entered the house. "I do have to tell you something," she said.

After his question about Aegwren, Kennick's mind immediately went to other men, but he had no notion who Meera could have possibly met since they had gotten together. "Do you want to go inside?" he asked. He felt the irrational desire to get Meera into the house like it would prevent her from leaving him again.

"No, I ... I need to just tell you," she said.

Kennick could see the anxiety in her face and her heart rate accelerating in her chest. A gaping pit of fear began to open in his stomach. He had no idea what she was about to say. He just looked into her eyes and waited.

Meera swallowed and took a deep breath. "Kennick, I ... think I'm pregnant," she said tremulously.

For a moment, he just stared at her, then the pit in his stomach closed up and sprouted wildflowers that tickled him from the inside. "Really?" he breathed. In all his years of lying with women, he had never even dreamed that he might father a child. Pregnancy was so rare among knell. He knew of people who had tried for hundreds of years before conceiving. Kennick had never even thought to fall in love, let alone have a baby with someone he loved. When Meera had expressed her desire to drink Soleille's tea, it had not bothered him because he had not thought it would make any difference. Now ... pregnant?

15

MEERA

Meera watched as Kennick's expression changed from one of dread to hope, and her own face tensed; it was hard for her to see all of his dreams come true and yet wish that they weren't. She wanted to feel the joy he clearly felt, but she didn't. When he cupped her face and kissed her, she tried to kiss him back but couldn't. Pulling away, she stared at her boots. She wished she could celebrate with him, but she felt so ... wrong.

He touched her cheek lightly to get her to look up at him. "What is it?" he asked.

"I ... didn't want this," she said, shaking her head and feeling tears flood her eyes. She wondered if Kennick would finally be angry with her—finally see something in her he couldn't love. He had been so welcoming when she'd returned, so accepting of her time away. She almost wished he would yell, so she could feel less guilty about the selfish decisions she had made.

"I know," he said softly. "Are you ... certain? Should I get Soleille?"

"No! Don't—please. I'm not ready for everyone to know. I'm not even ready for me to know. That's ... that's why I didn't tell you," she said.

"How long have you suspected?" he asked.

"Since the first time," she replied, wincing up at his shocked expression. "I felt something, but I didn't know what it was. I thought, maybe—but it was my first time ... I just didn't know what I was meant to feel. I thought I was being paranoid—I hoped I was being paranoid, but then Shaya said true mates are extra fertile. Then, later, she told me raeken know right away when they conceive, and I've been tired and nauseous and sore and even hungrier than usual. And I ... I should have told you earlier. I'm sorry," Meera said, letting it all pour out of her before studying Kennick's face, unsure how coherent she had been.

"What has it been—a month?" he asked, thinking back.

She nodded. It had been about a month. She put a hand absently to her stomach, then lowered it. He caught the movement, and his eyes snagged on the tear in her shirt. She grimaced, knowing what was coming next. "You fought a Champion's Challenge knowing you were pregnant?" he asked incredulously. His eyes kept returning to the cut in her shirt with horror. Clearly, he was imagining what might have happened.

Meera crossed her arms over her stomach. "I didn't know, exactly—I suspected. I hoped I wasn't, but when Lethian almost sliced my stomach ... I felt a surge of protective instinct. That's when I really knew," she explained. She could only suppose the rush of power and fierceness she had felt had also been a raek thing, but maybe it was just a mother thing.

Kennick nodded, frowning.

"It's ... all been a lot," she told him, her voice cracking.

He pulled her into his arms and held her tightly. "I have you,

Meera. I am here for you. If you would just run toward me ..." he said.

Meera knew he was right; she needed to stop fleeing every time things felt hard. She needed to lean on Kennick and share with him. She did lean into him, then, and they stood that way a long time.

"I love my ring, by the way," he said, pulling away to admire it. She knew he was being nice by changing the subject for a while. "I still want to see you in a wedding dress, though," he added, bending to kiss her.

"I don't want to be a pregnant bride, Kennick," she said, biting her lip.

"Why not?" he asked.

"It's embarrassing—for humans, anyway. I know that knell don't care, but I'm not all knell ... By the way, I'm a little terrified our baby will have feathers or something," she admitted, laughing. If she was part-raek, maybe the baby was too. It felt good to share her silly fear and to laugh. Telling Kennick was a relief, in a way, even if the joy he was so obviously trying to hold back was a little much for her to handle.

He laughed and shrugged his shoulders. "Feathers could be interesting," he said. "A baby with claws might be an issue."

Meera laughed with him, but her worries soon returned. She edged around him to look across the small lake behind their house. The sun was setting, and the sky was awash with pinks and purples. "I'm not ready, Kennick. I'm supposed to be trying to end the war! My body only just changed! I'm still figuring out my abilities! I don't know anything about babies! I don't even know if I like them ... Part of me ... Part of me wonders if I should make it go away—if Soleille might be able to shape it out of me," she admitted, unable to look at him—too afraid to see the inevitable disgust in his face. Knell didn't use contraceptives, let alone end pregnancies.

Kennick wrapped his arms around her and held her from behind. "You are not doing everything alone, Meera, and you have a long life ahead of you to do it all. I think you forget that your lifespan is no longer that of a human. We can raise our baby to an adult and then work to end the war before you are older than Soleille is now. You have eight months to get ready—we do, together—and if you truly did not want this baby, you would not have felt so protective in your fight with Lethian," he said.

His words comforted her—to an extent. But Meera wondered if he was right, or whether her protective instinct was separate from her desires. She felt like it was her body that had protected the pregnancy while her mind now wondered whether she should have let Lethian hit her. Then she would not be pregnant or the Queen's Champion, and two of her burdens wouldn't exist. But she didn't voice the thought. She leaned back into Kennick and let him hold her up.

They watched the sky slowly darken. Then Kennick scooped Meera into his arms and carried her into the house, kissing her as he went. It felt good to be held, and it felt good to be kissed. Shutting her eyes, she let herself focus only on Kennick and how right it felt to be back with him. She tried to block out all of her other thoughts, but she could not help but notice how gentle he was being, how reverent his touches felt, and how his hands kept returning to her stomach. When they lay spent, he fell asleep quickly, but she tossed with her thoughts long into the night.

———

THE NEXT MORNING, Meera arose to find Kennick making breakfast in the kitchen. He was already fully dressed and appeared to have gone into town to buy pastries as well. He stood over a pan frying eggs and had already laid out a plate with meat, cheeses, and fruit. It looked to Meera like enough food for all of the riders. "Are we having company?" she asked, wondering if she should change out of the silk robe she wore.

"I just thought you might be hungry," he said, turning and kissing her good morning.

"Well, I am, but ... I don't think I'm quite this hungry," she said, gesturing to the array of food.

"I just want you to have plenty to eat," he replied.

Meera stared at Kennick blankly for a moment before realization dawned, and she understood why he was acting so strange. She thought about saying something but didn't actually want to talk about the pregnancy again, so she didn't. Instead, she broke a jam pastry in half and started eating.

"What do you want to do today?" Kennick asked, putting a plate in front of her and sitting down to eat.

Meera shrugged. "The same as usual, I suppose. I'd like to run around the lake and train—maybe some hand-to-hand. We could try covering you in metal and seeing if you can catch yourself from a fall," she suggested.

He furrowed his brows at her. "Should you really be training so hard?" he asked.

She stared at him. "Seeing as I'm the Queen's Champion and most of the knell in Levisade think that I should be captured and detained somewhere, I really think I ought to keep training and stay in shape," she replied sourly, avoiding his true question.

He put down his food and gave her a serious look. "Meera, come on. You cannot keep pretending—" he started to say.

"I'm not pretending anything! I'm just living my life however I want to live it as I have the right to do. I'm still me," she said angrily.

"Yes, but you are not *just* you at the moment," he reminded her annoyingly.

"I'm hardly bursting with child, Kennick. I think I can keep training. It hasn't done any harm so far," she replied.

"Maybe we should ask someone who actually knows ... I really think you should see a healer. Sol—"

"I don't want to!" Meera snapped.

"Why?" he asked calmly.

"Because I don't want to be pregnant! Don't you get that?" Standing, she stormed out of the house, forgetting she was still wearing one of Kennick's silk robes. Blood was rushing through her body, and she wanted to scream or run or something— anything. Since it was plenty warm out and she wasn't wearing clothes, Meera settled for swimming laps in the lake.

By the time she cooled off mentally and physically, Kennick was waiting for her with a towel. Part of Meera thought it was nice of him, but part of her wondered if he was still coddling her for being pregnant. "Afraid I'll get a chill and lose the baby?" she asked nastily, snatching the towel from his hand, but the expression in his dark eyes was so loving and patient, it made her immediately regret her words.

"I just want you to be safe," he said quietly.

"I know," she sighed. "But I just want to be treated the same as always. You've been weird ever since I told you."

Kennick frowned at her. "If by weird you mean happy, excited, concerned, and guilty then yes, I have been weird. But I cannot unknow now that I know ..." he said, taking her hands once she had donned her robe. "I never thought this would happen, Meera. For that I am both sorry to have put you in this position and grateful to you for carrying our child. I wish you would let me take care of you."

Meera shifted on her feet and struggled to meet his eyes. He was being so sincere and probably handling the news exactly like he should be, but she could not help but wish he were a fraction as upset and scared as she was. His readiness and acceptance was exactly what she should probably want from him, yet it left her feeling alone. She was already an anomaly among humans and knell, and now she seemed to be the only person in Levisade not overjoyed to conceive a child.

"Can we just wait a few days before we tell anyone?" she asked. "Please? Give me a little more time, then I'll ask Soleille to scan me. Then I'll ... act happy and everything."

"I am not asking you to act, Meera, I am just asking you not to pretend it is not happening," Kennick said. She could tell he was getting frustrated by how he kept pushing his hair behind his ears even though it wasn't falling forward.

"That's the same thing! If I announce that I'm pregnant, I'll have to smile when everyone congratulates me and pretend to be excited. I'm not ready to do that," she explained.

"Do you really think you will be any more ready in a few days?" he asked incredulously.

She didn't, and she knew it—she was only stalling. "I can try," she replied, crossing her arms over her chest.

"Okay. A few days, then," he agreed.

Meera walked around him to go inside and get dressed. She still wanted to go to the peninsula and train; she couldn't stand the thought of bickering with Kennick about her pregnancy all day. When she eventually left the house, he walked with her. She could tell that he wanted to put their arguing behind them, but she could barely look at him—not because she was still mad, but because he knew; he knew, and she had to face the truth every time she met his eyes.

As they passed through the clearing where Shael and Isbaen

usually sparred, they were sheathing their swords. "Done already?" Meera asked.

"I am done for the day," Isbaen replied. "Gendryl and I have plans." Meera nodded at him, and Isbaen departed.

"Want to do some hand-to-hand, Shael?" she asked. She immediately sensed Kennick tense next to her, but she ignored him.

"Sure," Shael said, but his green eyes roved up to Kennick's expression and turned wary.

"I'll see you later," Meera told Kennick without meeting his eyes.

"Meera, please," he said, but she continued to walk across the clearing toward Shael, who looked as if he'd just knocked over a hornet's nest.

"I'll see you later," she repeated more forcefully.

Shael looked at his boots.

"No, Meera," Kennick said.

"No?!" she asked, whipping around in outrage. He was not in charge of her. She could train if she wanted to.

Kennick put his hands up placatingly. "Please, Meera. At least tell him. He could hurt you—then how would he feel? Is that fair to Shael?" he asked.

"Whoah! what is going on?" Shael asked, eyes widening.

"Nothing!" Meera shouted.

Kennick looked at her levelly, seeming to deliberate, but Meera didn't actually think he would tell Shael—not without her permission. She could feel Shael looking at her in concern and confusion and avoided his gaze, choosing instead to stare Kennick down. "Meera is pregnant," he said quietly.

Meera couldn't believe it. For a moment, she just gaped at him in shock, then anger replaced her shock, and she let out a howl of outrage. Her raek fire flared on her body with her primal cry. She was livid. "How could you?!" she shouted. Her flames flared even higher, encompassing her whole body and extending out for several feet.

"Leave!" she shouted, accentuating the command with a gust of air that knocked Kennick back a few steps. Her flames receded into her, but she shook with emotion. "Go! Go tell everyone! Throw a party, while you're at it—just know that I won't be there!" she shouted. Tears were streaming down her face, and she shaped them away in agitation.

"I would rather you be angry than get hurt, Meera," he said before turning to walk away.

She stared daggers at his back, and when he was about to be swallowed by the trees, she said, "No, you just care more about this baby than about me." Then she turned away and didn't see the stricken look on his face when he glanced back at her. His footsteps continued into the woods, and she fell to her knees and clasped her hands over her face to stifle her sobs.

16

SHAEL

Shael stood shocked while Meera and Kennick fought and watched in absolute disbelief when his friend walked away, leaving his—apparently pregnant—fiancé crying on the ground. After her recent fiery outburst, he approached Meera cautiously. "Meera," he said quietly, so she would know it was him before he touched her shoulder. He rubbed her back in a display of friendly comfort—he thought they had gotten enough of their friendship back for that.

As they sat in silence, Shael tried to puzzle out what had just happened. He could not tell if their fight had been about him, the pregnancy, or both. "Did you not want me to know?" he asked after a time.

Meera was calming down, wiping her running nose with the back of her hand and burning away the slimy detritus. She sat back on her butt and turned to him. Shael thought about taking her hand but decided that would be too much. She shook her head before she managed to reply, but he did not know if that meant "No, she had not wanted him to know," or "No, she did not care if he knew." He was not sure how he even felt about knowing. He was still wrapping his mind around Meera and Kennick, whose relationship both did not entirely make sense to him, having known them both beforehand, and yet made all the sense in the world when he saw them look at each other.

"It's not about you, Shael," she replied to his relief. "I just wasn't ready to tell anyone yet, and he knew that." When she said it, her face scrunched up again in hurt. Then he did reach forward and take her hand.

"I can pretend I do not know if you want," he said with a smile.

She laughed. "Can you teach Kennick how to do that? He's treating me like I'm made of glass," she replied.

Shael could not blame his friend but did not say so. He would avoid taking sides in this if he could. "Are you not happy about it?" he asked. "I would have thought with the whole ... true mates thing or whatever ..."

"He told you about that?" she asked.

"He thought it would make me feel better—you know, to know that you and I were never meant to be together," he admitted.

"Did it?"

Shael shrugged. "It did, actually," he said, then he waited patiently for Meera to tell him what was going on. It had not escaped his notice that she had avoided his question.

She looked down and fiddled with a piece of grass. "You're right—I should be happy, but I'm not. I'm overwhelmed and embarrassed," she admitted.

He nodded. He could understand that. He was also not at all surprised that Kennick—a knell—might not understand that. "I have not told you this yet, but I am now godfather to Caleb's twins," he said.

"What? Really?" Meera asked, gaping at him.

He smiled. He loved those babies and had already been back

several times to visit. "You know I did not plan to be a father of any sort, but when I met the twins, every reason I ever had for hating myself and not wanting children seemed unimportant. When you hold your baby, your reasons for not wanting to be pregnant will seem just as unimportant," he assured her.

Meera sighed heavily. "I know that's probably true. I mean, of course it's true—of course I'll love my baby. I just—I'm not sure it's what's best for me right now. Doesn't that matter too? Kennick doesn't seem to think so. He only seems to care about the baby," she said. "Am I being selfish? Am I a bad person?"

"No," Shael said with certainty. He knew Meera was never selfish and far from a bad person. "It makes you human," he said, grinning and giving her a light shove. She smiled too. "Do you really want to end the pregnancy?" he asked. "I will help you find a way if you do." He supposed he had just taken sides, but he felt he was siding with the baby. A truly unwanted baby should not have to come into the world.

Meera thought for a while before answering. "No, I don't. But thank you, Shael. I feel less alone in this now," she said.

He squeezed her shoulder, and when it seemed like Meera did not have any more to say, he asked, "Do you still want to fight, or should we go get lunch?"

"*Would* you still fight?" she asked.

"Poorly," he replied, and they both laughed.

"I'm not much in the mood to beat you up, so I guess we should get lunch," Meera said, but she grimaced.

"I doubt Kennick actually told anyone else," Shael assured her. "He only did that to protect you."

Meera did not answer. She still looked hurt.

When they approached Hadjal's table, it was already filled with the other riders who were eating a light lunch. Kennick had food in front of him but was not eating and looked uncharacteristically burdened. Shael tried to make eye contact with him, but he did not look up when they approached. Shael sat in his usual seat, but Meera remained standing at the head of the table. He peered up at her, and after a moment, the others did as well. She looked resigned.

"Everything alright, Meera?" Hadjal asked, sounding nervous. Meera always seemed to make Hadjal nervous these days.

"I'm pregnant. Kennick's happy about it, but I'm not. Now you're all caught up," Meera announced succinctly, throwing a scathing look at Kennick before taking her seat next to Shael.

For a long time, no one spoke. No one knew what to say to Meera's abrupt pronouncement. Kennick tried in vain to catch her eye, but she filled her plate then began eating with obstinate concentration. Shael wondered if he should start a conversation to ease the tension, but that was not exactly his strength.

Finally, Gendryl of all people spoke. "I was once pregnant before I transitioned. It did not feel like the right path for me, so I found a healer to end the pregnancy. I can introduce you if you would like," he announced.

Shael did not think he could be any more shocked that day. He had never heard a knell admit to such a thing. Almost everyone else looked surprised as well—including Isbaen, which Shael felt uncomfortable to see. Soleille, on the other hand, looked annoyed. "Meera has a perfectly capable healer right here," she replied. "For whatever you need," she told Meera pointedly.

At this point, no one was eating anymore. Meera looked touched and close to tears once more, but Kennick was clearly alarmed. Despite the obvious fear in his friend's dark eyes, he did not speak out against Meera ending the pregnancy, and Shael silently willed him not to.

"Thank you both," Meera said, wiping her eyes. "But I have decided to keep the pregnancy. It is the right path for me—I'm just there sooner than expected," she explained. Most of the table exhaled in relief.

"I will help any time, Meera. Children make good training weights," Katrea said.

Meera laughed. Shael did not; he was not sure he wanted to see Katrea using Meera's child as a dumbbell. Then the others proceeded to offer Meera and Kennick their assistance and congratulations. It was a fast lunch; everyone was clearly uncomfortable due to the obvious tension between the two soon-to-be-parents. Shael asked Meera if she still wanted to train, but she shook her head. He watched her and Kennick walk away with Soleille, and he realized that he was excited for his friends.

To Shael's surprise, he did not feel jealous or uncomfortable or self-pitying. He was glad that Meera and Kennick would be a happy family together—he was sure Meera would be happy given time to process her changed life. Shael was happy too. He still hoped to find love, and he even thought he might leave his vow behind him if he did.

17

MEERA

Meera walked with Kennick and Soleille to her old cabin for privacy. Despite the support the other riders had shown, she was still struggling to meet anyone's eye. She knew it wasn't rational for her to be so embarrassed about being unmarried and pregnant in a society that didn't care about such things, but she couldn't help how she felt; her human upbringing was affecting her perceptions.

When they entered the tiny cabin, she took a deep breath and told herself it was time to be brave; it was time for her to face reality and accept the imminent changes in her future. She felt inspired by Gendryl's fearlessness at lunch, which had surprised and moved her. Meera thought Isbaen's lover was a delightful host of contradictions to be so shy and yet so bold.

She avoided looking at Kennick, who was continually trying to catch her eye. She wasn't even sure if she was truly upset with him anymore—she understood why he'd done what he'd done—but somehow, it just felt easier for her to be standoffish than to play the part of the glowing expectant mother. She wasn't proud of her behavior and wished she could give Kennick the experience he deserved. She just couldn't. She was barely holding herself together.

"Ready?" Soleille asked, holding out a hand.

Meera nodded and averted her eyes. Soleille would only tell her what she already knew. The healer placed her hand on her stomach to sense inside her body, and a moment later, her hand fell away. "Yes, you are pregnant," she said quietly.

Meera did look at her then, hearing the emotion in her friend's voice. "What is it?" she asked. "Is something wrong?" She glanced at Kennick, whose face looked taught and strained, though he continued to hold his silence.

"No, it is just pretty amazing to feel," Soleille admitted, wiping tears from her eyes.

It was unlike Soleille to be so sincere and emotional, and it unsettled Meera. "Oh," she said. Why couldn't she feel some of the awe that showed so plainly in Soleille's face? Why wasn't she getting the warm, fuzzy feelings that everyone else seemed to be experiencing from her news? While she felt pregnant, she couldn't actually feel the baby growing inside her in any remarkable way. She didn't feel any sense of amazement or wonder. She didn't feel like she was some sort of miracle bringer of life—she just felt sick and tired and burdened.

"Do you know how far along you are?" Soleille asked. "It is too soon for me to tell."

"A month," Meera said.

"A month? You mean Genway? Your first time? How remarkable! I had just assumed you had not taken the tea I gave you regularly enough. Your union must truly be smiled upon," she replied.

Neither Meera nor Kennick said anything. What were these

greater forces that *smiled upon* loving couples with unplanned pregnancies just to cause a rift between them?

After a very awkward silence, Soleille asked, "Do you two have any questions for me? I do not specialize in pregnancy, but I could always find out if you do ..."

Meera stared at Kennick expectantly. He hesitated, looked into her blank stare, then asked, "Is there anything that Meera should or should not do—to keep herself safe?"

"She should get plenty of rest and eat well. She can continue running and shaping but should avoid anything that could result in a blow to the stomach," Soleille replied.

They both thanked her and shuffled out of the cabin. The second Soleille was out of earshot, Meera hissed, "I wouldn't have let Shael kick me in the stomach!" glaring at Kennick.

"It was not worth the risk," he replied evenly.

"I have been living as usual for a month without harming the pregnancy. A few more days would not have hurt anything!" she spat.

"Well, if you had told me a month ago that you thought you were pregnant, I would have tried to convince you not to fight then," he said, his voice finally rising just a little bit.

"I hadn't really known!" she said defensively.

"We are supposed to be sharing our lives, Meera—all of our lives, not just the parts we are sure about or happy about," he said very quietly.

Meera looked into his earnest eyes then away again. She knew she had hurt him and felt duly chastened. She would have been upset if Kennick had kept something from her that long or had run away to a cave without her—in fact, she would have been devastated. She knew that he was handling her behavior very well. "I'm sorry. You're right," she said. Taking his hand, she squeezed it. He squeezed back, but she still had trouble meeting his eyes.

THE DISTANCE between Meera and Kennick continued to stretch even as they walked home hand-in-hand. And over the following weeks, it widened and settled and festered. Neither of them seemed to know how to get back to one another; they weren't angry anymore but were both still hurt and unsure. Neither of them knew how to suddenly start celebrating the pregnancy that had started out with so much fraught emotion, so they settled on not mentioning it.

Meera stopped combat training, and Kennick stopped fussing over her. If anything, he seemed to go out of his way to try not to do anything overtly kind or caring lest it upset her, which only made Meera feel worse. She thought maybe she should start discussing the pregnancy and the baby as she came to terms with it in her mind, but she didn't know how to do so without sounding forced or fake after everything else she had said. She felt like she had boxed herself in, and now she couldn't feel or express joy even if she wanted to.

Meera found herself spending most of her time with Shael, who—for some reason—didn't make her feel as self-conscious as Kennick did. They exercised together and talked, and he even flew her on Cerun to visit Caleb and his family. Meeting Elise and her twins was eye-opening for Meera, who had never spent much time in the presence of babies before. She could see how exhausted Elise was and how busy the babies kept her and Caleb as well as how deeply in love they both were with their children.

She enjoyed watching Shael interact with his god-children and realized that she looked forward to seeing Kennick with their baby. She held the twins, too—awkwardly at first, but she got the hang of it. When little Sophia spat up on her, Meera startled Elise and Caleb by burning away the muck with her raek fire, but once Elise understood what Meera had done, she exclaimed, "That's going to come in handy! What a great ability for a mother to have!" Meera smiled to think that her shaping would be useful for parenting and thought maybe she was more prepared than she had realized.

However, even as she became more and more comfortable with the idea of her pregnancy and impending motherhood, she still struggled to close the chasm that had opened between her and Kennick. They slept side by side but didn't touch. They spoke but didn't connect. She saw the hurt in his eyes when she walked away to spend her time with Shael, but she went regardless; she needed support, and she wasn't getting it at home.

In addition to her other swirling emotions, Meera began to feel listless; she didn't know what she was supposed to be doing with herself despite the many responsibilities that closed in around her. Shaya kept asking what their next steps were in ending the war, but she didn't know. She was supposedly the Queen's Champion but had no idea what that entailed ... She felt like she should be doing something—anything—like the world was waiting for her to act, but she couldn't think where to start.

Meera expelled some of her nervous energy by running; she ran every day around the lake with Shael, sometimes more than once. Kennick watched her leave each morning without a word until one day, he could not bear it anymore. "Meera, spend the day with me—please," he begged her, standing in the doorway.

She had just laced her boots to meet Shael, and her chest contracted hearing the pain in Kennick's voice. She didn't mean to keep hurting him—she was just trying to survive; she was trying to get through each day without having a meltdown about everything going on in her life. "Okay, of course," she replied, kicking off her boots. She hated to leave Shael waiting for her, but he would live.

Then she and Kennick eyed one another awkwardly, and Meera wondered how they had reached this point when a matter of weeks ago they could barely keep their hands off each other. "What do you want to do?" he asked. "Do you still want to run?"

Somehow, Meera didn't think running in silence next to Kennick would do anything for her nerves. She shrugged her shoulders. "Maybe not," she said.

"Will you help me figure out how to catch myself from a fall?" he asked hopefully. It was something they had been talking about doing and looking forward to before the whole pregnancy business.

"Okay! The cliff?" she asked, meaning the cliff over the Riders' Lake.

Kennick smiled and shaped a blob of metal into his hand from across the room. Similar indistinct masses of metal graced the various nooks and corners of their house in case he ever wanted to use them for anything. Then they set out together through the woods, walking side-by-side and not talking. Meera had left her boots behind since it was a warm day, and it felt good to stretch her feet against the pine-needle trail they followed.

However, that was about all that felt good about the walk. Neither she nor Kennick spoke for a long time, and the air between them seemed to intensify. What once might have been an easy, companionable silence felt like a pressing weight upon them. Meera wracked her mind but couldn't seem to think of what they used to talk about. None of the topics she came up with felt safe. "What have you and Shael been doing?" Kennick finally asked. He tried for a light tone, but she could sense the urgency behind the question.

"Nothing!" she said quickly before realizing it sounded like she was hiding something. "I mean, not much. Mostly we've been running. We went to visit friends of his in Sangea last week. Shael's a god-father now, you know."

"No, I did not know," he replied sadly.

"I didn't either," she said, trying to make him feel better. "He took me to meet the babies. He ... thought it would help."

"Did it?" Kennick asked.

"It did," Meera admitted.

He smiled at her, but she averted her gaze. She felt like she was being inspected—like he was waiting for her to be fixed and normal. She had never said she wouldn't love their baby, after all. She could have chosen to end the pregnancy if she had wanted to. Sure, she had experienced a lot of emotions and doubts and had voiced them, but there wasn't anything wrong with her. Meera wished Kennick would stop waiting for her to act happy. She really was beginning to feel some excitement and joy at the prospect of their baby, but it was all tinged with uneasiness because of their recent inability to connect.

"Maybe we can babysit one day for practice," he suggested.

Meera gave Kennick a smile she knew didn't reach her eyes. She didn't need him watching her struggle to care for someone else's babies and judging her for her lack of mothering abilities.

They didn't say much else before reaching the cliff, at which point they discussed their objective for the day. First, they debated how much metal Kennick might need in order to catch his body weight. Then they whittled the hunk of metal down until it was as small as possible but still able to lift him off the ground when he held it in his hands and shaped it upward. Next, he would need to practice jumping and stopping the velocity of his fall.

"Why don't you start by holding it in your hands, so you don't hurt yourself," Meera suggested.

He agreed and took off his shirt in preparation for his jump. Normally seeing Kennick shirtless would give Meera a whole host of feelings and ideas, but she just stared at his sun-kissed, toned abdomen with relative indifference. Her inability to connect with him emotionally was affecting her desire for him, and she looked away feeling unspeakably sad and hopeless. She missed him even though he was right there, and she didn't know how to find her way back to him.

For the next couple of hours, Kennick jumped and climbed the wall repeatedly, making slow progress with his efforts. They realized he needed more metal to catch him in a fall than to lift him from standing still. Then he had to practice making the fall smooth and not jerking himself back up into the air. All the while, Meera watched and offered support and suggestions. She hoped learning to catch himself would help Kennick shed some of his fear of heights and falling; she wanted him to relish his raek riding as much as she did.

When they were about to move on to having Kennick wear the metal around his body, he sat down panting and dripping to take a break. Meera thought maybe she should jump in for a swim soon. She was sweating just sitting still in the moderate summer heat. However, she couldn't help but wonder if Kennick would throw a fit about her jumping from so high up in her current condition. Sighing, she stared longingly at the water below, unwilling to ignite a possible argument.

"How did you figure out how to catch yourself?" Kennick asked, regarding her. "You never told me."

Meera reclined onto her elbows and looked up at the blue sky above for a moment. The answer to that question was not her fondest memory. She glanced over at him. "Shaya threw me off her back far above the mountainside in the middle of winter," she replied wryly. She could still remember how stiff and freezing she had been from the whipping wind and her panic when she had fallen—technically she had let go, but Shaya had not given her any other option, threatening to throw them both into the mountainside below.

"That was it? You did not practice beforehand? She just threw you and let you fall?" he asked in disbelief.

Meera nodded. She hadn't shared much about her training in the mountains with him; it always felt like a personal, solitary experience that she wanted to keep to herself. But she was glad to have something to say to Kennick—something that hopefully wouldn't cause more discord between them. "I was terrified," she admitted, knowing he could imagine. "And I didn't fall gracefully, either. It hurt. I didn't talk to Shaya for days afterward, but ... she was all I had in the mountains."

"Raeken!" Kennick spat with a pointed sound of exasperation.

"Where's Endu?" Meera asked, suddenly realizing she hadn't seen him in a while.

Kennick looked down at the ground. Meera missed his usual confident smile, and as she waited for him to answer, she processed how sad he really looked. She had been so busy avoiding his gaze for fear that he was judging her all the time that she had not taken a moment to really look at him and notice how he was doing. She was used to him being so steady, but he didn't look steady now—or confident; he looked ... broken. "Kennick, where's Endu?" she asked again, sensing something was wrong.

"I do not know," he replied very quietly. "I have not seen him since your challenge. He ... He refused to fly after you, so I left with Shael and Cerun. I have not seen him since. I cannot even sense our connection ..." He paused, but Meera could tell he was not finished speaking and waited. She was finally getting a fuller picture of what it had been like for him when she had fled the fight, and she felt as if he were crushing her chest with a metal weight. She had not stood by him, Endu had not stood by him, and he had been left alone and waiting. She swallowed down her tears at the thought, not wanting to make his grief about her.

Finally, Kennick completed his thought: "I am not sure I am a rider anymore."

Meera sat up and groped for his hands. She couldn't stand how much she had hurt him, and she looked pleadingly into his dark eyes. "It's my fault. It was all my fault, Kennick. I'm sorry. I'm sorry I ran. I'm sorry I left you and that I put you and Endu in that position," she said.

He was shaking his head, but Meera kept talking, kept apologizing. She suddenly understood how he must have felt, and she needed him to understand her feelings too. "After the fight, everyone looked so scared of me—so disgusted. There was a whole stadium facing me full of fear and judgment, and when I looked at you ... I saw your fear, Kennick. I saw your face, and I just had to get out of there. That was why I ran. No one else's opinion mattered, but yours ... You mean everything to me, and your fear hurt," she admitted.

Kennick leaned toward her and cupped her face in his hands, wiping her tears with his thumbs. "I was not scared *of* you, Meera —I was scared *for* you. I did not know what the crowd might do or what Darreal might do. All I want is to have you safe and have you with me," he said. He pressed his forehead to hers, and Meera tangled her hands in his hair and held him there.

She understood all of it now—how all of Kennick's actions had been out of love and a fear of losing her: his overprotectiveness and his betrayal—telling Shael when he had said he wouldn't. He had lost his raek and had lost her for several long days, and he hadn't been able to bear the possibility of losing her again—or their baby. She understood. If she were ever afraid for him, she would do anything to protect him, even if he didn't want her to—didn't like her for it. Meera hated that she had been so absorbed in her own fears and emotions that she had overlooked the true depth of his. "You will always have me," she told him, still clutching his face to hers.

Kennick kissed her with a passion that sent liquid fire through her veins. She felt her body flicker with her raek fire and knew that anyone on the peninsula could probably see them, but she didn't care. She pulled him to her with stark need; she wanted him as close as possible and to hold him there until the distance between them was a long-forgotten memory. He was already shirtless, so she started tugging off her own shirt.

He laughed against her mouth and stilled her frenzied arms before picking her up by her backside and carrying her—straddling him—to their nearby private clearing. It was the clearing where they had gotten to know one another training, the clearing where they had first joined together, and the clearing where they would now find their way back to one another. When he knew they were alone, Kennick removed all of her clothes in a fevered hurry, tearing off his own pants in the process. Then he kissed and touched her with a hunger that mirrored Meera's urgency.

Gripping her butt firmly, he sent waves of tingling desire through her core, and he hoisted her back up to straddle him. Meera clutched him to her and groaned at the feel of his hardness bumping and slipping between her thighs. She was ready for him. Kennick pressed her back against the smooth trunk of a tree and ground into her, pinning her in place with the pressure of his hips while his hands cupped her breasts and teased her nipples.

"I think these are bigger," he said low in her ear, making her shiver.

"Get your fill before you have to share them," she told him.

He kissed her smiling face and gripped under her butt once more, kneading and spreading her until she ached. She wanted him closer—joined with her in every way. But instead of giving her the contact she craved, Kennick bent and took one of her nipples in his teeth, flicking his tongue against it. Meera arched and gasped. "Kennick—" she pleaded.

"Say it," he told her, before taking her other nipple in his mouth.

Meera looked down at him and found that the smug glint had returned to his dark eyes. She wanted him to always look like that; she never wanted to hurt him again.

"I want you inside of me. All of you. Now!" she said.

Grinning at her, he straightened up, and with one smooth thrust, he pierced her opening, burying himself inside her to the hilt. She cried out, and he continued to thrust into her hard and fast, pressing her against the tree in a frenzy of heated friction. Meera quickly toppled over the edge of her pleasure and Kennick with her. Then they both sagged, trembling and panting.

Kennick pulled himself free and lifted Meera once more to tip her down onto the soft grass of the clearing, sprawling next to her before gathering her to him. They reclined together in the warm air, breathing hard. Their sweat mingled where their skin touched, and Meera shaped a gentle breeze to tickle them. They didn't speak, but their silence was tender like the swirls Kennick traced over her bare body. Leaning into him, she shut her eyes, at peace.

Meera felt they were connected in spirit once more even if their minds had not touched during their joining. Opening her eyes, she smiled up at the man she loved in pure joy and contentment. When Kennick's breathing slowed, she reached over him and kissed him deeply, trailing a hand slowly down his body before following that hand with her mouth. Her desire was reawakened with their love, and she didn't think she would ever get enough of him.

Meera was ready for more and knew that with a little coaxing, Kennick would be too. When she took him into her mouth, she teased the skin of his thighs and stomach with her harmless flames and looked up into his eyes. He smiled lazily down at her, and his pointy canine showed over his bottom lip. With his dark red hair fanned out around his head, he looked like a lion basking in the sun, and Meera enjoyed licking and teasing him while watching the hunger in his face slowly build.

Once she had stroked and sucked him to life again, Kennick touched her face to bring her back up to him. Meera crawled up the length of his body and kissed his pointy tooth, resting her weight against him. She kissed him long and slow, trying to impart with her lips and her tongue that she would never leave him again. Their hair mingled across the ground in a clash of colors and textures that still somehow blended together.

Kennick ran his hands over her, stopping to touch her stomach with a tenderness that in no way bothered Meera. She covered his hand with one of her own, and they both rolled onto their sides. When they came together, they gazed into one another's eyes and felt the click of their mental tether fall into place. They took their time to make their pleasure and connection last, but even when both crested and fell away, their love and joy in one another remained. Meera felt like she had finally arrived home after a long absence.

18

MEERA

The next couple of weeks were blissful and uneventful. Meera still ran with Shael each morning, but otherwise, she spent all of her time with Kennick. They continued to talk through all of the feelings they had each had, but mostly, they just enjoyed one another's company: they trained and ate and swam in the summer heat, and they discussed their future child with increasing excitement.

With her life at home feeling stable, Meera was able to give more thought to her other responsibilities. She wrote to Darreal, thanking the queen for her show of support but requesting Lethian be reinstated as her champion. However, Darreal replied that wasn't possible—though she didn't expect Meera to perform her role. She also relayed that her council was still gathering information and deliberating about whether the knell should intervene in the war.

As it seemed Meera was not currently needed as Darreal's champion or for the war efforts, she enjoyed her peace and quiet at home and at the peninsula. She continued to wrap her mind and heart around the baby that would be in her near future, and Kennick started planning an addition to their house. Shaya was restless and bored hanging around the peninsula, so Meera gave her the task of finding Endu and scaring some sense into the raek.

Kennick was still living in limbo—unsure of whether Endu had truly disavowed him as his rider or not—and he did not yet want to share his concerns with the other riders. Meera understood his feelings, but she also assured him that he would always be a rider, raekless or not. She had not technically been accepted as a rider, but it didn't matter—they were a family. They were all a family, and Kennick was a huge part of that. Meera didn't think the others would abandon him in any sense if Endu left, but he insisted he would rather wait and be sure before saying anything.

She knew he was embarrassed, and it made her realize that her own embarrassment about being unmarried and pregnant was perhaps just as unfounded. On a whim, she wrote to Follaria about making them wedding outfits. She wanted to give Kennick the wedding of his dreams, and she would rather do it soon before her pregnancy showed. When Follaria arrived unexpectedly at the house and announced she was there to discuss Meera's wedding dress, Kennick's face was so full of delight, it was enough to make Meera want to succumb to whatever kind of ridiculous wedding he might want.

Before they could get far into making plans, however, they received an unprecedented letter from Kennick's parents inviting them both to visit. Andreena stated that she wanted to host their wedding for them. When Kennick handed Meera the letter, she had to read it four times to comprehend it. Why would Andreena and Destin want to host their wedding? They hated her. They hated all humans—but especially her. "What am I missing?" she asked Kennick, wondering what ulterior motive his parents could possibly have for suddenly accepting their relationship.

Kennick shrugged. He looked perplexed as well, but Meera thought he also looked a little hopeful. He had been extra vulnerable in Endu's absence, and she could see that he craved this contact with his parents, despite having long since learned to live without their love and support. She wasn't sure it was a good idea for him to get his hopes up, but she also wouldn't stand in the way of him connecting with his parents if that was what he wanted. Even if they were truly awful …

"Maybe they were impressed by your abilities at the challenge. Andreena loves power," Kennick suggested optimistically.

Meera wasn't so sure, but they were his parents. She had never wanted to return to Kennick's family home again after their last visit, but she would go if he wanted to. Alas, she would do anything for Kennick. She had already pledged herself to whatever wedding he wanted, so if he wanted it to be at his parent's house, then so be it. She only hoped it would be soon. She didn't know exactly when she would start showing but knew it would happen quickly.

Kennick drummed his fingers on their metal table while he thought, drawing Meera's attention to the ring she had made him. "Do you hate your ring?" she asked suddenly. "Does it just remind you that I left and didn't return right away?" She still felt bad for fleeing and leaving him to wait for her at home. She had made his ring out of love, but she had used it as an excuse to prolong her visit to the cave as well. She could understand if he had some negative feelings about it.

He touched the ring then took one of her hands, forcing her to look into his eyes. They were almost as black and gleaming as the diamond he wore. "I love this ring, Meera. It reminds me that even when you were overwhelmed and upset, you still thought of me and took the time to make it for me. It is also as strong and unique as you are," he replied.

"Don't forget as handsome and seductive as you are," she said with a grin.

Kennick smiled, but his eyes returned to his parent's letter in distraction.

"We're going, aren't we?" she asked, sighing.

"Would you mind? We won't stay if they are anything but kind and apologetic toward you," he promised.

"I'll see if I can call Shaya back," she replied.

THEY LEFT the next day when Shaya—somewhat miraculously—came to Meera's call. The raek had been surprisingly amiable lately. Meera didn't know why, but she wasn't questioning it.

"Did you find Endu?" she asked mentally.

"It was not hard. His red plumage is eye-catching," Shaya replied tonelessly. Meera was tempted to tease her about her obvious infatuation with the dark red raek but decided not to. Unfortunately, Shaya still seemed to sense the essence of what Meera might have said and snorted an irritated puff of smoke in her direction.

Kennick looked up from strapping their bags to her side, vaguely startled, but he didn't comment. It was considered rude to interfere too much in another rider's relationship with their raek —an old tradition Meera didn't exactly stand by.

"Well?" she asked Shaya mentally. "What did he say?"

"He communicated that he is contemplating his place in the world—something to that effect," Shaya replied.

"Do you think he'll come back? Did he mention Kennick?" Meera persisted.

Shaya merely grunted in answer.

Meera sighed and was glad she hadn't mentioned anything to

Kennick; she would have gotten his hopes up for nothing. Then she climbed onto Shaya's back and smiled as Kennick settled behind her. When they took off, she gritted her teeth and hoped for the best during their visit.

Andreena and Destin once again greeted their arrival by fanning all of their staff out in the front courtyard. Kennick must have sent his carrier bird ahead to let his parents know they were coming. Shaya took off the moment they untied their bags; she didn't like the feeling of being walled-in. Meera couldn't blame her, but she asked her to please stay close. The raek gave her a flippant mental tail swish in response that Meera interpreted as a shrug.

"Welcome," Andreena said—with her mouth, anyway; her eyes shone distinctly icy and unwelcoming.

"Mother, we were not sure we should come but decided to give you another chance to welcome Meera into the family," Kennick said as a preliminary first test.

Meera saw Andreena's jaw tighten. "We have taken time to process your choice in bride, son, and have decided to accept it," she replied. It was not an overt acceptance of Meera nor was it a friendly statement, so Meera thought there was some chance it was genuine. It was about as good as she might have hoped for anyway.

"Yes, we would like to host your wedding as a show of support and as an apology to you, Meera, for our previous resistance to your presence in our son's life," Destin added, sounding like he was reading a script.

Meera nodded in reply. She was always unsure of what to make of Kennick's father, who tended to look like his thoughts were elsewhere entirely, even when he contributed adequately to the conversation.

"Let us not loiter any longer," Andreena commanded sharply.

"We will have refreshments in the drawing room, then dinner will be at the usual time."

Meera and Kennick followed his parents into the house—which to her still looked more like a castle—and sat with them in the drawing room. Andreena and Destin didn't bother with small talk; they didn't ask Kennick how he was or what he had been doing lately, they just jumped right into discussing the wedding. Meera thought maybe Andreena simply liked hosting grand events.

"I was thinking a winter wedding with an outdoor ceremony and reception in the ballroom. A friend of mine who shapes water can make us snow for the occasion, and I have a large collection of furs waiting to be made into the most splendid coats," Andreena announced.

Meera glanced at Kennick, who looked back at her questioningly. She could tell he was amenable to the idea, but as much as Meera wanted to give him whatever wedding he wanted, she didn't wish to be a massively pregnant bride. Her baby would be born at the end of winter.

"I was ... hoping it could be sooner," she said tentatively.

"Sooner?" Andreena asked with a dramatic rise of her voice. "These things take time. Winter is soon enough as it is."

Meera bit her lip and looked at Kennick. The question was clear in her eyes: was he going to tell them, or should she? He sat up straighter, giving her the answer she was hoping for. "Mother, Father, Meera and I actually have news," he began.

"Oh?" Andreena inquired. Destin's focus seemed to be on a plant in the corner.

Kennick took Meera's hand and squeezed it. Andreena watched the display with the keen intensity of an apex predator. "Meera is pregnant. You are going to be grandparents!" he declared. He sounded so proud, Meera couldn't help but smile with him.

Andreena looked beyond shocked, and Destin appeared vaguely alarmed and disoriented. "Pregnant? And you are sure? You have had a reputable healer sense her?" Andreena asked Kennick.

"Yes, Mother," he replied tersely.

"And you are sure it is yours?" she asked.

Kennick glowered at her, not deigning to answer the question.

Destin put a hand on Andreena's arm—a quelling gesture, Meera thought. "What happy news! Congratulations!" he said rather loudly and with a large, fixed smile. Then he got up and gave Kennick a hug that made Meera cringe but seemed to make Kennick happy. He really did have the worst parents, she thought, feeling sad for him. Even the shell that remained of her father would still react more warmly than this—she expected. She supposed she would need to find a time to tell him soon. Andreena followed suit, offering wooden congratulations and hugging her son—though thankfully, not Meera.

When they all settled back into their seats, Meera explained, "I would rather not be showing at the wedding."

Andreena and Destin both looked baffled by her statement. "Why not?" Destin asked. "A woman full in bloom is at her most beautiful. A pregnant bride would garner the utmost admiration."

"It's a human thing," Meera explained vaguely, which did the trick of halting further argument.

Andreena and Destin both looked distinctly uncomfortable. "Well, we can discuss this more at dinner," Andreena said rather faintly.

They all rose and left the room. Kennick led Meera to the kitchen to get a snack, rightfully guessing that she was hungry; she was almost always hungry when she wasn't nauseous. Pregnancy really wasn't any fun whatsoever. Although ... She found herself almost looking forward to torturing Andreena and Destin with discussion of their future half-human grandchild at dinner. Kennick had once mentioned how he always tries to get his mother to make the candles flicker, and Meera thought the two of them could have a competition.

"I think that went well," Kennick said, giving her a beseeching look. He clearly wanted her agreement.

Meera didn't exactly agree, but she didn't want to dash his hopes either. "Your mother seems keen to plan the wedding," she said. It was the most positive thing she could think to say about the encounter that was also true.

"Andreena loves a party," he agreed.

Even if she hates humans, Meera thought, but she didn't say so. She ate some corn pudding that the cook had made for the servants. It was delicious, but even as they were stepping out of the kitchen, she already started to feel her stomach churn and roil in protestation. Breathing deeply, she tried to think of something else, hoping she wouldn't spew her snack all over the floor. Her morning sickness had been a pervasive nuisance lately.

"Where are we going?" she asked Kennick, who was leading her through hallways on a lower level she had never visited before.

"I am taking you to the vaults. While we are here, I want to pick out some gems to make into something for you to wear at the wedding," he explained.

"But I'm going to wear the necklace you made me," she said, still breathing deeply and trying not to think about her churning insides.

"Then I will make you earrings or something for your head," he replied, smirking.

"You're going to make me a crown, aren't you?" she asked, giving him an exasperated look.

He shrugged and winked at her, and she sighed dramatically. She couldn't help but think that if she did walk down the aisle with a swollen stomach, Kennick would make a crown for her protruding belly as well. No, she thought, she shouldn't think about her stomach —her nausea pressed upward, and she did her best to swallow down the feeling. She didn't understand how she was supposed to feed her growing baby if the baby didn't let her hold down any food.

"Can you just take jewels from your parent's house?" she asked Kennick, distracting herself.

"I can take my half of anything from the house," he said.

"Your half?" she asked in confusion.

He gave her a surprised look. "Meera, in knell law, offspring immediately inherit a fraction of their ancestor's estate at birth. I own half of all of this since it is only my mother and I who are descended through this line," he explained, gesturing around at the house. "Where did you think I got my money?"

"I thought your parents gave it to you," she said, flabbergasted. No wonder Follaria had once referred to Kennick as the wealthiest eligible bachelor in Levisade.

Kennick laughed at her surprise.

"But when they threw you out, you said Follaria had to take you in ..." Meera said, confused.

"I suppose they did not technically throw me out, considering I have a right to live here," he said, "But they made me unwelcome and made sure all of their friends also made me unwelcome. I paid Follaria to live above her shop, but she still lost all of her best paying clients when she sided with me against my parents."

"Why do knell inherit when they're born?" Meera asked.

"We live so long that waiting for inheritance became an issue long ago. The reigning monarch and their council changed the law for fear that younger generations would start killing off their elders for their wealth rather than waiting hundreds of years for them to die," Kennick said matter-of-factly. "Our child will immediately own a third of my family's wealth."

Meera's eyebrows rose up at that. She couldn't imagine Kennick's parents would be happy sharing their money with her baby. "I don't want to live here," was all that she said on the matter.

"The Riders' Holt is our home," Kennick agreed, but his face darkened. Meera knew he was wondering whether he was still a rider at all.

"It always will be," she said, squeezing his hand. Then her stomach gave a sudden heave. "Fresh air!" she gasped. It was her code for needing to vomit. He always offered to stay with her, but she would rather he not watch her puke repeatedly even if she always very efficiently burned away all evidence.

"That way!" Kennick said, hurriedly pointing to a far door.

Meera rushed out the door and promptly regurgitated her corn pudding all over the cobbled path outside. It didn't taste nearly as good coming back up as it had going down, and she felt sure she wouldn't eat corn pudding again for a very, very long time. Then she stood sucking in air to try to settle her still uneasy gut.

There were birds chirping and some human staff members speaking nearby, but Meera could also make out the quiet sounds of an argument. Looking around, she didn't see anyone. She quickly burned away all traces of vomit from the ground and shaped some water out of the air to drink. Ever since the challenge, she had found water shaping much easier. Being able to conjure drinking water was a skill that would surely always be useful—she certainly could have used it on her journey the year before.

She was about to go back inside when she heard a raised voice again, this time louder. She could have sworn it sounded like Andreena. Glancing up, she realized she was hearing Kennick's mother out an upper window. Meera couldn't tell what the woman had said, but she hadn't sounded happy. After a brief moment of uncertainty, she shaped an air current to waft the sounds from the upper window down to her. She wanted to know what Andreena and Destin were really thinking.

"Quiet, Andreena or you will be heard," Destin said. Meera smiled; he was right.

"I know, I know," Andreena replied, quieter, but Meera could still hear her easily as she shaped their voices through the air. "It just sickens me—the thought of our son fathering a little half-breed that we will then need to tolerate for the rest of our lives. I will not have it!"

Meera tensed. She may have taken some time to get used to the thought of her future child, but she would not stand for anyone else saying such things about her and Kennick's baby.

"Yes, I know, darling, but what are we to do about it? I agreed that hosting the wedding was necessary for keeping Kennick close, but that was when we thought this tryst with the human would quickly fizzle out. If she has his baby, how likely is our son to leave them both?" Destin asked.

Meera supposed marriage wasn't as permanent in knell society as in human society, and Kennick's parents had simply been biding their time, waiting for him to grow bored of her. They really didn't seem to know their son at all, she thought. Kennick truly meant to marry her and spend his long life with her—of that, she was certain.

"No, clearly we cannot leave this up to Kennick. We will need to find a way to end the pregnancy. With any luck, if the human loses his child, he will leave her before we even have to host their absurd wedding," Andreena said.

Meera's stomach flipped, and it wasn't morning sickness this time.

"How?" Destin asked.

"How? What do you mean, how? You are the plant expert, are you not?" she replied snarkily.

"Yes, but Andreena, Kennick would know it was me. Then we would lose our son for sure," Destin protested.

"You are right," Andreena conceded, sighing. "We will need to make it look like something else ... We will need her to not just lose the baby but be sick as well. We can give her a combination of poisons to make it look like she has an illness that happens to make her lose the pregnancy. We will call for Mastin and pay him to pretend he cannot heal her. He can say it is some foul hereditary human disorder. Then, surely, Kennick will be glad to be rid of the girl's baby."

Meera clutched the side of the building for support, feeling suddenly weak and exhausted. She couldn't believe what she was hearing—actually she could, she just wished it were otherwise. Kennick's parents not only sought to control him, they actually thought killing his unborn child was an acceptable means of doing so. What was wrong with these people? How could they pretend to care about him and plan to hurt him so egregious? Couldn't they see how excited he was to be a father?

"I know just the extracts to collect!" Destin announced.

"Is it too obvious if we do it tonight?" Andreena asked.

"I will choose slow-acting plants. They will be home by the time she feels anything amiss," he said.

"But what if they get another healer who finds her blood-stream full of poison?" his wife pointed out.

"Yes, you are right. I will make it act fast. We will have to just be very good actors and hope that Kennick does not suspect us," Destin replied.

"My heart does break for our son. He is so desperately foolish and easily led astray," Andreena simpered.

The two were interrupted by a knock on their door. Meera stopped shaping the air, pressed a hand to her still-flat stomach, and slid to the ground. Kennick's parents hated her—hated humans—so much, they were willing to kill their son's child in her womb. Despite her earlier uncertainty about whether she wanted to keep the pregnancy, the thought of someone else attacking the unformed child in her belly horrified and sickened her. She loved and wanted her baby now that she had had time to process her pregnancy. She wouldn't let them hurt it.

Meera positively seethed thinking about the despicable knell couple in the massive house behind her. Andreena and Destin's plans were unspeakable no matter what their motivations were, and Kennick would certainly never forgive them. Kennick, she thought sadly—poor Kennick had the worst parents and the worst raek. Meera couldn't stand the thought of telling him what she had overheard. She hated that she would have to be the person to take his parents from him—even if they were awful. She had to tell him, though; it wasn't as if she could now eat dinner with Andreena and Destin.

19

MEERA

Meera stood and wobbled, feeling faint. She really needed to eat something, but eating led to vomiting, which always left her even more exhausted. Not to mention, she would not be eating another morsel of food in that house. Opening the door, she walked down the dimly lit corridor toward where Kennick waited for her. Some of her burden must have shown in her face because he touched her cheek gently. "Bad one?" he asked.

She nodded, but before she could open her mouth to speak, he whisked her into an open doorway. "Come on," he said. "I want to get a sense of what styles you like." The excitement in his voice rang around the stone room where they now stood, bouncing off the many, many sparkling gems in the jewelry that lined the walls.

Meera gaped, overwhelmed by the sheer wealth that surrounded her. "Kennick, I—" she started to say, trying to tell him what she had heard.

"I know you do not need any of this, but I want to make you something for the wedding that you will truly like. I just want to know which pieces you think are nice and which you do not," he said, smiling.

"No, I—" she tried again.

"Please, Meera?" he asked.

Bewildered, she stared up into his hopeful eyes. "Okay," she replied against her better judgment. Then she looked around and started pointing to some of the crowns, necklaces, circlets, etc. that she thought were especially beautiful. "Does that help?" she asked.

"Yes," he said with certainty. "Do you mind if I go and get started right away? I will meet you at dinner," he said.

She started to open her mouth to protest, but he kissed her and turned to go. She followed, but when she shut the door to the jewel room behind her, she saw that he had used a key to open it, and it took her several moments to turn the key once more in the lock and pull it free. By then, Kennick had disappeared around the corner, and she wasn't sure where he was going. For a while, she wandered around looking for him, but she felt so tired, she couldn't keep it up. Instead, she returned to their room to wait for him.

To her amazement, Kennick didn't return to their room to change before dinner. Meera walked to the dining room—climbed up to the ridiculous dining room that was located three floors above the kitchen. She hoped to cut Kennick off before he got there—she had to tell him what she had overheard and get them both away from his parents—but he was not in the hallway. Her empty stomach about dropped out of her when she heard three voices in the dining room.

He was already in there, as were his parents. Meera approached the dining room feeling sick and unsure of how to proceed. Andreena and Destin were seated on either end of the long table, and she hesitated in the doorway, staring. It was the same dining room where Andreena and others on the Queen's Council had attacked her. The marble floor was smooth and seamless where it had closed around her ankles, and the large window had a fresh pane of glass. The walls were new and freshly papered. Meera swallowed her thoughts of that encounter and took her seat across from Kennick.

She gave him a look, hoping to convey to him that she needed to talk, but he seemed to interpret her look as sickness. "Are you still not feeling well?" he asked.

Andreena perked up at the question. "Not feeling well, dear?" she asked in a sappy sweat tone that made Meera's skin crawl.

"Some food might settle your stomach," Kennick suggested.

"Yes, let us eat!" Andreena cried loudly for the benefit of the waiting servants.

Meera opened her mouth and gaped in utter horror at the food that was put in front of her. How had she ended up here? Staring at the seemingly innocuous plate of salad, she wondered whether some or all of Destin's plant poisons were in it. Then she glanced side to side at Kennick's parents who sat calmly, cutting into the food on their own plates. How could they be so heartless? How could they eat when they planned to kill her baby?

Meera's blood suddenly boiled with her hatred for these people. The same overpowering protective instinct she had felt during her fight with Lethian rose up within her, threatening to burn the table and all of its contents to ashes. Sitting still and rigid, she tried to contain her emotions and power. She stared at her food but didn't touch it, her hands clenched in fists at her sides.

Kennick was watching her with concern that was quickly turning to confusion. "Meera, what is it?" he asked, putting his own fork down.

Andreena and Destin also stopped eating, and Meera glared at

Kennick's mother, sizzling with rage. She hated the woman for what she planned to do to her unborn baby, and she resented her for what she was doing to her own son. Meera didn't know a lot about being a mother, but she couldn't imagine a worse woman for the job than Andreena. Kennick deserved better, and he needed to know what his deranged parents were capable of. "Tell him, Andreena," she said, suddenly wanting her to have to say the words that would break Kennick's heart. She hoped Andreena would feel every inch of her loss when she looked into Kennick's beautiful dark eyes and watched as she lost her son for good.

"I do not know wha—"

"Tell him!" Meera shouted, flames licking down her bare arms in an unspoken threat.

"Meera, what—" Kennick started to ask.

"No! I want her to tell you! Tell him, Andreena!" she shouted again, staring the woman down. Clutching the table in front of her, she fought to contain her writhing fury. Then she watched as Andreena's dark eyes—so similar to her son's—glinted in a way much more devious than Kennick's ever would. She was so cold, so heartless. Meera knew the woman was opening her mouth to lie, so she acted—she shaped the air from Destin's lungs in a rush of passion and power.

Suddenly, Kennick's father was clutching his throat. His mouth gaped wide, but he couldn't draw in a breath—Meera wouldn't let him. He was a vile, despicable man, and she hated him like she had never hated before. In that moment, she felt no pity—no bounds to what she might do to Kennick's father. She thought only of protecting her baby from his poisons and getting Kennick the truth he deserved from his monstrous parents. Destin's eyes bulged in fear, and he started to bang on the table.

"Meera, stop! What are you doing?" Kennick shouted, standing and going to his father.

Meera only had eyes for Andreena. They were in a stand-off with her husband's life hanging in the balance, and Andreena continued to act and to lie. "Kennick, stop her!" she cried, putting a hand to her chest in mock horror.

"Tell him, Andreena," Meera repeated—this time in a low, dangerous voice. She and the red-haired woman eyed one another like wolves from different packs, each daring the other to cross the territory line. Neither one budged. Meera continued to hold her grip on Kennick's father, and Andreena refused to speak—to admit to her heinous crimes. Destin fell to the floor, unconscious. Kennick lunged across the room and gripped Meera's arms, forcing her to look at him instead of his mother.

When Meera finally met Kennick's eyes, she released her shaping. He looked afraid—afraid and horrified. She stood, stumbling back and away from him. What was she doing? Destin was gasping on the floor, and she looked at him with wide eyes, realizing she had almost killed him. What was wrong with her? She didn't want to hurt anyone! Why couldn't she control herself? Kennick stepped toward her, but she retreated, back and back until she hit the window she had once jumped out of. Meera turned to that window.

"No!" Kennick cried, but he was too late—she was already fleeing.

Meera blew out the window with a gust of air and leapt through it. Shaya was coming; she wasn't there yet, but she would be soon. Meera let herself fall straight down and caught herself just before she hit the cobblestone courtyard. Then she ran; she ran toward where Shaya would soon appear over the wall. She didn't know where she was going, but she was going. She couldn't look into Kennick's face again and see his disgust and disappointment—she couldn't do it. There was something wrong with her, and she just needed to get away.

When she and Shaya took to the sky, Meera didn't know what she wanted to do or where she wanted to go, but she had a brief thought: the last time she had lost control, Darreal had stood by her. Shaya latched onto the thought and flew to the Levisade Estate, depositing Meera behind the long, low building in the field of wildflowers.

Meera looked around in shock and disorientation. After her bout of anger and power, she had crashed; she shook from exhaustion and low blood sugar. She barely remembered their flight there. She couldn't think—she needed to eat, to rest.

Entering the estate, she wandered through the halls toward where she thought Darreal's room was, desperate for an ally—for anyone familiar who could care for her. Lethian stood outside the queen's door, giving her presence away. Meera nodded to the blonde former champion, who looked extremely wary at her approach.

"I'm sorry, Lethian. You should be champion," she said in a tremulous voice, then she turned to the door and knocked. Leaning her weight against the doorframe, she felt her legs shake and threaten to buckle under her. Lethian looked like he wanted to tell her to leave—that Darreal didn't want to see anyone—but he didn't.

Darreal called, "Coming, Lethian!" When she opened the door, however, she barely allowed her surprise at finding Meera to show on her face.

"Can I come in?" Meera asked, breathing hard. She didn't feel right. She needed to sit—she needed to eat. That was all she could think about. She wasn't even sure what she was doing there at the queen's door. She felt like she was having a complete meltdown.

Darreal gave her a hard, appraising look, then she stood aside and opened her door wider. Meera shuffled into Darreal's private room and collapsed into a chair in her sitting area without waiting for an invitation. Darreal was wearing a robe but seemed to be in the middle of eating her dinner. Meera stared longingly at the food. Her stomach felt cavernous, and her head spun. "May I?" she asked, reaching toward a basket of bread.

Darreal nodded, looking perplexed. "Meera, what are you doing here?" she asked, remaining standing and ignoring her half-eaten dinner. Her face was not so expressionless now that they were alone.

"I don't know," Meera replied around the food she was shoving in her mouth. "I shouldn't have left Kennick," she groaned, putting a hand to her face, she realized she had fled and left him behind again, without even a raek to follow her. Touching minds with Shaya, she asked her raek to fly back and get him. Shaya was not pleased, but she agreed.

Meera couldn't believe she had run again. She knew Kennick would be hurt, which was the last thing she wanted. What was wrong with her? Why was she so out of her mind? Was this the pregnancy, or was she just losing it? She kept eating and slowly started to feel more like herself.

Eventually, Darreal sat down and pushed her half-eaten plate toward Meera, who took it thankfully. "Meera, what happened? Where did you leave Kennick?" she asked.

Meera sighed and met the queen's golden-brown eyes. With her hair unbound and the circlet she normally wore sitting on her vanity, Darreal looked even younger than she normally did. She looked and sounded Meera's age even if she wasn't. Darreal was old enough to be her grandmother, but Meera supposed that in knell years, they were about the same age.

"I almost killed Destin," she confessed. Darreal's eyes widened in alarm, and Meera immediately tried to explain herself: "They wanted to poison my baby! They were going to make me sick and have me miscarry with Destin's plant poisons. Then they just sat there eating like they weren't horrendous monsters. Kennick had no idea. I just wanted Andreena to confess! I wanted her to be the one to destroy him—not me. Of course, then I did much worse ..."

Meera stopped eating and put her face in her hands. She needed to explain all of this to Kennick, not Darreal. What was she doing there? Maybe she should have gone back with Shaya, she thought, but she was so tired ... She felt ill.

"You are pregnant?" Darreal asked with wide eyes.

Meera "uh-huhed," a little surprised that Sodhu had not told her already.

"And Andreena and Destin tried to poison you?"

Meera "uh-huhed" again.

"Meera, that is punishable in our laws by death. I would not have even tried you had you killed Destin so long as there was proof to your claim."

Meera shrugged. That didn't matter to her. Kennick mattered, and she didn't think having his parents killed was going to help their relationship. "Can I stay here?" she asked pitifully.

"Of course, I will have a room prepared for you," Darreal replied, standing up. But Meera was already getting comfortable in her chair, kicking off her boots and curling up.

Seeing her, Darreal asked, "Are you well, Meera?"

"I'm pregnant!" Meera replied in exasperation with her condition. She felt tired, sick, and a little bit crazy.

Darreal went to a chest of drawers, pulled out something silky, and stood in front of Meera's chair. "Up," she said, holding out a hand.

Meera groaned and dragged herself out of the chair. Darreal proceeded to help her undress and redressed her in one of her own nightgowns. It was too big, and the shoulders kept slipping down, but Meera didn't complain. Darreal then walked her to the bed, pulled back the covers, and tucked her into them. Meera laughed despite her exhaustion. "Wow, being pregnant in Levisade is just like being a queen," she joked.

"Not quite," Darreal said, but she gave her a smile.

"Where are you going to sleep?" Meera asked.

Darreal shrugged her shoulders evasively. It was not a queenly gesture at all.

"I'm sure Lethian has space for you," Meera teased.

Darreal looked truly surprised at that. "Why would you say that?" she asked, biting into one of her girlishly pink lips.

"He obviously loves you," Meera said, incapable of discretion in her current state. Darreal's eyes grew wider yet, making her look almost comical. "You didn't know?" Meera asked.

"No," she replied.

"Do you love him?" Meera asked, curiously.

"Do you really think a queen would answer such a question?" Darreal replied indignantly.

Meera smiled and pulled down the covers on the other side of the bed, unperturbed. "Would the queen deign to sleep next to the commoner?" she asked.

Darreal tinkled a laugh. Then she actually climbed into the bed next to Meera, who grinned at her. As tired and upset and confused as Meera felt, she was overjoyed to have finally broken down some of the barriers between herself and Darreal. She had craved female companionship since she was a small, motherless girl. Soleille and Katrea always felt a bit to her like teasing older sisters, but she thought that Darreal could be the true female friend she had always wanted.

Meera and Darreal laughed and talked until Meera finally succumbed to the heavy weight of her drooping eyelids. She had not felt Shaya return yet, and her last thought before sleep was of Kennick.

20

KENNICK

When—for a second time—Meera leapt through his parent's dining room window, Kennick leaned over the sill and willed himself to jump. He wanted to follow her and had been practicing with the metal cuffs around his wrists and ankles enough to think that he could do so safely. But he hesitated, and his moment of hesitation was enough to ensure that he would not catch up to her. He watched her cut across the courtyard and gripped the sill when she flew away on Shaya's back. She was gone again. She had left him again.

Kennick turned on his parents. He did not know what exactly had happened, but Meera had been endeavoring to get them to confess something. He had known their desire to plan the wedding had been too good to be true. He had known they could not possibly be happy about Meera's pregnancy. Kennick was not fooled by his parents—they had raised him, after all. And yet, he had tried for his unborn child's sake to strengthen his blood ties and give his baby some semblance of a family. He had to remind himself that his child already had a family—more of one than

Kennick had ever had. His baby had him and Meera as well as Shael and the other riders.

Kennick looked hard at his mother, who was calm and composed despite Meera's near fatal attack on his father. He wondered whether Andreena would have even been upset if Destin had died or whether she would have just considered it a mild inconvenience. "Well?" he asked her. "What did you do?"

His mother put a hand over her heart, always a sure sign that she was lying—poorly. "My son, that woman is deranged!" she cried.

Kennick turned away and left the room; he had heard enough. He supposed he would be walking home. First, he retrieved his and Meera's possessions, frustrated to be doing so yet again. He knew she did not mean to keep doing this to him—he had seen the devastation in her eyes when she had looked into his face and seen his fear, and he knew that was why she had run—but it still hurt. He sighed uncharacteristically; they had just repeated their actions from only weeks before—actions that had left them both reeling.

Kennick had been afraid. He had been afraid Meera would not stop—that she would kill his father. But he had not feared for his father's life so much as he had feared for Meera; he had known she would never have forgiven herself for killing Destin even if he had no doubt done something to deserve her wrath. Kennick had not wanted to see his father hurt, but he knew what his parents were capable of. If they—as he suspected from Meera's reaction at dinner—had been trying to poison her, he would have forgiven Meera for killing Destin. His father had always been as wicked and conniving as his mother—he just let Andreena take both the credit and the blame for their actions.

As Kennick left his parent's home for what he decided would be the last time, he heard a raek's shriek. His first thought was of

Endu, even though he knew that was not the case; he still could not sense Endu at all. Then he thought perhaps Meera had returned for him. He ran across the courtyard to where Shaya appeared on the wall, but she was riderless. "Where is Meera?" he called up to her. He would not normally speak directly to another rider's raek, but he did not care about being polite in that moment.

"She is with the queen. She sent me for you," Shaya replied. The ancient wild raek's presence in his mind was more powerful and overwhelming than Kennick had expected it to be. He suddenly had a vague sense of where Meera's incredible abilities came from. While he did not know why she would have gone to the queen, he accepted that she was at least safe and had thought to send Shaya back for him.

Before he could respond, however, he suddenly felt Endu in his mind for the first time in weeks. His raek seemed to have sensed Shaya's immeasurable presence through their tether and radiated with alarm. Kennick could not speak to Endu directly at such a distance, but he attempted to reassure his raek through their bond. Regardless, Endu was coming for him—Kennick could tell. He was shocked but not unhappy to have his raek return to him. He supposed he would wait for Endu rather than flying Shaya to the estate, and he told her so. Shaya responded with an irritated huff and flew away. Her slashing tail sent several stones cascading from the top of the wall.

Kennick waited late into the night for Endu to arrive. And when his raek finally appeared, they regarded one another awkwardly. Kennick did not feel as if he could immediately ride Endu to the estate; they had matters to discuss. He felt Endu had betrayed him by refusing to fly him after Meera and by disappearing. They either needed to come to an agreement about their relationship, or they needed to go their separate ways. He did not want to live with the uncertainty of whether Endu would refuse him or leave him again, and he expressed as much to his raek in thoughts and feelings.

"I suppose your mate conveyed to you that I was away to contemplate my place in the world," Endu said.

Kennick expressed his confusion. Meera had known where Endu was? Why had she not told him? In that moment, he felt like everyone in his life was constantly lying to him and running from him; he had always been easy-going and confident, but he could only take so much. He was getting worn down. He was loyal—why was no one loyal in return?

"And what have you decided?" Kennick asked Endu, dreading the answer.

"A raek should stand by his rider above all else, and I have not done so. I took all I learned from my mother to be fact rather than respecting your judgment. I chose you as my rider because I could sense that you were good and just, and I should have trusted myself and trusted you. A raek's bond with his rider should hold above all other oaths and laws," Endu replied, emanating sincerity and gravitas.

His words struck deep into Kennick's soul. He had never known why Endu had chosen him and had thought it had something to do with him coming from an Old Family—Endu was something of a snob as far as raeken were concerned. Kennick could hardly believe what his raek was saying. Yet, he was glad, and he was grateful. He let Endu know how he felt and forgave him for their previous differences.

"If the human woman is your true mate, then she is worthy of my respect and protection," Endu added.

Kennick walked forward and put a hand to his raek's scaly jaw. They were not usually affectionate with one another, but he decided it was time for them to be different; it was time for them to reforge their partnership and start anew. He rubbed Endu's neck and thanked him. "I am to be a father," he told his raek.

He felt Endu's warm glow of pride at his words. "Then I will protect your young as my own," he replied.

Kennick looked into the raek's dark red eye and felt a surge of hope for their future together. Then he mounted Endu, and they flew to the Levisade Estate to find Meera.

———

THOUGH THEY ARRIVED at the estate very early in the morning, Kennick nonetheless roamed the halls, asking everyone he met whether they had seen Meera. Still, he could not find her. When the sun finally rose, he requested to speak with the queen but was told she was in a meeting. Frustrated, he continued to wander and search, poking his head into the many random rooms lining the estate's hallways. Eventually, he came across Lethian. "Lethian!" he called down the hall, halting the blonde warrior in his tracks.

"Kennick," Lethian replied with a grin, and the two men clasped forearms in greeting.

"Have you seen Meera?" Kennick asked.

Lethian's face appeared uncharacteristically closed at the question, and his grey eyes darted to the side.

"Where is she?" Kennick asked.

"The queen's room," Lethian replied quietly lest anyone else in the hall hear him.

Kennick did not understand. Why would Meera be in the queen's room? Why was Lethian acting so unlike himself? Lethian told him which room it was, and Kennick set out for it, taking long strides to get there quickly and work off some of his frantic energy. By the time he reached the right door, he had convinced himself that something was wrong. He was sure Meera might be hurt in some way.

He pushed into the room, not bothering to knock—he knew Darreal was in a meeting. Then he whipped his head back and forth, scanning the space. He did not even see Meera at first—until her disheveled head popped up from the bed. "Kennick?" she asked groggily as she sat up. Her hair was loose and wild, and she wore some sort of silky nightgown that fell open to expose her breasts.

Kennick stared at her disbelievingly. He could not quite comprehend what he was seeing. He had thought Meera might be hurt or ill or distressed, and the reality of the situation was almost beyond what his mind could process. She was half-naked in the queen's bed, which was rumpled on both sides. She had clearly slept there and not alone. Is this why Lethian had whispered her location?

His heart plummeted as understanding slowly dawned. He forgot all about Meera nearly killing his father and fleeing. She had slept with Darreal! She had left him behind to spend her time in another's bed! Kennick had never thought Meera would hurt him like this, and he froze—his whole body tensing and shutting down in an entirely unfamiliar way. Was he breathing?

Seeing his face, Meera leapt out of bed, running toward him. He could not face her; he tried to turn to leave, but she grabbed his arms. "Kennick, I can explain—your parents, they—" she started to say.

"My parents are horrible, but what have you done, Meera? How could you?" he asked, his voice cracking.

"I didn't mean to hurt him! Is he okay? I'm sorry! I don't want to hurt anyone—I was out of my mind!" she cried.

"I am not talking about that! I am talking about this," Kennick said, gesturing behind her to the bed.

"I know! I ran again, and I'm sorry! I didn't mean to!" she said. There were tears in her eyes, but Kennick was teeming with too much of his own hurt to care.

"You said you would run toward me, and you ran to Darreal —" he said, voice dripping with disdain. "With my child in your stomach!"

"I didn't know where I was going. I—" she tried to say.

"You did not know whose bed you fell into?" he asked.

"I was sick—I ... Wait, what do you think happened? Kennick, I was sick and exhausted, and Darreal let me sleep in her bed," Meera said, beginning to look alarmed.

Kennick did not want to hear it—did not need another person lying to him. He turned away from her, unable to handle this right now.

"Kennick, stop! Where are you going? Let me explain!" she called.

He did not stop. He did not turn. He did not want to stick around to be the fool packing their bags again. He dropped Meera's things with one of the knell who volunteered at the estate, and he and Endu left for home. As they flew and he processed, he calmed somewhat. He was still hurt—he still felt Meera had betrayed him and lied unnecessarily, but a part of him understood.

He supposed Meera had never gotten to experience being with anyone else and was curious. He thought maybe her impending motherhood was making her want to explore new things before the baby came. That was fine, he thought; he could understand that. She could have her time with Darreal, he decided. He would give her the space and time she needed, and he would wait for her at home. He knew he would forgive her when she returned; he would probably forgive her for anything. Still, he felt lost and alone and heartbroken.

21

MEERA

Meera didn't know what was happening. She had thought Kennick was upset about her episode in his parent's dining room, but he'd left seemingly under the impression that she had slept with Darreal. She supposed she *had* slept with Darreal ... but she had not had sex with her! Meera found the idea ridiculous—though she knew in knell culture it was not entirely ridiculous. Glancing down at the silky gown falling off of her, then over at the rumpled bed, she saw what Kennick must have seen.

She could almost laugh at the absurd misunderstanding, except that Kennick had looked both so certain and so hurt. How could he think that she would do that? He wouldn't even let her talk—let her explain. She had made plenty of mistakes in the past twenty-four hours, but she had not been unfaithful. Her stomach lurched, and she sat down rather than running after Kennick half-naked.

She didn't want to make a spectacle of herself—not again. Instead, she ate some breakfast that Darreal must have left out for her and got dressed. Then she calmly left the room to find Kennick. However, try as she might, she couldn't find him, nor could she find Shaya. Shaya, Meera assumed, had gotten bored of ferrying people around and left, but she had no idea where Kennick was. Would he have left without her?

She plunked down on a patio chair, tired and spiraling into despair. Kennick had finally had enough of her, she thought. She couldn't exactly blame him after how she had behaved the last two months, but she was still angry that he could think she would cheat on him of all things. They had just found their way back to one another. How could they have been torn apart so quickly?

Lethian walked across the patio, and she waved him over. She thought he looked reluctant, but he came regardless. "Lethian, have you seen Kennick?" she asked.

"He was looking for you earlier. I told him where to find you," he said, and Meera thought he sounded a little smug.

"Have you seen him since? He … got the wrong idea and left angry," she said, beginning to wonder whether Lethian also had the wrong idea.

The blonde warrior eyed her like he was trying to decipher something.

Meera sighed. "I'm pregnant. Last night I got sick, and Darreal let me sleep in her bed," she blurted.

Lethian's eyes widened, and his posture changed somehow, like he shifted from being ready to fight her to ready to defend her. Meera almost rolled her eyes. What was with the knell and pregnant women? "What wonderful news!" he said, sounding genuine. Meera knew he meant her pregnancy, but she thought he might also mean her not having a physical relationship with Darreal. "I have not seen Kennick since earlier, nor his raek."

"Endu?" Meera asked. "He was here?"

"He was in the back field earlier," Lethian replied.

Meera was surprised but pleased. Then she realized that Kennick had, in fact, left her there, and her pleasure dissipated. She hung her head in her hands. Kennick had left, Shaya was gone, and she was definitely not riding one of Darreal's horses home.

"Are you alright?" Lethian asked, sounding concerned.

"Yes, fine," she said. "You know, Lethian, I really am sorry about the challenge. I wasn't trying to win or to hurt you. You ... you almost hit my stomach, and I freaked out a little bit. I wish you were still Darreal's champion. You should be the one looking after her." Lethian stared at Meera's stomach in frank astonishment, clearly realizing the implication of her words. "It was my fault for fighting," she assured him, not wanting him to feel bad.

"I challenged you, and you won. You are Champion by right. I can continue to protect Darreal as I please," he replied.

Meera smiled at him. Despite her own problems, she would enjoy seeing Darreal and Lethian find happiness with one another and hoped they would. "Now that you're not her champion, maybe you can tell her how you feel," she suggested.

"Darreal has more important concerns," Lethian replied. Meera had no doubt that was what the queen told herself.

When she and Lethian parted ways, she went back to Darreal's room to find a pen and paper. She wrote Kennick a long letter, explaining everything she had heard and done—and not done. She told him she wanted to go home but that Shaya had left, and she hoped he and Endu would fly back for her. She really didn't feel well, and she wanted to be home and to hug Kennick and make things right between them yet again.

Meera waited all that day for a reply and got settled into a room of her own where her possessions waited for her. Packed among her clothes was the tiara Kennick had made at his parent's house. It was beautiful and understated and matched her necklace, and as much as she didn't envision herself as a tiara person, Meera loved it and put it on her dresser with a sigh. She knew Kennick should have received her letter by then and felt so helpless not being able to go to him. The next day around noon, she finally got his reply:

Dearest Meera,

I want you to know that I have read and understood everything in your letter. I believe you, and I am not angry. That said, I cannot help but feel that there is some reason you keep running away from me. If you need the space to figure something out or explore anything on your own, then I am giving it to you. I love you and trust that you will come home when you are ready to be with me. I am having work done at the house anyway, so you will be more comfortable at the estate.

Love,
Kennick

Meera read the letter over and over again, each time experiencing some new emotion. First, she felt disbelief. Then anger. Then she felt hurt, thinking that Kennick didn't want her home. Each time she read it, she thought she would fly home the second Shaya returned. Then she read it one last time, and on her final read-through, she began to think that maybe Kennick was right. Maybe there was something she needed to work out so she would stop panicking and fleeing. The trouble was, she didn't know what that was. It certainly wasn't sexual in nature, she thought with a laugh.

Meera ate with Darreal that night and spoke to her about the situation. Unfortunately, while Darreal was sympathetic, she didn't have any relationship advice to offer her. After a long bout of silence, she asked, "Are you preoccupied with something else, Meera? I often put aside my personal relationships when I have work on my mind."

"You mean always?" Meera asked on a hunch.

Darreal smiled guiltily. "Always ... except when incoherent pregnant humans storm through my bedroom door and make themselves at home," she teased.

Meera laughed; she was enjoying getting to know who Darreal was in private when she was not being the poised, ever-patient ruler of Aegorn. "What could I possibly be preoccupied with? Maybe it's that I ... I don't know, pledged myself to ending a war that has waged for over seventy years and kills more humans every day? I couldn't possibly feel the weight of that burden ..." she said sarcastically.

Darreal hummed sympathetically. She of all people under-stood. She had been living with that burden and more for forty years, while Meera hadn't even lived forty years. "We are making progress, though it is slow," Darreal assured her.

"We? Maybe you are, but I'm not doing anything other than making a mess of my personal life," Meera lamented. "What can I do, Darreal? Should I fly out to the border and shape a giant wall and moat between the lands? That wouldn't stop Terratelle from hunting raeken, but it would end the fighting, I suppose. Or should I just go to the palace alone and kill the royal family? I'm not sure I could do that ..." she said honestly.

She had no love for King Bartro, but she didn't think she could kill him. She didn't even think she could kill Prince Phineas, the biggest monster in all of Terratelle. Her stomach churned thinking about her attack on Destin. Kennick hadn't mentioned it specifically, and she wished that he had. She hated that he had seen her that way.

"I have almost gotten the council to agree to having peace talks with Terratelle. They adamantly refuse to send knell warriors to the war—or riders—but they are considering sending a peaceful envoy to negotiate an end to the war and a ban on raek hunting," Darreal said.

"Really? How soon will they decide?" Meera asked. She would like to go and support Darreal while she negotiated for peace and had the sudden, crazy idea that maybe she could help end the war before having her baby. Then she, Kennick, and their child could live happily ever after and never worry about anything else. It wasn't likely, but it wasn't impossible, either.

"I am pressuring them to decide soon, so we do not end up traveling in winter," Darreal replied, eyeing Meera thoughtfully. "Would you go in your condition, Meera? I understand if you would not, but I cannot lie and say I would not feel safer with you by my side."

"I would go," Meera said with certainty. She saw no reason why she should not. Humans would be easy to defend against with her abilities.

"I will let the council know that tomorrow," Darreal replied.

Meera hoped it would help. She wasn't actually sure if the war was the reason she kept running from Kennick, but it would definitely help her concentrate on their family if her monumental task was behind her. She thought about asking Kennick to go with her, but a part of her wondered if it was he who needed space. She did not want to be apart from him, but he clearly didn't seem to want her home at the moment.

Meera decided to stay at the estate until he asked her to return. She wanted to give Kennick time if he needed it. She knew she had hurt him a lot lately and didn't want to force herself on him. The second he wanted her home, she would be there, but until then, she would focus on the war.

Meera also resolved to go with Darreal if she left to negotiate with Terratelle. Either way, she may not see Kennick for a while, and she ached at the thought, already missing him. She was missing her father as well, who she had not seen since being back at the estate. However, she was anxious about telling him her news; she feared both that he wouldn't care and that he would be disappointed in her for getting pregnant before she was married. She wasn't sure which possibility she dreaded more.

Eventually, Meera racked up the nerve to see her father. Darreal had set up a large workspace for him and provided him with two knell assistants in addition to Ned. Orson Hailship seemed to be single-handedly in charge of organizing the estate's entire collection of manuscripts. Plus, he was making copies of those he thought were historically significant and taking copious notes on everything he learned. Meera felt overwhelmed by his task just walking into his space; it seemed almost as large and unruly as the one she had taken upon herself.

Ned ran up and hugged her hello. She was surprised by the gesture but hugged him back. "Miss Meera! How good to see you!" he exclaimed. He proceeded to gabble on excitedly about how Darreal had made arrangements for his mother to move to the estate and had given her a job as well before telling her all about their latest discoveries and the other two assistants, even though the man and woman in question were well-within knell hearing range.

Meera nodded and smiled and listened with as much enthusiasm as she could, but she hoped to get her father alone for a minute.

"That's enough, Ned!" her father finally called, tearing himself away from his work to come over. "Meera, I didn't know you were here," he said, hugging her.

She hugged him back and held on an extra moment after he

had already let go. "Can you come outside and talk for a minute?" she asked.

Her father glanced regretfully at his work, making her stomach flip and her throat burn with acid. Why couldn't he have a purpose *and* take time for her? "Of course," he replied, following her outside. "Is everything okay?" he asked, but he didn't really look like he wanted to know.

Suddenly, Meera felt a rush of anger. "Do you even care if it isn't?" she asked. "I've barely seen you—barely heard from you. I don't feel like I ever got you back from the war, Father," she said, her voice breaking. She put a hand to her mouth to suppress her grief. Her emotions had been all over the place, and she cursed her changing body.

Her father adjusted his wire-framed glasses and looked down at the ground. "Meera, I care, but you are this other person—this changed, powerful woman—and I don't exactly know how to be your father anymore. I can't help you learn how to use magic or win fights ... I feel I am living in the ocean, and I study the fish in the water for lack of the ability to integrate myself amongst them. I study this place and these people for you, Meera. It is all I know how to do for the person you have become. I barely even see your mother in your face anymore," he added, touching her cheek.

Meera flinched at his words and touch. She accepted that he was doing his best, but his comment about her mother stung. She tried to swallow her pain with the acid in her throat, and hesitantly, she said, "Father, my body has changed—my face has thinned—but I'm the same person I always was. I live my life differently, but I am the same at my core. I wish you could see that, and I wish you could see me for all that I am and not just what remains of my mother."

Pausing, she cleared her throat and swallowed her tears once more. Then she continued: "I just wanted to tell you that I'm pregnant. You're going to be a grandfather. I hope you figure out how to do that in a way that doesn't involve research." She didn't wait to learn how he reacted to her news; she left.

Meera went to Darreal's room and waited for her friend to appear, hoping a decision had been reached by the council. The queen eventually entered with an uncharacteristically wide smile on her face. "I was hoping you would be here," she said first, making Meera's heart soar. At least someone wanted her around, she thought. "The council has agreed that we should negotiate for peace. We leave this week," Darreal announced.

22

KENNICK

K ennick went home, oversaw the construction at the house, and ate his meals at the peninsula with the other riders. He felt at peace with the letter he had written to Meera. He thought it was right to give her the freedom she needed when she still had the chance, but he missed her. He missed her, and he hated not being with her to experience every moment of her pregnancy. Even so, he felt he had done the right thing ... until he received her reply:

Kennick,

I miss you. I hate to be away from you, but I understand that you need space from me right now. Thank you for handling the addition, but please wait for me before decorating the baby's room. I don't want to come home and find a metal crib—there's something not right about that. I told my father about the baby. He continues to work on his research.

Anyway, since I don't seem to be needed in Levisade, I have decided to travel with Darreal to try to negotiate peace with Terratelle. We leave tomorrow. I would stop home before leaving, but Shaya has still not returned. She will need to meet me on my travels. I will miss you terribly, but perhaps I can accomplish something in our time apart. I promise I will not take any undue risks, and I will be back well before the baby is due.

Love,
Meera

Kennick stared at the letter in confusion. Meera seemed to think he needed space, and he had thought that she did. He sighed. However, despite their obvious misunderstanding, he knew she would want to go with Darreal to negotiate the end of the war regardless. He knew there was no point in asking her to return now. Still, he would have gone with her if she had asked ... Should he go anyway?

Kennick went into the house to pack his belongings, but instead, he read the letter again. Meera promised to be careful. He had annoyed her and offended her fussing over her pregnancy before, and he did not want to do that again; he did not want to be overbearing and overprotective again. He wanted Meera to know that he trusted her. Instead of packing, he wrote back:

Dearest Meera,

I would prefer not to be apart from you and to join you on your journey, but I trust you to take care of yourself. I wish you and Darreal speed and success in your venture.

Love,

Kennick

P.S. If not a metal crib, how about diamond? You will have to return in time to shape it.

Kennick sent the letter, and he also asked Endu to escort Meera until Shaya reached her in case she needed or wanted to return to Levisade—or to him. Then he did his best to occupy himself and survive the days of wondering where Meera was and whether she was okay. He knew Darreal would travel with her best warriors and protection, and he knew none of them was nearly as powerful as Meera. And yet, he could not help but worry. Two agonizing weeks later, he received a letter:

Kennick,

I thought we were going straight to the border to negotiate with Terratelle, but that, of course, would have been too simple and too efficient for the knell. Instead, we have been meandering through Aegorn while Darreal meets with human leaders to discuss what they would hope to gain in a negotiation. It's been incredibly tedious.

I've been trying to get to know Endu better, but he's about as sociable as Shaya, who I might add, I still have not seen or heard from. I continue to feel sick, but I've been keeping down more food lately. I'm spending all of my money on food from vendors and taverns because knell travel food is even worse than regular knell food.

I hope you are being more productive than I am. By the way, is a wooden crib really too traditional? If so, I think we should get Isbaen to weave one for us. Do you think he can weave plant fibers as well as he can his own hair?

Love,
Meera

Kennick smiled at the letter and wrote back:

Dearest Meera,

The addition is coming along nicely. I cannot say I am sad to hear you are not doing anything more exciting. I am sure Darreal has her reasons and a plan in mind. Thank Endu for remaining with you for me, and tell him he has my permission to make conversation as well.

I think if I mention a crib to the others, a competition may ensue. Should I do it? It could be a bloodbath, and we would not want to sully our child's bed with carnage. On the other hand, it could be an amusing distraction from the long hours I spend missing you. Please come home soon.

Love,
Kennick

The next week, Endu returned alone once Shaya finally joined Meera. Kennick's raek did not have much to say about Meera's travels, however. "She said she has nothing new to report to you and sends her love," Endu relayed. He did not express his irritation at being used as a carrier bird, but Kennick sensed it and thanked him profusely for accompanying Meera for so long.

Now that Endu had returned, Kennick had to resist the urge to jump on the raek's back and fly to Meera himself. He did not think he would be unwelcome, but he wanted to continue proving his trust to her. She did not say so, but he knew she was hurt by his earlier accusations about Darreal. Assuming the worst, he had not paused to consider other possibilities. As difficult as it was,

Kennick would stay home and continue to support Meera from a distance.

Summer gradually changed to fall—not that Levisade changed much. The leaves began to turn colors, and Meera finished her third month of pregnancy somewhere without him. Soleille informed Kennick that her pregnancy would begin to show soon, and he hoped she would be back in time for him to see the first emergence of a bump. It was then that he received the news he had been both expecting and dreading:

> *Kennick,*
>
> *We're finally going to the border to meet with Prince Otto and a group of generals to discuss negotiations. Otto has promised only a discussion since he must relay everything to the king for final approval. He assures us it will be peaceful. There's no real precedent of trust for this kind of meeting between Aegorn and Terratelle, but we all feel confident that they couldn't hurt us even if they tried.*
>
> *I will be at the meeting to protect us all, as will Lethian and a group of warriors under his command. Darreal feels she has a fair offer to make Otto (one that I would explain if I had bothered to keep up with all the split hairs these many days). Shaya is tempted to eat the prince to show Terratelle what wild raeken think of their royals. I can only hope that Otto is nothing like his brother.*
>
> *It feels incredibly strange to be this close to Terratelle again— mostly because it does not feel like home anymore. When I think of home, I think of you, the other riders, and the Riders' Holt. Hopefully, our task here will be accomplished in the coming days, and I'll be home again soon.*
>
> *Did you opt for a bloodbath? I'd like to put money down on*

Katrea. I have no idea what she would make, but I'm sure it would surprise me.

Love,
Meera

It was happening, Kennick thought; Meera was at the border, about to cross into Terratelle and face some of their leadership. He knew the knell had every advantage against their human opponents, and he knew Meera was the most formidable of them all ... But he also knew the burning in his chest would not subside until he heard from her again—or maybe not until she was safe at home. Kennick left for the peninsula to tell the others the news.

"I cannot remember the last time one of our monarchs crossed into Terratelle," Florean said wonderingly.

"Darreal is certainly taking a stand and making her own way as queen," Isbaen added.

"It is good to see," Gendryl remarked. "The knell should not fear change so much."

"Caution and fear are not mutually exclusive," Isbaen replied.

Hadjal nodded her vehement agreement to his statement, but Kennick shifted in his seat uncomfortably. Things between Gendryl and Isbaen had been strained since Gendryl had announced that before his transition he had ended a pregnancy. Isbaen was obviously uncomfortable with the knowledge, and Gendryl clearly knew it. And yet, they were both too even-tempered to have the confrontation they needed to get past their differences. The tension between them continued to linger and corrode all of their interactions, spoiling many of the riders' meals of late.

"When is the meeting?" Shael asked.

"She wrote the letter this morning. It is probably happening right now," Kennick replied.

"Will you stay here until you get word from her again?" Shael asked, looking about as anxious as Kennick felt.

He nodded and smiled gratefully at his friend. Lately, their shared love of Meera had gotten between them, but in that moment, Kennick felt it was drawing them together. It comforted him to know that Shael was as worried for Meera as he was. And so, they all sat and waited, unsure of how long it would take to receive news.

23

MEERA

Weeks of travel and frustration had worn Meera down. Her pregnancy made her unendingly tired and was also a constant reminder that her time was running out—her time to help end the war, that is. She pressured Darreal every day and night to move faster, to do more; she needed this time away from home and away from Kennick to mean something. She couldn't bear the thought of it all being a waste. Now, they were finally at the border to try to negotiate peace, and she was a bundle of nervous anticipation.

The border didn't look at all like she had expected it to, but Meera supposed it was an immense stretch of land, and they were only staring at a small chunk of it. There was nothing there. It was just a large field of grass where a forest had long ago been felled for wood. They were camped several miles from the nearest platoon of troops on either side. That was the point, really; they were supposed to be meeting somewhere safe, quiet, and neutral.

Since knell were inherently stronger and more dangerous than humans, Darreal had offered to cross the border into

Terratelle. It was a calculated show of good-faith, but one that none of them actually felt good about. Meera didn't know Prince Otto, but she had known his father and brother and didn't trust the prince for a second. She would be going into the meeting fully prepared to fight if she had to.

She had been dressed and waiting the entire day, wearing one of the fitted outfits Follaria had made her in dark purple. She tugged at the shirt uncomfortably. While her baby bump was not yet showing, her decreased activity and increased appetite were quickly shrinking her clothes. She knew it wouldn't be long until they didn't fit at all, but she thought she would be home in plenty of time to have new ones made.

Meera supposed she and Kennick had never managed to plan their wedding. But she still wanted him to have the wedding he desired and decided she would just have to get used to the idea of walking down the aisle with her stomach sticking out. Kennick would love that, and the thought of his gleaming eyes waiting for her at the end of the aisle brought tears to her own. Meera's emotions were still all over the place—although she suspected she would be crying for Kennick even if she wasn't pregnant.

Darreal abruptly entered her tent, where Meera awaited her. "What now?" she asked, seeing Meera's tears. "Did Lethian hold a tent flap open for you and offend you again? Did Shaya say you were getting soft? Did one of the assisting knell offer you venison jerky that may have once been a deer with parents and a family who missed them?"

Meera laughed. She supposed she had been a bit ridiculous lately. "I'm just missing Kennick," she said, wiping her eyes.

"Focus on the meeting," Darreal told her. "If all goes well, you can fly home tomorrow."

Meera nodded. It was only an hour until they were to cross the border—just a divot in the field—and enter the large tent they had been watching the Terratellens erect. Darreal proceeded to change her practical travel clothes for a golden gown that was laid out for her.

"Shouldn't you wear something that would be easier to fight in?" Meera asked.

"No, that is the whole point. I will arrive in formal, impractical clothing to show that we trust and respect them," Darreal replied, turning so that Meera could help her lace the back of the dress.

"But we don't trust them ..." Meera pointed out unnecessarily.

"No, but I trust you and Lethian and the others. I am not a fighter, nor am I capable of much shaping, anyway," Darreal admitted to her.

Meera had wondered but had never asked. The knowledge in no way detracted from her respect for her friend, however; Darreal had her own strengths. As a finishing touch, the queen loaded herself with jewelry and her usual gold circlet. They were her armor in this war of politicking. Meera wished she had her sword with her—not that she could bring it to the meeting. Both sides had agreed to no weapons and a set number of guards.

"Meera, I know that you are more than capable of protecting yourself, but if anything does happen at the meeting, try not to let them see that you are shaping. I do not want them to target you for any reason. I would sooner die than risk your unborn child," Darreal said.

Meera didn't ask her friend if she was serious—she was always serious. Tears flooded her eyes once more. "I will not let anyone harm my baby or my friend," she assured Darreal, reaching out to stroke her delicate, angular face.

Together they left the tent to gather for their departure. They were allowed five leaders for the discussion—including Darreal— and were also taking a member of her council and three human leaders of Aegorn to show Terratelle that knell could work alongside humans. The three humans Darreal had chosen for the task were the three that had been the least afraid of her when she had knocked on their doors these past weeks and the most willing to discuss an end to the war. They were all men, but Meera had assured her that the leaders representing Terratelle would all be men and would be less receptive to negotiating with a group of women.

In addition to their five leaders, they were permitted five guards. Meera, Lethian, and three of his warriors were to be the unarmed guards. In total, there would be twenty people present in the tent: ten at the table and ten on the outskirts. Meera assumed there would be a table, anyway. Once their group gathered together, they walked as one across the field toward the tent. Meera stayed close to Darreal on one side and Lethian on the other. Her heart beat in a nervous gallop in her chest.

When none of the group's keen knell senses caught anything amiss, they entered the open flap of the tent. As Meera passed under the flap, she shut her eyes to better sense her surroundings. She would be much more attuned to threatening movements and activity outside the tent with her eyes shut. Sensing the ten men already present, she found five standing by their chairs and five lining the canvas wall behind them. There was, in fact, a large oval table for the leaders to sit around.

"Queen Darreal, welcome," a deep voice said—presumably Prince Otto's.

"Thank you for hosting us, Prince Otto," Darreal replied, though hosting the gathering was more of a privilege than a burden.

"I'm pleased to finally be discussing peace. Even in my young life, this war has felt much too long and costly," Otto replied.

Meera felt an overwhelming curiosity about the prince and longed to observe him, but she kept her eyes shut and focused her attention on the movements all around the tent instead. There was a moment in which everyone stood silently around the table, then Otto said, "Please, Queen Darreal, after you."

Darreal was not accustomed to being deferred to at tables as a woman, but she acquiesced and took her seat first, followed by the male leadership present.

"Before we get started, I must ask whether I might have servers enter with refreshments. They are all young boys—not soldiers, of course, just servers. Would that be amenable?" Otto asked.

Meera immediately tensed. This had not been previously agreed upon, but now Darreal would have to say yes; she couldn't appear not to trust Otto or to be afraid of young boys. "Very well," Darreal said airily.

Meera knew better than to assume that the queen's light tone meant she was not on full alert. She sensed three small figures enter the tent, and the boys proceeded to place food and beverages around the table. Then the Terratellen leaders made a show of drinking and eating to prove that the refreshments weren't poisoned—an unnecessary gesture, considering one of Lethian's warriors was a water shaper and had honed her abilities to sense poisons.

It was Tara—the dark-haired, stern-faced knell woman who often acted as a guard around the Levisade Estate and had led Meera into the estate on two separate occasions. Meera had been practicing with Tara to learn the ability but had not yet mastered it. It was one she wanted to have if she ever dined with Kennick's parents again.

Darreal took some food and drink as another show of good-faith, and the other leaders from Aegorn followed suit. Eventually, they began to discuss possible terms for a cease-fire, but Meera didn't listen. As interested as she was, her role was to keep them all safe. Darreal could handle the negotiating.

Meera sensed Shaya flying around in agitated circles across the border, high in the sky where the Terratellens wouldn't see her. "What is happening?" Shaya asked.

"Don't distract me," Meera told her mentally. She was in the process of sensing the room for anything that might be used as a weapon and was also keeping tabs on the figures that moved around outside of the tent, though no one came close except the three young boys who occasionally walked in and out to bring in more food. Each time one of them reappeared, Meera scanned them for hidden weapons, but she didn't sense anything amiss.

When Darreal suddenly raised her voice, Meera shifted her attention to the conversation at the table. "We are not flexible on that stipulation," she was saying forcefully. Meera hadn't caught which stipulation that was.

"Do you see my general here?" Prince Otto asked, apparently gesturing to one of the present generals. "He's had first-hand experience with raeken, as you can see, and he assures me that they're as soulless and monstrous as I've ever thought to imagine. We won't allow them to fly undeterred over the innocents of our land."

"Tell me, General, was the raek in question perhaps being attacked or detained in any way when it assaulted you?" Darreal asked pointedly.

Meera didn't listen to the general's reply; she forced herself to tune out the conversation at the table. What she had heard doused whatever small hope she'd had for this meeting, but she would not let her disappointment distract her. She felt a sudden, stabbing cramp in her stomach, but she ignored it, trying to focus. She didn't feel right, she realized, but her pregnancy often waged war on her body. She shifted subtly on her feet but didn't otherwise move; she didn't want to alarm her companions or the human guards across the tent.

As the meeting wore on, she felt a little weak and light-headed and cursed her pregnancy for distracting her at such an important time. However, she did her best to disregard the sensations within her and do her duty. The conversation at the table continued. Eventually, the leaders had finished multiple bottles of wine, and the three boys left to retrieve more. While Prince Otto hadn't exactly agreed with Darreal on anything, he did seem genuinely open to discussion and negotiation. The meeting, at least, may not have been a complete waste of time.

Meera kept having occasional cramps, but she was used to ignoring such things—she had been pregnant for three months and a woman for much longer, after all. When the serving boys returned, each with a fresh bottle of wine, she once more searched their bodies for anything unusual but didn't notice anything. The boys each approached the table from different angles and pulled the stoppers from their bottles. Then, in unison, they put the supposed stoppers to their lips, turned toward Darreal, and blew.

Meera was so startled, she reacted on instinct; she immediately incinerated the stoppers, the minute projectiles leaving their hollow cores, and the boys that were holding them. Her pale flames devoured them all in an instant of still shock before pandemonium tore loose in the tent. Meera finally opened her eyes, dazed. Then she doubled over as an especially intense cramp wracked her abdomen.

Lethian lunged for Darreal, shaping a rock wall up around her in unnecessary protection. "Retreat!" Darreal shouted, a direct order to leave rather than fight. The knell in the room were tense and poised to shape, but they held back. The Terratellen leaders and guards looked terrified and scrambled to get out of the tent— all but one, who seemed to be striding toward Meera.

Staring fuzzily at his red general's uniform, she wondered how he had known she had done it? She hadn't moved—she had just shaped ... She had just burned three young boys with her raek fire, she recognized in abject horror. Then another violent cramp seized her body, and she acknowledged the feeling she had been repressing all day—the feeling of imminent, impending loss.

Meera suddenly knew. The same instinct that had alerted her to the moment of her conception, alerted her to what was now happening within her: she was losing her baby. Right then and there, her womb was expelling her unformed child from her body —casting it out long before it was ready. She could feel it in a way that she hadn't been able to feel the baby growing within her. She could feel it in every cramping, cringing inch of her flesh.

As knell and humans alike rushed around her to leave the tent, she fell to her knees. "Meera!" Darreal called, but she ignored her queen and friend. Lethian had her; she was safe. Meera could only focus on the feeling within her—the horrible, soul-crushing feeling of violent loss. Now that she had let it reach her, she couldn't pull away. Bits of ash particles stirred in the air before her, and she stared at them blankly. They were all that remained of the boys she had burned. She had never even seen their young faces.

Meera's heart cramped and died with the rest of her, and she felt like it would erupt from her gasping mouth. She was a child-killer. She had ripped three young, innocent boys from the world, and the world was draining away her own child as penance. She reached a trembling hand to touch the ash, but her movement caused a current that pushed it away. Abstractly, she wondered if she should get up—if she should leave with the others—but she couldn't make herself move.

When the general reached her, he bent and gripped her arm as if to detain her. Meera didn't struggle. She didn't shape. She didn't even look at him. She didn't care. She was lost with her baby. She deserved it, she thought; she deserved whatever awful thing they thought to do to her. She had killed her baby and those boys. She was a monster—a child-burning beast.

She felt Shaya in her mind—felt her raek reaching out to her, coming toward her—but for once, she managed to block her out. She closed their connection, overpowering Shaya's mysterious ancient strength. She just wanted to be alone—as alone as her emptying womb would leave her. Curling in on herself, she put her face to her knees and clutched her legs. The general maintained his grip on her arm but didn't otherwise bother her.

Meera's body cramped and heaved to force out the baby she had learned to love—her baby. Kennick's baby. The baby that had a new room waiting for it at home and possibly a plethora of crib options. The baby that might have been but was now nothing but a slow seep of blood and tissue. Meera felt the warm slickness coursing from her, and she burned it as it left her body. She was a child-burner.

24

KENNICK

Kennick and the other riders waited all day for word that never came. He supposed it was a long way for a carrier bird to fly, but still, he could not sleep that night; he had an overwhelming, irrational feeling that something was wrong. He considered getting on Endu's back and flying to the border over and over again, each time telling himself to wait, to be patient. The meeting was long over by then, and if he left, he would likely fly past the carrier bird on its way to him with Meera's letter.

The bird finally came the next morning when Kennick was at breakfast at Hadjal's house, but the letter he opened was not from Meera. Standing, he read the words with shaking hands:

Rider Kennick,

During our meeting with Prince Otto, three young boys made an attempt on my life. Meera killed them, and when we retreated, she did not exit the tent with us. I can only assume she was too consumed by her guilt to leave. As much as I want to stay and fight for my friend, my council is insisting we return immediately to Levisade.

I have no reason to believe Meera is hurt. I expect she will make her way across the border at any time. I can think of no Terratellen force that could prevent her from escaping, and so, I can think of no viable reason why I should command our warriors to risk their lives retrieving her.

Your actions are, of course, under the purview of Hadjal.

Darreal

"What is it?" Shael asked, rising from his seat and skirting the table to read the letter in Kennick's hand.

Kennick shoved it at him, processing Darreal's words. His first reaction was anger with Darreal for not forcing Meera out of the tent or going back for her, but he knew the queen had had other responsibilities. Also, he—like Darreal—could not think of a cage Meera could not easily break out of. She must be devastated, he thought. Children? Meera had never wanted to hurt anyone—let alone kill.

Kennick knew she struggled to view herself as being more important than anyone else, even though she was more important to him than everyone in the whole world combined. Yet, she was fiercely protective of their baby; he thought she must have acted out of instinct. While she often shut down after such outbursts, surely she would get herself to safety ... She would not allow herself or their baby to be hurt or held captive, would she?

Shael handed the letter to Isbaen, who proceeded to read it aloud. Everyone appeared as shocked and stumped as Kennick felt. Darreal's last line was clear, however, and he looked to Hadjal. "We have no reason to believe Meera is in danger, and I will not risk any of you to cross the border and find out," she said. "We will all stay here and wait for more news."

Kennick shook his head. "No," he said, without really thinking about what he was saying.

"Kennick, Meera can protect herself," Hadjal insisted.

"What if she cannot? What if she is hurt or sick?" he asked. He was going—of course, he was going. He glanced at Shael, who gave him a subtle nod.

Hadjal did not miss the exchange. "You will both stay here, or you will break your oaths to the riders," she announced in a low, commanding voice.

"Then we will break our oaths," Kennick replied. "I will not make the same mistake twice."

"Cerun and I are coming," Shael told him.

They both paused a moment, waiting to see if anyone else would join them. Kennick would not beg or petition his fellow riders to break their oaths with him, but he still thought that they might.

"Falkai and I will go as far as the border in case Meera needs me," Soleille said, looking to Hadjal for approval.

Hadjal sighed but nodded her consent.

"Thank you," Kennick said to Soleille. Then he picked up his and Shael's swords from where they had dropped them and sharpened both blades.

"Kennick, please," Hadjal begged, coming around the table. "I know you love Meera—we all do—but keeping the riders safe is more important than any one person."

"What good are we if we do not even fight for our own?" Kennick snapped. "The riders used to fight for peace and justice, and now you have us all cowering here for fear of losing our lives! I would rather die than abandon my family or my beliefs!" He handed Shael his sword, and they both walked into the field where Cerun and Endu would soon retrieve them.

"Take me!" Gendryl cried, running after them. "I will go across the border with you to find Meera."

Kennick looked at the slight, unmuscled man in surprise. Isbaen stood from Hadjal's table, eyes wide. "That is kind, Gendryl, but you cannot fight. You would only get in the way," Kennick told him.

The man nodded, not bothering to argue.

Sodhu came running out of the house and pressed bags of food and supplies into Kennick's arms. "Bring her back," she said, hugging them both. "And be safe." Kennick squeezed her tightly, knowing she was supporting them rather than her partner. It meant a lot to him.

The other riders remained at the table and watched them mount their raeken and fly away. All except Soleille, who had gone to her house for supplies and would follow them. Kennick was not entirely surprised that the others had chosen to stay behind considering none of them had gone after Shael, but he was disappointed. They all knew what had befallen Shael in the hands of the Terratellens, and he hated that they would not stand and fight so that the same would not happen to Meera.

KENNICK AND SHAEL flew most of the day to reach the border. Then they flew along its length to find Darreal. Kennick supposed they should learn as much as they could before charging into enemy territory. Meera may have even walked back to her tent by the time they reached it. The small strip of land where Darreal's camp was located was now surrounded by swarms of soldiers and knell warriors, protecting their queen and defending their country. Many of the humans stared up at them warily when they flew overhead. Endu and Cerun found a clear patch behind a cluster of tents in which to land.

Now that Kennick was close to where he knew Meera had been, he felt a sudden rush of urgency. The situation was starting to feel real, and it felt even more real when Darreal appeared, walking briskly toward them. He could tell by her gait that Meera had not simply extricated herself from the Terratellen troops and walked across the border. "Any news?" he asked, running up to her. Lethian stood protectively at her side, but Kennick ignored him.

"No, Kennick. I am sorry," she replied. "We are packing up to leave." She sounded regretful but resigned.

"What exactly happened?" Shael asked, coming up behind him.

Darreal looked vaguely surprised to see him there but did not comment. "Prince Otto used three young boys as seemingly harmless servers. The boys blew air darts out of hollow wine bottle stoppers, and Meera incinerated them. It happened so quickly, I doubt she gave it any thought. When I gave the order to retreat, she remained where she was.

"I saw her fall to her knees as we left the tent. I called to her, but she did not react. I am sorry. I wish I had done more," she admitted, giving Lethian what Kennick thought was an irritated look. Kennick imagined Lethian had prioritized getting Darreal to safety and had not spared Meera a second's thought. He shot the blonde warrior a scathing look of his own.

"What should we do?" Shael asked Kennick, who was wondering the same thing.

"Hadjal let you come?" Darreal asked, looking skeptical.

"No," Kennick replied. "And you will not stop us either."

Darreal gave him what he thought was probably the first

genuine smile he had ever received from the queen. "Meera is my friend. I wish you both luck, as the humans say," she responded.

Just then, Shaya's shimmering bulk dove toward them from above. She landed close to Endu and Cerun with several quick, successive flaps that whipped them all with wind. Then she hit the ground with a thump that rattled the bones of the surrounding troops. Kennick could not usually gauge much from the eyes of the wild raek, but he could see Shaya's fury now. Running up to her, he noticed she quivered in agitation. "Where is she? Why have you not gotten her?" he asked.

Shaya huffed a hot burst of smoke right in his face, and he coughed and waved his hand to clear the air. "She has blocked me out. I feel her only faintly. She is moving farther away," Shaya replied, making Kennick's mind buzz with her overwhelming presence.

"Why have you not gone after her?" he asked again.

Shaya opened her great toothy maw and shrieked at him. Endu and Cerun both reacted, but Kennick held up a quelling hand to calm them. Then he stared Shaya down and waited for a real response. After she had clawed the ground and swished her tail a bit, she finally answered. "She was meant to be a warrior! At the first sign of conflict, she fell to the ground like a sniveling weakling!" the raek shouted in his mind, making him wince.

Kennick could not tell if Shaya was truly disappointed in Meera or just scared for her. Either way, he was angry. "Can you at least tell me where she is, so Endu and I can retrieve her?" he asked.

Shaya turned to Endu, peering at him as if weighing the odds of his success. Endu fluffed his dark red feathers and spread his wings indignantly.

"Enough!" Kennick shouted at them both. He really did not think riders got enough credit for putting up with such temperamental creatures. "Where is Meera, Shaya? Can you tell? Is she hurt?"

Shaya rounded on him, eyes sizzling. "Hurt? No! She is not hurt, yet she lets them drag her away! She does not even seem to care. I do not know where they are going, but it seems to be a place she is familiar with. She is blocking me out, and I cannot overpower her. That is how she chooses to use her immense strength," she cried in his mind. Kennick could not tell, exactly, but he suspected Shaya was hurt by Meera's rejection.

"She shuts down and runs when she is upset, Shaya. It is not about you or me. We need to find her," he said calmly.

"You find her if you want. I will go in search of a true warrior," Shaya retorted before launching herself aggressively into the sky. Kennick was sad to see her go—sad for Meera; he knew what it felt like to have your raek give up on you. However, Shaya had at least given him some useful information.

"What did she say?" Shael asked, coming up beside him.

"She said Meera is unhurt and letting the Terratellens take her somewhere familiar. Would that be the palace?" he asked.

Shael nodded, looking grim but determined. They both thought in silence for a minute.

"We could try to head them off, but we would need daylight to search the roads and would be exposed ..." Kennick mused.

Shael nodded. "We should wait and let them get her to the palace," he replied, confirming what Kennick already thought but hated to say. "When she is at the palace, we will be able to fly there directly at night when we will not be seen. I know the way to the dungeon," he added grimly.

Kennick was glad Shael was there with him. It was comforting not to make these decisions alone and to have someone familiar with their destination. He wished they could leave right away—fly straight to Meera regardless of the risk, but he would not do that.

Kennick was many things, but he was not brash; he would not risk his life, Shael's, Endu's, and Cerun's unless he was sure Meera was in danger.

As far as he could tell, she was not in danger so much as she was distraught—destroyed by what she had done. He ached at the thought of her pain. He hurt for his beloved Meera who had killed children to defend her queen and friend. She would not recover from this easily.

"She will defend herself if she needs to," Shael reassured him.

Kennick grabbed his friend and pulled him to his chest in a tight embrace.

"We'll get her back," Shael said quietly.

Kennick nodded and swallowed his fear. Even if they retrieved Meera, he worried her mind would not recover from her trauma. "Have you killed, Shael?" he asked his friend, pulling away to look into his eyes.

"I have," he replied. "But only fully grown men who were trying to capture me."

Kennick nodded. He, too, had killed when he was at the border, but the men he had killed had been trying to kill men he knew and cared for. He could live with that—even if their faces clouded the periphery of his mind at times. He wondered if he could live with it had they been children bearing swords ...

25

MEERA

Meera opened her eyes and stared uncomprehendingly at the blue sky overhead through wooden bars. Her body rocked and jimmied from the movement of the wagon beneath her. She must have passed out, she thought. It didn't take her any time to remember what had happened—it sat heavy as a mountain on the forefront of her consciousness.

Staring at the lazy white clouds above her, she reached up to them. She would rather be in the sky than on the ground. Her problems always felt small and insignificant from so high up. But she didn't deserve that, she thought; she deserved to be right where she was. She let her hand drop back down to the rough wood of the wagon.

She was thirsty, but she didn't shape herself water to drink. She let herself be thirsty. She let herself be hungry. She let the chill of the cooling autumn air seep into the sleeves of her shirt and prickle her skin. She let the wagon bump and sway under her body, taking her wherever it would take her. She just couldn't care—not for herself. She was a monster, a child-burner.

Eventually, the wagon stopped, and Meera sat up slowly to observe her surroundings with vague disinterest. She was in a large wooden cage fitted into a wagon bed. Stretching out a hand, she touched the wooden bars that were like crib bars. It was fitting, she thought. A man stepped up to the back of the wagon and looked in at her. At first, Meera had trouble focusing on him; her thoughts kept straying and her eyes wandering. Then, when she finally looked, she thought maybe she really was where she belonged. "Am I dead?" she asked Linus.

"No," he replied.

She supposed he was right; he looked too worn to be enjoying the afterlife he deserved. Linus's honey-brown hair was longer and tied back. He could only be eighteen now, but he looked older. It was his eyes, she thought; his eyes didn't have any of their old joy and charm. His jaw was more pronounced, too, and he had grown a short beard which covered most—but not all—of the burn scars on the left side of his face.

Meera crawled closer to the bars to gaze at him, and he stared back, his eyebrows furrowed. She saw that his left hand was gone. It must have been removed, too damaged by Cerun's flames to heal. He, in turn, studied the silver swirls that graced Meera's neck, chest, and shoulder. Their scars were night and day: hers were orderly and even-toned, beautiful even, while his were haphazard and uneven where parts of his flesh had healed faster than others, where sections had festered and been cut away.

Meera noticed his red uniform and realized that he'd been the general in the meeting—the one who had spoken about his experience with a raek, the one who had grabbed her. She wasn't angry; she deserved it. She smiled at her friend, glad to have this chance to see him again even if she didn't deserve such a gift. "I'm so glad you're alive," she said, reaching a hand through the bars to touch his face.

He flinched away from her. Returning her hand to the bar, her sleeve slipped down, revealing Linus's bracelet on her wrist. It was old and a little worse-for-wear; some of the purple glass beads were cracked, and others had fallen off, leaving the strand sparse. Linus stared at the bracelet, his expression unreadable. "You're still wearing it," he said quietly. His voice was deeper and gruffer than she remembered it. He scratched at his short beard with his only hand.

"Always," she told him.

When his eyes focused back on her face, they darkened. She could see his mistrust, his hate even, but she didn't mind; she deserved it. Then his eyes shifted back to her hand. "That's some ring," he remarked.

Meera squeezed her eyes shut for a moment. She didn't want to think about that. "How's your mother? And your sister?" she asked.

Linus looked angry at that. "Don't talk about my family!" he hissed.

"Okay," she said, and she gazed and gazed at him. She couldn't get enough of his face. She had really thought he was dead, and here he was—so beautiful, if scarred. She felt her eyes fill with tears and wiped them away. She couldn't let herself do that. If she started, she would never stop.

"I don't need your pity," Linus snapped.

"Pity?" Meera asked with a laugh. "I thought you were dead, and here you are! You're alive and so handsome."

He glowered at her. "You will not be able to manipulate me that easily," he told her.

She laughed again, which seemed to unnerve him. "I'm just

happy to see you, my friend. I know you won't let me out. You're loyal—Loyal Linus," she replied.

He seemed perplexed like maybe she was mad. Maybe she was. "Why were you at that meeting? Why were you acting as one of the queen's guards?" he asked, looking genuinely confused. He couldn't tell, of course, that Meera was changed. She looked different from training but not so different that she appeared knell.

"Darreal is my friend. She and I have been trying to end the war together to put an end to all of the suffering," she replied.

"You're friends with the knell queen," Linus repeated incredulously.

"You're friends with the human king," Meera parroted, gesturing to his uniform.

Scowling, he shifted his stance, and she noticed he always kept his missing left hand down by his side, tucked in tight so that it would go unnoticed. "Can I see?" she asked, pointing to his left arm. He tensed. "I'm sorry, you know ... I shouldn't have let you be there. I should have protected you better. I never meant for either of us to be there. Of course, it doesn't matter what I meant—I still deserve this," she told him.

He frowned at her. Then another man approached from behind him. "Have you gotten the prisoner talking already?" he asked Linus.

Meera recognized Prince Otto's voice from the meeting, though he looked enough like his father that she would have known anyway. He had the same smooth brown hair and close-cropped beard as King Bartro, but his skin was a light beige—more like Phineas's—and his eyes were grey rather than his father's striking blue-green.

"Is he more like his father or his brother?" Meera asked Linus.

Linus stiffened and didn't answer either of them. However,

Prince Otto chuckled at her question. "Which would you prefer?" he asked.

She considered the question thoughtfully. "I suppose if you were like your brother, I could kill you without much remorse and hope that whoever took your place was more willing to negotiate," she replied.

He laughed again. "If you kill me, another one of my father's pawns will take my place," he said indifferently.

"Is it really all him?" she asked, considering Otto closely. She had never known a powerful man to willingly refer to himself as a pawn.

"It is the world we live in," he told her. Then he turned to Linus. "Make sure she doesn't escape and that she survives the journey. My father will be interested to see her again."

Linus nodded, and Otto sauntered away to do whatever it is princes in charge of armies do. Meera watched him go and swallowed, feeling how dry her throat was. Then she did it again, enjoying the small pain and its momentary distraction from her thoughts. Linus noticed and held out a water flask. She shook her head. He frowned but put it back on his hip belt. "Are you planning to refuse water until you die?" he asked warily.

"I don't have any plans," she replied honestly.

"No? Then what's the ring for?" he asked, pointing to her diamond ring once more.

Meera removed her left hand from the bar and covered it with her right. "I don't want to talk about that," she rasped. Then she started to rock back and forth, trying to think about something else, focusing her eyes on the wooden bars.

"Okay, okay!" Linus said. Sighing, he unclipped his water bladder again, once more holding it out to her. "Please drink, Meera," he implored.

She bit her lip but reached out to take the water, drinking her fill from the bladder. When she handed it back, she grasped his hand in both of hers. He flinched but didn't pull away. "I'm so happy to see you again," she said.

"I wish I could say the same," he spat, and he walked away.

———

MEERA SPENT the rest of the day bumping along in the back of the wagon, alternating between staring up at the sky, trying not to think, and curling up around herself, trying not to think. Occasionally, she felt Shaya batter at the edges of her mind, but she continued to block her raek out. She hoped Shaya would leave her to her fate and not show up, burning and tearing at the men around her.

Linus seemed to be in charge of her and sat at the front of the wagon to drive the horses. He periodically gave her food and water and a pot to pee in. Otherwise, they traveled in silence. Meera didn't bother to ask where they were going; she knew. She watched the sights pass by her wooden crate and stared back at the people who ran up to gawk at her. It felt strange to be back in Terratelle, surrounded by people as brown and as human-looking as her. She let them all think she was like them, even though she wasn't.

For several long days, they travelled. Linus barely spoke to her, and Meera barely spoke in return. She never asked for anything, and she never complained. When soldiers came to leer at her and made rude comments, Linus gave them a look to scare them away, but Meera just lay in her cage. At night, she shivered but did not conjure her fire. During the day, she grew thirsty but did not slake her thirst unless Linus offered her his bladder.

On their fourth day moving north toward Altus, something happened to frenzy the camp, but Meera couldn't tell what it was.

Linus left for a while, then returned to the wagon looking pale and shaken. The group continued to move but at a much quicker pace than before. "What's going on?" she asked curiously. She was looking at the back of Linus's head where he sat steering the horses in front of her.

She saw his jaw clench at the question. "We have to get back to the palace," he replied evasively.

"Why? What happened?" she asked. She couldn't help but wonder if it had something to do with her, if the riders were possibly storming the palace looking for her—not that Hadjal would let them leave the peninsula. Meera knew Kennick would come anyway, but she didn't want to think about him—she couldn't bear it.

"The king is dead," Linus replied. Meera let that soak in for a moment. Before she could ask how, he added, "Phineas killed him."

Meera laughed. She didn't actually find Bartro's death funny, but there was something ironically comical about his monster son striking him down. "He once admitted to me that he struggled to keep Phineas on a short enough leash," she said thoughtfully. Linus looked back at her with his usual frown. "I'm sorry for your loss," she added. She didn't know how close Linus and the king had become after her escape. She supposed Otto now had to run home, deal with his brother, and become king himself.

"Why were you at the meeting as one of the queen's guards?" Linus asked again.

Meera sighed. "To protect her," she said.

"Protect her how?" he asked.

Meera thought about how she had protected her queen. She thought about the three young boys who had been following orders they should never have been given. She thought of how easy it had been for her to burn them to nothingness. She had never even seen their faces—only ash. Then her thoughts were too much for her, and she started to rock and hit her hands against her face. When that wasn't enough to dull her feelings, she smacked her head into the wooden bars.

Linus pulled the horses to a stop and ran around the wagon, scrabbling with his one hand to get the key to the cage and open the back door. He reached inside and grabbed her, pinning her arms to her sides and holding her. Meera knew he wasn't really holding her, but it still felt so good and so comforting to have his arms around her. She cried and shook and rested her sore forehead against his shoulder, leaving a little smear of blood. Red against red.

"What did they do to you, Meera?" he asked.

Her sobs turned to laughter as she realized that he still didn't see it—he still didn't see that she was the monster. He pushed her away from him and stared at her. "Shut the door, Linus. I belong in here," she told him.

"Why? For letting the prisoners go?" he asked.

She supposed that was why he thought she belonged in the cage. She shook her head, over and over again.

"Why then?" he asked. He stood with the door still open, leaning in toward her. Meera crawled forward to look into his eyes. She saw him inhale and sway back a bit uncertainly, but he held his ground.

"I killed those boys, Linus," she breathed, barely able to say it. She needed him to hear it, though. For some reason, she needed him to understand that she deserved this—that he didn't have to feel bad for caging her.

Now he was the one shaking his head from side to side. "No. No you didn't," he said. "They were killed with magic."

"I killed them," she repeated. Her face scrunched and her body shook with her sobs.

Linus continued to stare at her in disbelief.

"Is there a problem, General? We need to make haste!" Otto called from atop his fine horse as he passed.

"No problem, Your Highness!" Linus called back. He shut Meera's door, locking her in. Then he eyed her a moment before walking back to his seat at the front of the wagon and urging the horses onward.

Meera fell back and stared at the sky. She stared and stared and willed her mind to clear, but it kept turning and returning to the boys she had burned. Curling into a ball, she tangled her hands in her hair and screamed, but she couldn't drown out the sound of her thoughts; she couldn't forget her actions and their devastating consequences. She screamed and screamed as the wagon rattled onward until she lost her voice and eventually hyperventilated herself to unconsciousness.

26

MEERA

M eera awoke to the sounds of shouting. Sitting up in her wooden cage, she peered out the bars to find that they were at the palace, moving slowly through the front courtyard. The palace inhabitants were filing out of the doors, cheering the arrival of their new king. Meera stared blankly at the cheering, clapping people, many of whom she recognized from her past. She remembered the night Shael was brought through the courtyard in a similar wooden cage to jeering and applause, and she thought how strange it was that she was now in the same position.

When the wagon stopped, Linus got down from his seat and walked around to her door. He looked tired and burdened; there were purple smudges under his eyes and lines on his young face. Meera gazed calmly back at him. With a frown, he lifted his only hand and the iron manacles he held. She smiled reassuringly at him. "Home sweet home," she joked.

"Put these on," he told her, slipping the manacles through the bars.

Meera crawled to them and picked up their dense weight. She wasn't sure if she would be able to shape them off or not, but she didn't care. Pushing back her sleeves, she carefully moved Linus's bracelet out of the way before clasping the manacles around her wrists, squeezing them shut until they clicked into place. Linus continued to frown at her and opened the back door. Then he grabbed her elbow to help her down from the wagon and led her into the palace.

Meera knew where they were going and walked the winding way to the dungeon automatically. On the way, she smiled at the servants and palace guards she recognized and marveled at how nothing had changed in her absence. But she supposed that wasn't true if the king was dead—that much had changed. She wasn't sure how she felt about King Bartro's death. She had almost looked forward to seeing him again, but she didn't think Terratelle would be any worse-off without him.

"Will they hang Phineas?" she asked as they began to descend the steep staircase into the cool dungeon.

"I don't know," Linus replied.

It occurred to Meera that Phineas might be in one of the cells, but she didn't think so—Linus had to light the lamps as they slowly crept down the stairs. She would be all alone in the dungeon. The thought didn't bother her; she had left Shael all alone in the dungeon, after all—she deserved it. Even so, the cool air and echoing drips sent shivers of remembrance down her spine, and she dreaded being locked away without sunlight.

Her breathing quickened, but she kept moving; she walked down the row of cells until she reached number 39—Shael's cell. Her cell. She waited while Linus retrieved the key and returned to lock her in. Then she stepped willingly into her cell and watched his face while he fumbled to lock the door behind her. "It's okay," she told him. She didn't want to be the cause of any more pain in Linus's life.

When he had locked the door, he reached in to remove her manacles. He struggled to do so with just his right hand, so he stretched out his left stump to steady Meera's arms. Meera grabbed ahold of it and pushed back his sleeve. Linus flinched violently, but he let her look. They had cut halfway down his forearm. The amputation looked clean, but scars licked up his entire arm, and Meera felt like she could read the story of his long, fevered recovery in them. "It should have been me," she said, peering up into his shadowed eyes. "We're alone here, Linus. You can tell me how much you hate me—yell at me for betraying my king. It's okay, I can take it," she told him.

Linus choked out a laugh. "You can take it? You seem like a mess to me," he replied. She shrugged her shoulders. "I never hated you, Meera. I wish I had. It would have made life much easier—still would," he added in a strained voice.

"I love you too, Linus," she said. Her chest ached with feeling; she had missed him so much—was so glad to find him alive and well—and grieved that this was how their story ended. "Now go home to your family. Kiss your mother, and live your life. Forget about me," she told him. She didn't want him to watch her rot in there.

"Forget about you?" he asked, his lips trembling. Meera could see that he had not forgotten her—that he had perhaps loved her more than she had ever realized ... But that was not what he said. "I'm in charge of questioning you, Meera! I'm your captor, and I'm to be your torturer if need be," he said.

"No," she replied, her heart breaking for him. She didn't want him to spend any more time in that horrible place.

Linus removed her manacles and stepped away from the bars.

"I'll make sure the lamps keep burning, and I'll bring you food later," he said.

"Just ask me what you need to know now and don't come back," she told him.

He merely looked at her, then turned and walked down the row of cells to the stairs.

"No," she said quietly to herself, before sitting on the cold damp floor. She didn't want Linus to suffer because of her. Maybe she should leave, she thought. She probably could, but she didn't try to shape the iron bars.

Meera curled up on the stone floor and let the cold from below permeate her body and seep into her bones. She had lain like this once before, and here she was again. Only this time, she was alone. Shael was not feet away breathing steadily beside her. She was alone in the cell and in her body. Clutching her stomach, she let herself feel the absence of her baby, tortured herself with it.

It was her fault, she repeated in her mind over and over again. She had not wanted the pregnancy. She had not protected her baby. She was a monster—a child-burner. Meera was still burning the blood that seeped from inside her over and over. Her clothing was full of ash like the boys she had burned. She deserved this, she told herself, pressing her face into the stone floor. She wanted to be punished; she wanted to be duly penalized for her crimes so she could move past them. She had lived with her guilt over Linus and the duke, but she didn't think she could live with this ... It was too much.

She smacked her hands against the stone floor to feel the sting of her pain. Then she cried until she felt the pull of exhaustion. She wanted sleep to claim her; she wanted to fall into blackness and forget herself, but she couldn't. Sleep didn't relieve her of her grief and guilt. The blackness didn't swallow down her consciousness. Instead, she lay staring wide–eyed at the moving shadows the lamps cast on the walls as they danced in a lurid rhythm that called to the flames flickering in her soul.

She ignored their call. She ignored her abilities. She ignored Shaya's persistent pestering, and she fell deep into the well of her despair. When Linus returned with food, she didn't rise to greet him. She didn't answer his questions. She didn't eat or drink. But she didn't sleep, either. All night, she lay awake, staring at the shadows on the wall. Linus tried for a time to rouse her, but eventually, he gave up and left.

27

LINUS

L inus bolted from the dungeon and stormed the halls to his room, where he went straight for the rum bottle in his cabinet. Twisting the top off with his teeth and spitting out the cap, he took a long drink. Drink had gotten him through the pain of his burns and amputation, and drink had seen him through every pain since. Linus felt like he was drowning, and he gulped his rum instead of air. He had seen and done a lot in his year as a general, but imprisoning Meera might be more than he could handle.

He should tell Otto he couldn't do it, but the prince—king, he reminded himself—had more than enough going on. But ... Meera? How was he supposed to be in charge of Meera? He was the last person who should be trusted with the job, and he had told Otto that. Otto, of course, had said that Linus's admission was exactly why he trusted him. Linus put down his bottle and scrubbed his hand over his face, scratching at his beard. He hated having a beard, but it covered his scars, which were too tricky to shave over anyway.

He lay back on his bed, too tired to even kick off his boots. He still couldn't believe Meera was there—that she had been at the meeting with the knell to begin with. He had never in a million years thought that he would see her again. He had hoped ... When she had first walked into the negotiation tent, he had thought he was imagining things. Then she had just stood there, absolutely still with her eyes shut. And now she was here, lying in the dungeon.

Linus had been angry with Meera for a long time, but he had also missed her. Now she was there with him—although, he wasn't sure she was all the way there; Meera's bizarre behavior since he had found her made Linus wonder whether she was deranged in some way. But if she was mad, why would the knell queen have used her as a guard? Had she really killed those boys?

Linus took another long drink. He wasn't sure he could forgive Otto for the boys. He had watched and helped his prince do plenty of questionable things over the last year, but he had begged Otto not to use the boys. They were his father's orders, though, so he had done it. Otto always did as his father commanded no matter how odious he found his tasks. Linus should have done more to stop him—should have tried harder. He couldn't stop picturing their scared faces when Otto had explained their orders or the way they had just disappeared into that white fire—there one second, then gone. Had Meera really made that fire? How could that be?

Pacing his room, he wondered whether he should return to the dungeon. Meera had just been lying there, so still, practically lifeless. Linus had spent so much time blaming her for his crippled arm and his hurt feelings, but it was hard to stay angry with her when she was clearly so broken. What was wrong with her? It pained him to watch her hurt herself and scream. He took another drink. It was not his job to fix her, he reminded himself; it was his job to get answers.

And yet, Meera had offered him answers, and he had walked away. Was he afraid to know? Or was he just afraid of what Otto would do to her once he had the answers he needed? Linus kicked his boots off, then, and took off his uniform. He needed rest. He needed to think. However, just when he got under his covers, a knock sounded at the door. "Who is it?" he asked.

"It's me."

"Come in, Your Highness!" Linus called mockingly, knowing the title annoyed him. Then again, he supposed it should be *Your Majesty* now.

Otto burst through the door, holding his own bottle of liquor. His hair was loose, and he looked distinctly rumpled and un-kingly.

"Shut the door before anyone sees you looking like that," Linus told him.

Otto obeyed his command and plopped down on the end of his bed. "I don't want to be king! I didn't even want to be a prince ..." he complained, already sounding rather drunk.

"As you would tell me, that's what makes you the best man for the job," Linus retorted.

Otto groaned in response.

"Where's Phineas?" Linus asked.

"Locked in his room with guards on his door," Otto replied. "My mother is beside herself, and everyone keeps asking me questions I don't want to answer. I take orders, I don't make them!"

"Are you going to hang him?" Linus asked, knowing that was one of the questions Otto didn't want to answer.

"He killed my father—the king. The law is clear when it comes to treason," he replied.

"You *are* the king, now," Linus reminded him. "You *are* the law." He wasn't actually thinking about Phineas, though; he was thinking about Meera. Otto could decide to do whatever he wanted with her.

"What has your girlfriend said?" Otto asked, clearly sensing Linus's train of thought.

"Not much," he replied evasively.

"This is the girl that set the prisoner free and got you burned, remember? You hate this girl!" Otto shouted.

Linus shrugged and took a drink. "Love and hate are a double-sided coin my mother would say," he said.

"What's in your bottle?" Otto asked, eyeing Linus's rum.

"Something far cheaper than what's in yours," he replied, not offering to share. They were both silent for a moment. "You shouldn't have used those boys, Otto. Damn you for using those boys!" Linus cried.

"I know. Damn me," Otto said tonelessly. "You know, I think the gods did damn me by killing my father."

"Get out, Otto. I need to sleep, and you need to rule," Linus told him.

Otto grumbled a bit, but he eventually stood up, gave Linus a mock-bow, and left the room.

THE NEXT MORNING, Linus got up and went to the kitchen to get his breakfast and a tray for Meera. He would make her eat today, he told himself. Whatever she had done—whatever she was— when she looked into his eyes, he still saw her there. Linus had met enough royals and generals to tell the difference between those who enjoyed violence and chaos and those who didn't. Meera may have ruined his life and killed those boys, but he could tell she was good. Vaguely, he wondered if she had thought the same about the prisoner ... if that was why she had set him free.

Linus served himself a plate of food from the large table in the center of the kitchen, and when he caught Cook's eye he said, "A tray for the prisoner, please, Cook."

Cook nodded succinctly but proceeded to follow him to where he sat down and linger until Linus looked back at them. "Is it true?" they asked, appearing uncharacteristically nervous.

"It's true," he replied.

"How's she doin'?" Cook asked.

Linus sighed. At least he wasn't the only person in the palace who remembered Meera for who she was. "I couldn't get her to eat yesterday," he replied. It was about all he was willing to admit. He didn't mention Meera's fits of screaming, hitting herself, and uncontrollable sobbing. He didn't want Cook to think he had abused her in any way.

"I—I'd like to go down with you," Cook said haltingly.

Linus looked at them in surprise but nodded. He supposed Meera might listen to Cook.

28

MEERA

Meera never slept. She didn't know how long it had been since Linus had come and gone, but it had felt like days. Her stomach rattled at the confines of her body for sustenance, but she ignored it. She didn't eat the food Linus had left and never even rolled over to see the pile of blankets next to her. Touching her beaded bracelet repeatedly, she wished her friend were somewhere else, with someone else. She didn't touch the ring on her finger—she still couldn't bear to think about him.

When she heard the sounds of approaching footsteps, she didn't bother to move; she could sense that there were two people coming. She wondered whether they would try to torture her. Would she let them? She didn't think she had the willpower for that. The figures approached her cell and stood staring at her. "You's skin and bones, girl," said a voice she recognized—one that made her stomach and heart do flips of joy.

Meera sat up very slowly, peeling her stiff, aching muscles from the stone. Then she turned and saw Cook for the first time in far too long. They looked the same, if greyer and sadder in the light of the dungeon. "Better skin and bones than ash," Meera rasped.

Cook and Linus exchanged a look like she was speaking in tongues. "I brought you a special tray," Cook said.

Linus unlocked the cell with a lot of clanking and jimmying. It had never been an easy door to open, and the task looked even harder with one hand. Eventually, he swung the door inward. Cook seemed hesitant, but they stepped inside to put the tray down. Meera quickly stood with the innate knell swiftness that remained in her muscles despite her long bout of stillness. Cook jumped at the movement, but when Meera wrapped her arms around them, they hugged her back.

"It really is you—it really is. How'd you end up here, girl? How'd you end up here?" Cook murmured.

Meera began to cry, and Cook patted her back. "I belong here," she told them.

"You never belonged anywhere in this palace, Meera. You never did," they replied.

Meera laughed. Then she stepped back and wiped her eyes to really look at Cook. She felt like seeing Linus and Cook again was an offering she didn't deserve but one she accepted, nonetheless. Cook studied her in return; their eyes lingered on her scar and traveled down her body. "Look at you in pants. And all muscle! Where have you been, girl, and how'd you end up here?" they asked again.

Meera glanced at Linus, wondering if this was his way of inter-rogating her. "I've been in Levisade," she told them both. "Then I went on a trip with the queen to try to end the war. I just wanted the killing to stop."

Cook nodded heartily like what she had said made all the

sense in the world. "I got's to go up, but I'll come back later," they told her. "You eat what I left you. Hear?"

Meera smiled and nodded.

When Cook left, Linus shut and locked the door, but he remained, staring at her. Meera stared back for a while, but then she caved and sat on her pile of blankets to eat Cook's food. Cook made the best food, and every bite tasted like warm memories.

Linus watched her eat. "I don't understand," he said finally.

She regarded him, pushing her tray aside. If he was ready for answers, then she was ready to give them to him. "What?" she asked.

"Any of it," he admitted.

"What do you want to know?" she asked warily. She would give him his answers, but she didn't feel much like talking. Now that her stomach was full, she thought she might actually sleep, and the promise of oblivion pulled her in like a tide.

"Why did you free them?" he asked.

"I didn't think they were monsters. I didn't think it was right to keep them here," she replied simply.

"You told me you were a spy for the king, but he never mentioned it after you left," Linus said.

Meera shrugged. "I was a spy for the king, and because of what I told him, someone died. I didn't want to do it anymore."

"And ... the prisoner—" he started to say.

"Shael," she told him.

"He just took you with him to Levisade? You lived with the knell?" Linus asked, his nose wrinkling. He looked disgusted at the thought.

"Yes."

"Does the queen really want to end the war?" he asked, and in that moment, a small light of hope shone in his eyes, making him look more like the Linus she remembered.

"Yes," she said. "What about Otto?"

"Otto wants to follow orders, not make them," Linus replied bitterly. Then he seemed to remember himself and pressed his lips together in a pale line. "Did *he* give you that?" he asked, pointing to her ring again, presumably referring to Shael.

Meera covered the ring from sight and shut her eyes. "No," she said very quietly. She didn't want to talk about this.

"Who did?" he asked.

She shook her head.

"Meera, is there someone who might come to get you?" he asked quietly and urgently.

Her eyes flew open. Was Linus trying to save her? Did he not realize yet that she belonged there? "Why don't you hate me?" she asked.

He crouched down to be at eye-level with her. "Everything you said before you left, Meera—you were right. You were always right, and I was too naive to see it. I was a child playing with toy soldiers who became a general commanding real ones," he said.

"It doesn't matter. I told you what I did," she replied.

"Did you really kill those boys?" he asked.

She nodded, biting her lip to try to dam the tears that started to flow.

Linus sighed. "You killed them, but Otto put them there, his father sent the command, and I watched it happen. We're all to blame. At least you were protecting someone you care about," he said.

Meera gaped at him. This was not the Linus she remembered. That Linus would have yelled and condemned them all to the dungeon; he had seen only good and bad, black and white. "You're different," she remarked.

"So are you," he replied.

"I'm tired," she told him, hoping he would leave. She had said enough—thought enough. If he wouldn't yell at her for what she had done, then she didn't want him there anymore.

"How did you do it?" he asked.

"What were their names?" she bit back.

"How did you do it?" he repeated.

Meera lay back down, putting a rolled blanket under her head and spreading two others over her cold body. She supposed she could get on the old bedroll, but she liked feeling the hard stone under her bones. It felt like atonement. After a while, she heard Linus walk away, and she shut her eyes. Moments later, she opened them and blinked in confusion. She was in a different cell. She was with Aegwren, she realized.

Meera looked through Aegwren's eyes at the wooden bars caging him. Why was he in a cell? Last she had seen him, he was leaving the mountains. What had happened? Unlike her, she could feel that he was filled with anger and indignation. She could feel that he didn't think he should be jailed. Lucky him, she thought. Though she supposed his human body prevented him from simply tearing open his cage and leaving whenever he felt like it.

"Coltran! Coltran!" he shouted, banging his right hand against the bars. His left arm was out of its sling, but Meera could still feel the twinge of hurt where his forearm had broken and healed poorly. She doubted he would ever have full use of it again. The thought brought Linus back to her mind, but she pushed him aside as well as her own life. She would gladly inhabit Aegwren for a time even if his body hurt, and his mind roiled with emotion.

It was not Coltran who appeared at the cell door, however, but Aegwren's mother. The thin, middle-aged woman screwed up her face at the sight of him. "My son, you live!" she cried.

"I live, Mother. For now, anyway," he said bitterly.

"They say they found you luring a raek to the village to exact revenge, but I told them they must be wrong. You would not do such a thing!" she said, reaching through the bars to touch Aegwren's haggard face and patchy beard. Meera leaned into the touch with him, wishing she could remember the comfort of a mother's hand.

"I was not luring her anywhere! She just follows me. She followed me from the mountains. I tried to tell them—to tell Coltran, but he would not listen. I only wanted to see you, Mother. I only wanted to come home," he said, his voice cracking. He had been alone and struggling for so long. Meera ached with him for the homes they both missed.

"I will get you out, my son. I will do it! I will come back tonight and get you out! They want to hang you!" she whispered, now sobbing. "They said I could come in to say goodbye, but I will not! I would rather die than watch you be hanged!"

"Quiet, Mother! Hush! Someone will hear you," Aegwren said, fearing for her. "You will not come back tonight—do you hear me? I am not afraid to die, but I would rather not hang with the shame of knowing my mother hanged too because of me. Do not come back! Do you hear me? Please, Mother," he begged, clutching her hands through the bars.

"How will I go on without you? How could I possibly?" she asked.

"As you always do, Mother," he told her, leaning his forehead against hers.

"Time to go, Meera," Coltran said, walking around the corner and grasping Aegwren's mother's shoulder.

Meera jolted. She had never known anyone with her name before. Why did everything in the past seem to come back to her?

"I love you, Aegwren! I love you!" his mother shouted as Coltran dragged her away.

"Coltran! Coltran!" Aegwren yelled, unable to get the man to listen to him. He released a strangled cry of anger and frustration. Then, to his amazement, he thought he heard the shriek of a raek in response.

Meera sat with Aegwren in his cell for the remainder of the day while he waited for evening ... and to hang. He was given a last meal, cooked by his mother, but he had no appetite for the food. The grey raek with the green eyes was somewhere outside looking for him, and while he did not know why she followed him or what she wanted, he was certain she was near. The knowledge gave him equal parts hope and fear.

Aegwren hoped the raek might save him. He was not afraid to die, but he was not ready to either; his journey had left him with the certainty that there was still much for him to learn and to explore, and he wanted the opportunity to do so. And yet, he would not trade the lives of others to save his own. He feared what the raek would do if she came for him. He had seen villages destroyed by raek fire—houses and people left in scattered ashes, and he did not want these people hurt ... even if they did not understand him—even if they shouted and strained in the village center to see him hang.

These people may not understand him or see the world as he did, but they were not bad people. They were his people—his mother's people. Could he stop the raek from harming them if she came? He did not know. He did not even know if she would really come for him, but he suspected she might. Anxiety lay in his gut like a furled cat ready to pounce, and he sweated and rocked in agitation like he did not know whether the cat pounced in earnest or in play.

A cell door rattled, but it was Meera's, not Aegwren's, and she opened her eyes in frustration, wanting to stay in the memory. It was Linus bringing her food again. He put the tray on the floor, but this time, he sat across from her. Meera rubbed her eyes, sat up, and scowled at him for waking her. "I thought we could eat together," he said.

"Why?" she asked, vaguely self-conscious of her breath and her unwashed body: her clothes were grimy—though their dark color hid it relatively well—her hair had fallen out of the bun it was in and hung around her face in frizzy, stretch-out curls, and her scalp was itchy with grease.

"Why not?" he asked, starting to eat from the tray.

Meera shrugged and joined him. She wasn't sure she deserved Cook's amazing food, but she didn't have the energy to turn it down. For a while, they both ate in silence. Then Linus surprised her by pulling a flask out of his pocket and drinking from it. "For the cold," he explained, shrugging. He offered her some. She shook her head. "If you can't drink when you're sitting in a dungeon, then when can you?" he asked.

She supposed he had a point and held out her hand for the flask. She took a swig and nearly spewed it all over him. Whatever it was, it was awful—not nearly as palatable as the sweet, fruity wine favored by the knell. Linus chuckled at the face she made. "That's disgusting. I prefer knell wine," Meera said.

"Oh yeah? What else is better in Magicland?" he asked.

"Levisade has more forests, though one of them tried to kill me ... But for the most part, people are people and towns are towns," she replied.

"Really? You're not going to preach to me that the knell queen should rule the whole world?" he asked snidely.

"Darreal is a fine queen, but no one person should have that much power," Meera said, and she couldn't help but think of herself; she had far more power than any one person should be rightfully allotted.

"Do you think power corrupts people, or are all people just horrible to begin with?" Linus wondered aloud.

"All people aren't horrible," she replied.

"No? You're probably one of the nicest people I've ever met, and you killed children," he said flippantly.

The food in Meera's mouth turned to ash, and she went suddenly still.

Linus stared at her unapologetically. "What about the man who gave you that? Is he not horrible? I've never met a person who could afford a diamond like that who isn't," he remarked.

Meera glared at him; he could say what he wanted about her, but she wouldn't hear a word against Kennick. "No, he isn't horrible. Don't talk about him!" she spat.

"Why not? You're in love with one of them, aren't you?" he asked, his nose wrinkling at the thought. "You couldn't love me—I was ... too young? Too naive? Too ordinary? But you can love one of them even though they aren't even human?" he asked.

"I thought you didn't hate me," Meera replied, eyeing him. He quickly deflated and took another drink from his flask. "We don't choose who we love, Linus. Obviously, you already realize that."

"So, are you married or not yet? How's it going to work when you grow old, and he doesn't?" he asked. Meera couldn't tell if he was being curious or attempting to be cruel. She couldn't tell if he was really this disillusioned by the world or if it was an act, a shield.

"I'm not going to grow old, Linus—not for a very long time, anyway. I've changed. I told you: I killed those boys. If you want to hate me for what I am, hate me. If you want to hate me for what I did, go ahead. I'm not overly fond of myself at the moment," she said, and she started eating again, feeling a new numbness settle over her. She supposed numb was preferable to raw.

"What do you mean? What did they do to you?" he asked, looking alarmed.

"Do *you* really want to know or does Otto?" she asked. She

wanted to know if she was talking to her friend—former friend, anyway—or if she was talking to her interrogator.

"What difference does it make?" he asked.

"Where's Cook?" Meera asked in turn. They had said they would be back.

"Cook wasn't comfortable coming back down here," Linus explained.

Meera nodded and sighed. She was disappointed but not surprised; Cook spent their whole life in that kitchen, and Meera had always figured they preferred their orderly little nook in the world to the messiness of real life. "You weren't either once," she reminded him.

"I've been on battlefields," he replied dryly. Meera couldn't imagine what that was like. "You know, those boys were soldiers. They probably would have died anyway, only in much more horrible ways," he added.

"Is that supposed to make me feel better?" she asked.

"Would you rather your precious queen had died?" he asked in return.

"Those weren't the only options. I just ... overreacted," she said quietly.

"Oh? What else could you have done?" Linus asked.

"Burned the darts and not the boys, for one," she said.

"So, you really made that fire?" he asked.

"Yes."

"Then why haven't you burned me and run?" he asked, gesturing to the open door behind him.

"Because I would never hurt you, Linus—not on purpose—and because I belong in here! I'm a monster!" she shouted, losing her patience.

He just stared at her evenly. "Speaking of monsters, would you like to see Phineas hang?" he asked.

Meera gaped at him. "No, of course not!" she cried.

"You don't want to see a monster punished? One that hurt countless people, attacked you, and killed his own father?" Linus asked smugly. She got the point he was making and didn't bother to answer. "Come on, Meera, you're no Phineas," he said in a quieter, kinder voice.

Looking down at her hands, she touched her ring. Maybe he was right—maybe she wasn't a complete monster just because she had done one rash, monstrous thing. But that didn't make her feel any more ready to face her life. She had never even made amends for what she had done to the duke or to Linus—how could she make this right? How could she atone for the three boys she had burned? How could she face Kennick and tell him she had killed their baby?

Meera clutched her right hand over her ring until it bit into her skin, squeezing her eyes shut. Why hadn't she stayed home and taken better care of herself? Why hadn't she wanted the baby to begin with? What would Kennick think of her? She couldn't face it. She couldn't go home. She didn't know how to make any of it better. She was a child-burner!

Suddenly, Linus's arms were around her, holding her. He stroked her hair and patted her back and made shushing noises while she cried as he might have once done for her. Burying her face in his bony chest, she left snot on the bear emblem of his uniform. "Meera, I'll let you out if you tell me you'll go to safety," he whispered to her. "I'll let you out. Just tell me you'll get away, that you have somewhere to go—someone to take care of you."

"Linus, that's treason," she said.

He laughed, and she huffed a laugh too; they were having a major role-reversal. "I don't care, Meera. You don't belong in here. You don't," he said.

She was starting to believe him, and yet, she couldn't leave now. Even if Linus didn't let her out, everyone would think he had. "Linus, I could get myself out of here—easily—but I won't. I already ruined your life once. I won't let you be hanged because of me," she told him. "I'm fine. Just get stationed somewhere else, and after you've been gone a while, I'll leave. I promise. When you won't be affected, I'll leave."

"This is my role now, Meera. Otto wants me in charge of you, and more than that, he wants me with him. Now that he's king, he'll keep me here," he replied.

"Why?" she asked, pulling away to look at him.

He shrugged. "We're friends."

"Well, if you're friends, ask him to send you somewhere else," she insisted.

He laughed like she was being ridiculous. "We're not friends like that," he said.

She furrowed her brows at him in confusion. "You mean you're lovers?" she asked.

Linus jumped and about fell over. "What? No!" he cried. "I just mean that I'm a friend to Otto, and he's a king. He doesn't have to be friends with anyone in return."

Meera scrubbed the tears from her face and wiped her nose, burning the snot automatically. Linus jumped again at the sight of her fire. "That really was you," he said in disbelief.

"I told you it was," she replied, irritated.

"What are you?" he asked, backing away looking frightened.

"I told you: I'm a monster. Now, leave. I want to go back to sleep," she said, exasperated.

He backed all the way out of the cell and shut and locked the door behind him, looking wary and uncertain. When she turned away and lay down, he left.

29

LINUS

Linus rushed back to his room to change uniforms before the hanging. His hand shook from what he had seen—hearing Meera say she could create fire out of nowhere was one thing, but seeing it was another. What was she? What had happened to her? He wondered whether he *should* leave her locked in that cell indefinitely. Could she really leave whenever she wanted? He figured if she wasn't lying about the fire, then she probably wasn't lying about that. Would she actually stay just to protect him?

When he reached his room, he hurriedly put on clean clothes and refilled his flask, drinking straight from the bottle while he was at it. Otto expected him by his side when he hanged his brother. Linus would not be sad to see Phineas die—Phineas was as violent and inhumane a person as ever he had met—but hangings were never fun.

He sometimes wondered what his life would be like if he hadn't followed his brother into service to the Crown. Would he have a happy, peaceful job? Or would he be just another nameless, faceless soldier in the war? Probably that, he thought, but he wasn't sure this life was any better. He supposed he at least sent plenty of money home to his family, but he rarely visited them; he hated for them to see what he had become.

Thinking about his family earned him another drink. Linus drained the rum bottle and left his room for the front courtyard. He sidestepped servants and nobles alike, who jockeyed in the halls to get to the spectacle in time for a good view. Linus could almost understand the servants' excitement; Phineas had been truly heinous to those beneath him his entire life. The nobles, however, had shifted from loving and admiring the charming, golden-haired prince to chanting for his death in a matter of hours. Linus didn't care what Meera thought; he knew all people were horrible.

As he strode across the courtyard, people stepped out of his way. He wasn't especially large or commanding, but his red general's uniform spoke for itself. Otto wasn't there yet. The royal family always walked out last, just before the condemned. They were too important to stand around waiting, after all. Linus took his place next to the raised hanging platform, tucked his hand and lack-thereof behind his back, and waited for his king. Otto's coronation had not technically taken place yet, but he was king, nonetheless. The coronation was just a formality and an excuse to get drunk.

Eventually, the crowd parted for the royal family. Otto led the way, followed by his mother and hoard of siblings. Bartro really had made himself plenty of heirs. Linus hated that the young ones had to be there, but it was policy, and Otto was not one for breaking policy. To Linus's continual frustration, his friend clung to the rules and regulations of other men in order to absolve himself of any guilt for his crimes. Then again, Linus supposed they all had to cope with shit in their own way. He took a quick drink from his flask before the procession reached him.

As they drew nearer, he could see and hear that Otto's fair mother, Queen Magda, was openly sobbing and pleading with him. The new king was not so much leading his mother to the platform as he was dragging her. Most of his younger siblings were also crying and carrying on, but they followed their brother and mother to stand next to the platform. Linus gave Otto a reassuring look and pat on the back.

"I hope my brother rots in hell for what he's doing to our mother," Otto hissed in his ear.

"Did he order his own execution, then?" Linus quipped.

"We all know the penalty for treason," Otto replied loudly so that others could hear. Linus supposed it wouldn't behoove his friend to let others think they could murder him without consequences.

"My baby!" Queen Magda wailed over and over again. She was tearing down her pale blonde hair, and her usually lovely face was red from crying. Linus hoped the woman could retire comfortably to a country home now that Bartro was dead. She had never handled palace life well, be it cultural differences or personality deficits.

Once the royals were in place, two guards led Phineas through the courtyard. The spectators yelled, cheered, cursed, and spat, but the golden prince smiled as broadly and handsomely as ever. Linus had often wondered how deranged Phineas was, and apparently, the answer was: very. His hair shone in the sunlight as he tipped his head to those nearest him like they were applauding his actions and not his death. His performance was so endearing, some in the crowd actually quieted their shouting and laughed instead. Otto didn't like that.

Linus could feel his friend shifting uncomfortably. Otto didn't want to be the one to order Phineas's death if he was still beloved. He stepped forward as Phineas was brought before him. "Prince

Phineas, Brother, you are charged with the brutal murder of our father, King Bartrothomeer Altusroll. You were found with his bleeding body, holding the weapon that ended his life. You are, therefore, sentenced to death by hanging. Do you have any last words?" he shouted for all to hear.

From where Linus stood behind Otto, he could see Phineas's confident sneer and could tell his friend was already regretting the age-old custom of allowing last words before Phineas even opened his mouth to speak. But Otto would always follow tradition. Linus could only hope he married a woman with both a kind soul and the ability to manipulate him. However, he wasn't sure what the odds of that were; he had met his share of noble women and found most of them to be as foul as their male counterparts.

"Brother, I would say only that I humbly released our father from the burdens of his crown, and I hope that someone will soon do the same for you," Phineas said loudly. Then he bowed very formally and handsomely, impeded only slightly by the two guards hanging off his arms.

Otto's hands clenched at his sides briefly before he gestured for the guards to take Phineas up the ramp to the platform. Phineas went willingly. If anything, he seemed to be enjoying the attention. Linus noticed he didn't spare a glance for his bereft mother or frightened younger siblings. Even when the hangman put the rope around his neck, he continued to smile and wink at the crowd. By the time the lever was pulled to retract the floor out from under him, some were even shouting for a pardon. But prince or not—handsome or not—Phineas died at the end of the rope, same as any other man.

Linus made himself watch and gripped Otto's arm when he swayed next to him. But when Otto went to lead his mother inside, he bolted for the palace doors. He was so sick of it all: this palace, this land, this life. Without knowing where his feet were taking him, he found himself going to the dungeon. When he reached Meera's cell, she was asleep.

Rather than wake her or leave, Linus slid down the adjacent wall and stared at her sleeping face. Of all the ugly, brutal things in the world, Meera was not one of them. Gazing at her beautiful face in the shifting light of the oil lamps, he let the even rise and fall of her breathing soothe him. He soon found himself dozing off, numbed by his rum and comforted by Meera's presence.

Sometime later, he awoke to the sounds of footsteps and voices. Startled, he slid sideways into the blackness beyond Meera's cell and crouched in readiness. He was not a proper soldier, but he would not let anyone harm her if he could help it.

30

SHAEL

hael and Kennick waited at the border for as long as they could stand to. Neither one of them knew exactly how long it would take Terratellen soldiers to travel from there to Altus, but after days of waiting, Shael did not think he could hold Kennick back any longer; his friend was more anxious and ruffled than he had ever seen him before. Being strong for Kennick was the only thing keeping Shael together when he would normally succumb to his darkest thoughts and crumble.

They waited until dusk to leave. Soleille had stayed with them at the camp, but she and Falkai were going to remain behind—despite Kennick's desperate pleas for her to go with them. Shael was not surprised; none of the riders had gone for him when he was imprisoned, after all. He was not bitter about it. If anything, knowing how much they all loved Meera was reassuring; Shael was selfishly comforted by the fact that the riders did not run to her rescue when they had left him to his fate. Normally, he would hate himself for such a thought, but he was slowly learning to be kinder to himself, more forgiving.

People were complex, he reminded himself. Not every thought defined him. His actions defined him, and he—for one—was going to help find Meera. He was supporting Kennick, and he was willing to give up his life as a rider for his two best friends. That was who he was, he told himself as he packed his bag and strapped his new sword onto his hip. It did not quite fit him the way his old one had, but he was learning to live with it.

"Ready?" Kennick asked as he exited his tent.

"Ready," Shael confirmed.

Their plan was simple: fly straight to the palace, find Meera, fly away with her. If they had to fight, they would fight. But if Meera's security was as relaxed as Shael's had been, they probably would not even need their weapons. The real, unspoken unknown was whether Meera would willingly leave with them. As far as they knew, she was unhurt and had not escaped on her own. It was possible she was in chains or behind metal bars and could not shape herself out of them, but Shael doubted that; he thought it was much more likely she was punishing herself for the boys she had killed.

"Kennick, what if she does not want to come?" he asked. He had been avoiding the question but felt they needed to discuss the possibility before leaving.

Kennick was braiding his hair out of the way, and his face tensed. "I will not leave without her," he replied.

Shael sighed. "Okay, then I will hit her over the head, and you can carry her," he said. He was not leaving without either of them.

Kennick pulled him in for one of his prolonged hugs, which Shael tolerated with a few pats to his friend's back. Then he kissed his cheek—something Shael knew he only did to embarrass him. "Enough, let us go," he said, flustered. He and Kennick mounted Cerun and Endu, respectively, and the four of them leapt into the dark night and flew high above the land.

Shaya, to their amazement, had left days ago with Darreal. After her first conversation with Kennick, she had refused to talk to him. According to Darreal, the raek insisted on escorting her safely back to Levisade to continue to try to negotiate for peace from there. Shael had been shocked that she would abandon Meera but supposed he did not know the wild raek well enough to really have an opinion about her actions. He was glad he could always count on Cerun.

"You and Meera can both always count on me," Cerun said in his mind. "Even if her raek is a spineless salamander." Shael laughed despite himself. Cerun almost never insulted other raeken.

They flew late into the night until they reached the palace, at which point Cerun hovered over Endu so that Shael could jump down to the other raek's back. From there, he and Kennick were both going to fall to the ground below, and Kennick would catch them with his metal shaping. They both wore metal cuffs around their wrists and ankles as well as plates of metal attached to their belts. They had been practicing for days, but Shael was still nervous; they had not practiced in the dark or from quite so high up.

Standing on Cerun's back, he looked down to Endu's. Kennick was peering up at him, ready to assist him if he fell astray. However, Shael jumped and landed squarely on Endu's back, bending his knees to balance on the shifting raek. Without speaking, Kennick gripped his hands and looked into his eyes to prepare to jump. Even in the dark, Shael could see his friend's fear, which heightened his own. Still, he trusted Kennick to catch him.

When Endu tipped to the side, they both jumped. For a brief moment of freefall, Shael's stomach jolted into his chest, but as soon as Kennick started to shape, the feeling dissipated; instead, Shael felt pressure on his wrists and ankles as they descended to the palace's back gardens. When their feet hit the ground, they both stumbled before balancing one another and quickly releasing each other's hands to check their surroundings.

The gardens were deserted as far as Shael could tell. Involuntarily, he glanced down to the canal where Cerun had spent many weeks chained. That time felt immeasurably distant now that he rarely had nightmares about his torture. Kennick drew his attention and beckoned for him to lead the way, so Shael led him through the gardens to the back doors he had exited on the day of his escape. He only knew one way to the dungeon, but it was not one he had forgotten; every nerve and tissue in his body had been on full alert that day—he could still smell the garlic that had emanated from one of his guards.

They entered through the door, watching and listening carefully. They had not bothered to try to disguise what they were; two men in black hoods with swords would have been just as suspicious as two knell warriors. They just moved very slowly and strained their ears for movement. The few times someone walked toward them or stood in the way, Kennick shaped something metal to move or fall or otherwise distract their attention.

They were almost to the dungeon door, and Shael could not believe how well everything was going. But then Kennick stopped him with a hand. Shael gave his friend a questioning look, wondering if his full-knell ears had heard something he had not. Kennick pointed down a hallway, but Shael shook his head; that was not the way. If they got lost, they could waste a lot of time wandering around the maze-like palace. Kennick pointed again. "Trust me," he said with a hint of a smug grin.

Shael had no idea what he was doing, but he followed him

regardless. Kennick led him down hallways and up flights of stairs, until Shael started to wonder if he was planning something crazy like single-handedly killing all of the royals and taking over Terratelle. He dismissed the thought, however. Kennick was not stupid. No knell could ever force dictatorship over Terratelle; the people's hate and distrust of their kind ran too deep. Shael's thoughts were distracted by the sounds of drunken laughter, and he and Kennick slipped into an alcove and remained very still, hoping not to be noticed.

"Where is General Backer?" one of the men was shouting, banging on doors at random and calling for the general. The men with him laughed and did not try to shush or inhibit their companion in any way. Shael assumed the man was important enough to do whatever he wanted and held his breath, hoping not to be discovered. The men passed without a glance in their direction and continued to make a lot of noise until they were well out of sight. At which point, Kennick urged Shael onward.

Eventually, Kennick stopped at a door and tried the knob unsuccessfully. Then he shaped the locking mechanism and turned the knob slowly. Shael gripped his sword as he threw open the door—unsure of what they would find within—but the room was empty. It looked like a study with a back wall of tall windows, letting in the moonlight. A desk stood to their left and a sitting area to the right. Kennick walked toward the desk, stepped around it, and grabbed something from the wall. Suddenly, Shael understood what they were doing there: it was his sword.

Kennick handed him his old sword, white teeth flashing in the dark. Shael held his lost weapon with reverence and watched as Kennick sharpened the blade. "Thank you," he breathed.

"I will never make up for not rescuing you, Shael, but I hope this is a start," Kennick replied quietly. "Now, let us find Meera."

Shael nodded, and they left the study. Kennick locked the

door behind them, and they carefully retraced their steps. "It is beneath us," Kennick murmured as they walked through a deserted hallway. He could apparently sense the iron bars below.

"The door is this way," Shael replied, leading him around a corner. One more turn and they would be there, but when they paused at the corner, they heard the breathing of two guards stationed in the hall. "How do you want to do this?" Shael asked almost inaudibly.

Kennick lowered his eyebrows in concentration, and Shael heard the sound of a door open and close loudly further down the hall, past the dungeon entrance.

"What was that?" one of the guards asked loudly.

"Beats me," said the other.

Shael and Kennick waited until they heard both men walk away. Then they slipped soundlessly around the corner and ran to the dungeon door. The door creaked, so Kennick made more noise further down the hall, banging a door and knocking something onto the floor.

"Who's there?!" they heard one of the guards yell toward their diversion.

"Should we have just knocked them out for our retreat?" Shael asked.

Kennick shrugged in the lamplight. "Someone might have found them unconscious and raised an alarm," he replied.

Shael supposed that was good logic. Then he looked down the narrow staircase that led to the dungeon, and all of his thoughts fled his mind. Suddenly, his body revolted at the prospect of descending the stairs: his heart raced, and he gulped in desperate breaths like the air rising up from below could not fill his lungs. He knew that air—he had breathed that air for so long and while in so much pain. He gripped the railing to remain upright.

Cerun was monitoring his thoughts and actions and

attempted to send him soothing energy, but Shael's fear was too pressing and immediate; he could barely concentrate on his raek's presence in his mind. Kennick cupped his face in his hands and forced Shael's eyes to his. "You are safe, Shael. I have you. Just breathe," he said, taking slow deep breaths of his own for Shael to mimic.

Shael grabbed the front of Kennick's shirt with his free hand, rooting himself to his friend—incapable of embarrassment in his state of panic. Kennick pressed his forehead to Shael's, and their breaths mingled, warming Shael's face despite the chill rising to them from underground. After several long moments, his breathing evened and slowed, and he released his grip on Kennick's shirt, taking a step back on the narrow staircase. They were there for Meera, he reminded himself.

Shael nodded at Kennick, who nodded back, and they both descended the stairs. The oil lamps on the wall were lit up to Shael's old cell, and they strode forward until they stood in front of it. There she was. Meera was lying on the stone floor under several blankets, asleep. Shael's chest ached at the sight of her slight form on the floor. He wanted to get to her—to hold her— but he looked to Kennick; he would leave this part up to his friend.

Kennick swallowed as he stepped toward the cell door, gazing down at the woman he loved—the woman they both loved. Shael looked away, wishing he could give them privacy for their reunion, and it was then that he noticed movement to his right and turned quickly, raising the sword in his hand. A man stepped from the shadows into the light, holding up his hands—well, he held up one hand and one empty sleeve. "You," the man said.

Shael looked closer and recognized Linus, Meera's friend from the palace—the boy who had stepped in front of the king and been burned by Cerun's flames. "You," Shael said in return. Kennick was tense and ready to fight behind him, but Shael lowered his sword. "Kennick, this is Linus. Meera would not be happy if you hurt him," he said.

"No, I wouldn't," she agreed, sitting up in her cell.

31

MEERA

Meera opened her eyes to find herself once more in Aegwren's wooden cell. He was just where she had left him—slumped on the floor, his mother's food uneaten and cold in front of him. It would not be long now, he thought. Meera could feel his growing fear, but she was bolstered by the knowledge that he would survive, even if she didn't know what would happen. When Coltran came to retrieve him, Aegwren stood and held his head high; he did not plead or beg or try to explain himself any longer.

Aegwren had come to the conclusion that Coltran would not listen no matter what he said. The grey-bearded leader of the village was making an example of him; he was showing the villagers that if they were not against raeken, then they were with them. Aegwren knew the man had his reasons for his war—he had lost most of his family to attacks made by raeken and against them—and he knew Coltran's hate justified his actions in a way that reason could never invalidate.

Raising his chin, he took heart that he had lived his short life by his own beliefs. Coltran bound his hands in front of him, and Aegwren followed him out of the shed-turned-jail and into the road where the whole village had gathered to watch him die. His friends and neighbors were, at least, not cheering for his death; it was a solemn affair. He looked into the faces of the people he had known his entire life, and even as they stood by and failed to defend him, Aegwren nodded to them—he sent them silent thanks for the good times they had spent together and wished them farewell. He felt relatively steady, at ease; his doom had not quite sunk into the depths of his mind.

However, as Coltran led him to where the noose and ladder awaited, Aegwren heard his mother's desperate cries, and his panic finally rose like a wave within him, churning up a primal need to survive from the bottom of his being. He did not want to die! He was young—there was so much he still wanted to do! All of his steadiness deserted him; his heart raced, and his legs trembled and slowed until Coltran had to drag him forward.

Aegwren wracked his mind for a way to live. He could fight! But he could not fight off the entire village—not with his hands bound and his left arm weak. Gaping to the left and right for options, he found none, so he shut his eyes and prayed to his uncle to show him a way out. He was not ready! As much as he wished to see his uncle and father again, he was not ready to leave the known world. Stubbing his toe, he pitched forward and opened his eyes to catch his balance.

Coltran prodded him ever onward, creeping toward the swinging noose just visible in the torchlight, and Aegwren's insides roiled with fear. He was suddenly glad he had not eaten his mother's food, sure it would be coming out of him from one end or the other. The faces of the people he had recognized and loved moments before seemed to close in menacingly—flickering and gawping grotesquely at him. Averting his gaze skyward, he searched the night for the raek in desperation. He could have sworn he had heard her earlier, but he could not see her. Where was she?

When they finally reached the stepladder, Coltran shoved him roughly up each step. Aegwren tripped and nearly fell over—unable to balance with his shaking knees and his bound wrists—but Coltran held him steady with the strength of his determination and forced him up the last step of the ladder. Aegwren could see his mother in the crowd now—crying for him, held back by friends and neighbors. Her eyes and hair were wild, and her hands twisted before her, reaching out to him. He shut his eyes to block out her image, then he opened them and peered up at the sky again, searching—beseeching; please, he thought.

Only faint stars and the moon shone above him, distant and oblivious to his anguish. No flash of feathers or flap of wings met his eyes. Coltran reached for the dangling noose, and Aegwren stretched out his own hands in a silent plea to his bestial friend; please, he thought again. For a moment, all was still and silent, and he thought he was lost. Then—as Coltran teetered on the ledge beneath him and strained to wrap the rope around his neck —a screech rent the night air, drawing every face upward in fear. The grey raek with green eyes dove into the torchlight for Coltran, snatching the grizzled leader with her deadly claws.

Aegwren was knocked sideways by a wing and fell off the ladder and onto the road below. He hit the ground hard, unable to catch himself with his bound hands. Struggling for breath, he fought to raise himself from the dirt. He could not see what the raek did to Coltran—for which Meera was grateful—but he heard the man's undignified screams of agony until they abruptly died. As Aegwren pressed himself up, chaos erupted around him; villagers ran in every direction—some fled, some tried to rush the raek, and others attempted to get to him.

Scrambling to his knees, he battled to stand. He needed to stop the raek—he could not let her destroy the village! This was not what he had wanted, he kept thinking; this was not right! Just as he staggered to his feet, a group of men charged to restrain him. Jostled among them was his mother, fighting to get to him—to free or defend him. Aegwren saw the resolution in her eyes just before the raek rose up and unleashed her sphere of green fire.

Aegwren screamed, but he could not hear the sound of his own horror over the fear of the other villagers. He squinted into the green fire, but when it finally yielded, there was nothing left of those who had rushed toward him—there was nothing left of his mother. He blinked and blinked, clearing his eyes of the shadow flames that haunted them and staring at the blank space where she had been. A wound tore open in his chest as gaping and empty as the stretch of road before him. Meera didn't want to be there anymore—Aegwren's guilt and grief felt too much like her own. "No!" he cried, but no one listened.

Men with weapons ran toward the raek. She crouched in readiness and drew her head into her neck, parting her mouth in preparation to burn them all. Make it stop, Meera thought; make it stop! Aegwren could not hear her, but he, too, had the same thought and ambled forward in a sloppy, staggering run. Putting himself between the raek and men, he held up his bound hands once more in another seemingly futile gesture. "Stop!" he shouted. "Enough!"

The raek did not understand his words, but the men did. Without Coltran to lead and spur them on, they hesitated, afraid to die as their friends had. The raek continued to slash her tail and bunch her legs in agitation, but she did not attack, nor did she fly away; she stared at Aegwren through her bright green, curious eyes as if trying to understand him. "Stop!" he called, turning to her. "Please, do not hurt them! They are my people!"

He touched his bound hands to his heart and gestured to the men behind him.

The raek swayed her head side to side and puffed a cloud of smoke from her nostrils in obvious confusion, but she remained where she was, eyeing the villagers as they eyed her in return. Slowly, the screaming and chaos quieted as raek beheld human and human raek, and Aegwren stood in the middle, turning and scanning for movement—desperate to end the violence. Neither side moved. For a long time, they stood in a standstill, stalemated. Eventually, people began to trickle from their homes and the nearby woods where they had fled, and the villagers gathered in the road once more, hushed and hesitant.

Suddenly, all eyes were on Aegwren; he was the center of everything—the middle-ground between man and raek. He had no idea how he had gotten there, and he had no idea what to do. Aflame with heartache, he wanted nothing more than to collapse and curl in on himself, but he could not—he could not allow any more violence and killing. He could not abandon this mess of his own making.

All night he stood in the center of the road to hold the raek and villagers at bay. Had the raek left, he would have desisted— would have allowed the villagers to do whatever they wanted with him—but the raek did not leave. She settled herself on the edge of the road under the still swinging noose and observed the crowd before her. The villagers, in turn, watched the raek and talked amongst themselves, wondering at her behavior—at her docility.

Finally, dawn broke, and Aegwren felt as if his legs would crumble beneath him. An elder stepped forward—a woman named Brienn who had always been a friend to his mother. "How did you tame this beast, Aegwren?" she asked so that all could hear.

The raek perked up, tilting her head and focusing on the woman as if she sought to understand her.

"I did not," he said simply. Rolling his shoulders back, he tried to release the cramps bunching his muscles from having his hands bound for so long. "I met this raek in the mountains. She could have killed me, but she did not. I do not think raeken are as monstrous as you all believe ..." he added tiredly. Even though the raek behind him had killed his neighbors, Coltran, and his mother, Aegwren could not find it in himself to hate her. He *knew* her. He knew she had acted to protect him even if he did not understand why. He knew she was not a blood-thirsty creature, eager to burn and destroy.

Talk broke out among the villagers behind the woman. He heard disbelief and accusation, but Brienn held up a hand for quiet. When she did, the raek shifted behind Aegwren. He turned to look at her—fearing she felt threatened and would attack. Women in the crowd bundled their children to their breasts, and men raised their weapons. But the raek did not attack; unfurling one of her great wings, she lifted it, mirroring Brienn's raised hand. For a moment, raek and woman stared at one-another, unmoving.

Then the old woman laughed in awe and delight. She waved once more, and the raek imitated her, moving her wing back and forth in an approximation of the human gesture. Aegwren recalled her once waving to him, and despite his grief and exhaustion, he smiled at his curious raek friend. He had long since learned how intelligent she was, but he was amazed to find her so willing to communicate with his people—people who had spent generations hunting her kind.

The villagers were delighted. Many others raised their hands to wave at the raek. An excited small child ran forward—his mother was not fast enough to stop him, nor was Aegwren. The young boy ran right up to the raek and patted her leg like she was a dog. The crowd held its combined breath, but the raek did not move. She simply observed the child and let him touch her scaly foreleg. When the boy returned to his mother, she gathered him to her to take him home, but then she hesitated; before she turned to leave, she held up a hand to the raek in acknowledgement, and the raek waved in return.

Slowly, the villagers dispersed to resume their lives, mourn their dead, and take care of their families. These were people who had survived before and would move on, hoping to survive again. Aegwren sighed to see that it was over—that no one else would fight and die because of him. Brienn stepped forward to cut his hands free. Then she patted his arm briefly in condolence and returned to her home and her life. Aegwren was left standing in the road with the raek.

"Thank you," he said to her, knowing she did not understand. Reaching up, he scratched her jaw in a show of gratitude and affection. She had killed, but she had killed for him—she had also stopped for him. Aegwren stood back, expecting her to leave, but she remained. And when he wandered back to his mother's house, she followed.

Later that night, a meeting was held to decide on a new leader, and Aegwren was named head of the village. He could not believe it; he had thought the villagers might still decide to hang him. The deaths of the men killed by the raek lay heavy on his conscience, and the death of his mother stood teetering atop his shoulders, threatening to unbalance him. He had called the raek there; he had asked for her help, knowing what she might do. It was all his fault.

Aegwren wanted to decline the position. He wanted to wander back into the mountains to leave what traces of ash he had managed to collect from the road with his father's and uncle's remains. He wanted to hide away and grieve and not allow himself to live comfortably among people again. Meera understood his desire—it felt like her own. Then she watched as he did the opposite.

She watched as he accepted the leadership position. She watched as he helped his village mourn their dead and supported the families who had lost their providers. She watched as he packed away his mother's things, giving most to those who needed them and keeping a few of her prized possessions as reminders of the woman she had been and the man he wanted to be. And she watched as he and Isabael—as he named the raek—learned to communicate with one another and slowly forged a deep bond.

Aegwren led those around him not with power or speeches but by example; he showed the villagers that raeken could be friends, not just enemies. He lived with his grief and his guilt, and he tried to make amends for his actions. Meera wondered how she could do the same. She wondered how she, one person, could show all of Terratelle that raeken and knell were not monsters. She wondered how she could learn to live with her grief and her guilt and make amends for the lives lost because of her actions.

She and Aegwren were climbing onto Isabael's back for his first flight when she heard voices—voices from her life, not his. Meera didn't want to leave Aegwren, but she had watched him face his life and knew that she must now do the same. Closing her eyes to the sleek grey feathers in front of her and the large, male hands gripping them anxiously, she opened them to her cell. She blinked several times at the scene before her.

"Kennick, this is Linus. Meera would not be happy if you hurt him," Shael was saying.

"No, I wouldn't," she agreed, pushing herself up to sit.

When the three men turned to her, Meera immediately regretted speaking; she was overwhelmed by their intense attention—by the weight of their presence in her dungeon. She didn't know what to say or do. Then she looked into the familiar dark eyes before her, and no one and nothing else seemed to exist anymore. All of her emotion flooded to the surface in a torrent she couldn't suppress. "Kennick," she sobbed.

32

LINUS

L inus could only assume that the tall man with the dark red hair and jewelry had given Meera the ring she wouldn't talk about. They were gazing at one another with so much raw feeling, he felt uncomfortable bearing witness to their reunion. Still, he was glad the strange men had come for Meera; he was glad that he wouldn't have to keep her in the dungeon anymore. He pulled the key out of his pocket, but no one bothered to ask him for it.

"Come on, Meera. It is time to go home," the man with the jewelry said softly.

Meera didn't move from the stone floor. She was crying and shaking her head and seemed to be struggling to speak. Her hands gripped the legs of her pants like she was in pain. Linus shifted awkwardly, hoping she wasn't about to have another episode of smashing her head and hands against the bars. She already had a bruise and gash on her forehead. The red-haired man seemed to notice the small wound because he whirled on Linus. "Did you hit her?" he asked in a deadly low voice.

Linus had no doubt from the look of the man that he could easily kill him if he wanted to. Even so, he shook his head unconcernedly. "She did that," he said. He thought he might have to explain, but the man turned back toward Meera and didn't give him a second glance.

"Meera, I know. Darreal told us what happened. We know. You do not have to say anything. Just, please come out. I will not make you—I want you to do it on your own," he pleaded with her.

Linus wondered if any of them even noticed the solid iron bars holding Meera in. She continued to shake her head and sob. "You don't know," she choked out, and she put her face into her hands, digging her nails into her skin.

"Meera, look at me!" the man said, kneeling down to her level and pressing his face to the bars. She didn't look up, but he kept talking anyway. "Come home, Meera. We have a crib to pick out and a room to decorate."

Linus was stunned. He had seen the ring on her hand, but for some reason, he had not actually thought she would have married one of them. Meera was pregnant with one of their babies? No matter what she had said, Linus still thought she looked human, and he found the idea of her carrying a knell child a little sickening. Then again, the man crouched before the cell seemed to truly care for her ... Even if he was bizarrely angular and beardless and even a little feminine looking with his long hair and ear jewelry.

The man had said the wrong thing, however, because Meera really lost it then; she started keening and rocking. The man gripped the bars of the cell like he was tempted to rip them apart, but Linus didn't think knell were that strong. The other man hadn't been able to escape the dungeon, after all—Shael, Meera had said his name was. Shael was standing unnaturally still, watching the exchange alongside Linus.

Meera buried her hands in her filthy hair, continuing to rock, but she was saying something between her sobs. It took Linus a moment to realize what it was: "It's gone," she kept saying. It didn't dawn on him what she meant until the red-haired man started to cry with her. "It's my fault, Kennick! It's my fault! I should have stayed home ... I just stood there. I just stood there in that meeting while our baby was dying. I—I didn't do anything! I just stood there! Then—then I killed those boys! I killed them all! I killed them all!" she shouted.

Linus's stomach dropped at the thought of her in that awful meeting having a miscarriage. He had watched her almost the whole time, standing perfectly still with her eyes closed. "Shit, Meera," he said under his breath, but no one acknowledged him. He pulled out his flask and took a drink. The black-haired one—Shael—shot him a look, so he offered him the flask, but Shael turned away in disgust. Shrugging, Linus took another drink.

The red-haired man had tears streaming down his face, and his hands shook where they gripped the bars, but he was still looking at Meera. "These things happen, Meera. It was not your fault. Please," he said, reaching for her through the bars. Linus, again, thought to offer them the key, but he didn't want to interrupt.

"Get her out of there, Kennick. I can't take it!" Shael said, and Linus noticed for the first time how upset the man looked.

"No. It has to be her decision," the other man—Kennick—replied very quietly. "Please, Meera. I love you. I am here for you. Run toward me," he begged, still reaching for her through the bars.

Meera looked up at that, seemingly roused from her anguish. Very slowly, she uncurled herself. Her whole body quaked with emotion, but she pressed her hands into the stone ground and pushed herself unsteadily to her feet. Kennick stood as well and stepped back from the bars. Linus only had a second to wonder why when the iron suddenly bent and deformed to create a gaping hole that Meera then stumbled through.

Once she was out, Kennick gathered her to him and held her, kissing her face and whispering things into her ear that Linus was glad he couldn't hear. This scene was all a bit much for him. Shael put his hand on Meera's back, and Kennick pulled him into the hug as well. Linus turned away then—that was definitely too much for him.

"We should go," Shael said.

"You really should," Linus confirmed.

Meera was still shaking and breathing hard, but she wiped her face and attempted to pull herself together. She and Kennick broke apart, but the man kept a hand on her at all times. Linus couldn't tell if he was possessive or just really relieved to have her back. "No, we can't just leave," she said. "What about Linus?"

"What about him?" Kennick asked, finally giving Linus another look.

"He'll be hanged for treason! They'll think he let me out," she told him.

"No one will think I did this, Meera. Just go," Linus said, gesturing to the misshapen bars.

"What if they hang you anyway? You know they'll need someone to blame," she argued.

"Then I will be honored with a noose that just graced the neck of a prince," Linus joked. While he was more than a little afraid of hanging, he didn't usually acknowledge his fears—that was what rum was for.

"What prince?" Kennick asked.

"Prince Phineas killed Bartro and was hanged for it," Meera explained quietly. "Otto is king." The knell men looked vaguely surprised by this news but didn't comment further.

"I told you, Meera, Otto is my friend. He will not hang me,"

Linus assured her. He wanted her to go—to save herself. He was already living in hell and wasn't overly concerned by his future prospects.

"Actually, you said that you're a friend to Otto, but he's not a friend to you. He hanged his brother today," she added, giving him a surprisingly clear and penetrating look considering her recent behavior on the cell floor.

"Meera, I know he was once your friend, but he is a general and can take care of himself," Kennick said, trying to coax her toward the stairs.

"And he is a lousy drunk," Shael added.

Linus shrugged. He was guilty on both accounts. Meera pulled away from her knell men and walked up to him. She gripped his arm and stared into his face. He was a little uncomfortable with the contact considering what he had just seen her do, but no matter how she had changed, when he looked into her eyes, Linus saw the Meera he knew—scars, muscles, puffy eyes, and messy hair notwithstanding. He sighed; he didn't like the determination in her face.

"Linus, are you really safe here? I don't want to ruin your life again. I'm not leaving unless you convince me you'll be okay," she said.

"Meera, we do not have time for this!" Shael groaned, looking anxious.

She ignored him, and Linus couldn't help but grin; he was glad to see that Meera was as independent and strong-willed as ever. "Go, Meera. You have not ruined my life," he told her. He had done that all on his own—he and the rulers of Terratelle. He couldn't blame her anymore, not after seeing how much she just wanted to do the right thing and be a good person.

"Come with us," she breathed.

His eyes widened. That was a proposition he hadn't been

expecting. "Go with you to Magicland?" he asked with a laugh. Maybe he was drunk, he thought; this suddenly seemed extremely funny. "I should go with you and these two and—what? Be your third husband? Be made into something ... inhuman?" he asked.

"There's somewhere else I want to go, actually. Somewhere in Terratelle. You could start over there, or you could come with us to Levisade. Come on, Linus, you can't tell me you're happy being Otto's favorite general," she said, looking down at his red uniform.

Linus squirmed under her intense gaze. Of course, he wasn't happy as a general. Every new order he followed was more detestable and foul than the last. He supposed he didn't see his family much anyway ... Could he make a life somewhere else? His hand—or lack-thereof—made him awfully recognizable.

"Come!" Meera pushed him. "You can help us try to end this war, or you can be a fisherman or something."

"Fisherman?" he asked. "Where are we going?"

Meera beamed at him, and it was truly refreshing to see after all of her crying. Linus was glad to go just to see her so happy. It was probably the happiest he'd made anyone in a long time. "To Harringbay," she said.

"Where?" Shael asked.

"Meera, what are you talking about?" Kennick asked.

"To Harringbay!" Linus agreed, raising his flask and taking a swig of rum.

33

MEERA

Meera looked pleadingly into Kennick's eyes. There was so much they needed to talk about, but in that moment, they just needed to agree on a destination. She wanted to go to Harringbay—to talk to the duke's family and try to make amends for her part in his death somehow. She needed to do some good, and she needed to start right away. Otherwise, she thought she might just collapse back onto the cell floor and never get up again.

"Can we at least go to the border first? Soleille is waiting for us there. I want to make sure you are okay," Kennick said quietly even though Shael and Linus were clearly listening.

"I'm fine, Kennick. I mean, I'm not, but Soleille can't help me. I just want to start making things right—please," she begged.

"I think you are running again, Meera," he replied, touching her cheek lightly.

She knew what he meant, and he was probably right; she was running from her feelings—she was once again pushing into a new plan to avoid dealing with her emotions. It was what she always did, and she knew it; she knew she was running away, but she had to—she had to keep moving toward something lest she be tempted to lie down and die. "Maybe," she said. "But I'm asking you to run with me this time."

Kennick gave her a hard look. His eyes were still clouded by his devastation at her news, but he managed a small smile that showed his pointy canine tooth. She loved that tooth. "You know I will follow you anywhere," he said. "Shael?" he asked, looking over at Shael's patient figure.

Meera noticed for the first time that Shael had a sword belted to his hip and one in his hand. He must have retrieved his old weapon, she thought, and she was glad he had gotten something out of coming to find her. Shael brushed his already smooth hair back with his free hand. "Might as well. We already broke our oaths," he said.

Meera was shocked at first, but when she gave it a moment's thought, she realized that of course they had gone against Hadjal to be there. Hadjal would never risk the lives of the riders for anyone or anything. "I'm sorry," she said to Shael. Then she almost laughed because they had such a long history of apologizing to one another.

Shael caught her look and rolled his eyes in imitation of her. "Come on," he said. "We should get out of here."

"Wait—" Meera said, getting an idea. She turned to Linus. "Give me your uniform jacket!" she said.

Linus shrugged out of his red general's jacket and handed it to her. The plain black shirt he wore underneath had the sleeves rolled to his elbows and revealed his scarred stump. "Cerun is sorry about that, by the way," Shael said flippantly, gesturing toward Linus's arm. Meera wasn't sure how sorry Cerun actually was, but she supposed if Cerun and Linus were about to come face-to-face again, it was a necessary gesture.

Linus didn't answer, but his face paled. Meera suspected he was only just realizing that they would be flying away from the palace.

"Shaya?" she asked Kennick.

He shook his head. Meera felt a sting of pain but pushed it aside with her other pain. Then she lifted Linus's jacket and burned a portion of it away, trying to make it look like it had fallen off of his burning body. Otto had seen what she'd done to the boys, after all. "There," she said. "Hopefully they'll think you're dead," she told Linus.

He looked grave but didn't argue. They all started toward the staircase, but the same moment Meera stepped onto the bottom stair, the door above opened. A figure began to descend toward them, and they all froze. The figure kept walking down the stairs, seemingly unaware of their presence. The person was focusing on the rattling tray in their hands. They passed under an oil lamp. "Cook?" Meera called.

The men behind her were still and tense, waiting to see how they should react. Cook jumped and the dishes on their tray clanked and clanged, echoing off the stone walls. They gaped down the stairwell with eyes like saucers. "It's okay. Please don't scream," Meera said.

Cook opened their mouth but didn't scream and didn't manage words for a few moments either. Finally, they said, "I—I couldn't sleep. I said I was gonna come see you, and I didn't. I was —I was just comin' to see you."

Meera smiled and walked up toward them. She took the tray from their shaking hands, put it on a step, and gave Cook a hug. They hesitated, trembling, but they hugged her back. "Thank you for coming. It was so good to see you again," Meera said, and when she pulled away, she looked into Cook's terrified eyes. "Cook, I'm leaving now. We're not going to hurt anyone; we're just going to leave. Do you think you can take this tray and go back to the kitchen?"

"Meera, no!" Shael said behind her.

Cook jumped at the sound of his voice.

"Will you go back to the kitchen and not tell anyone what you saw?" Meera asked. Cook had always been straight-forward with her, and she trusted them. Cook nodded, and that was good enough for Meera. She picked up the tray and handed it back to them. "If the guards ask, just say you forgot something, okay?" she asked.

Cook nodded again, swallowing. Then they turned and walked back up to the top of the stairs, but before they opened the door, they glanced back and said, "Be well, Meera."

Meera nodded, feeling tears fill her eyes once more. She knew she would never see Cook again. Swallowing her tears, she was glad she didn't have to say goodbye to Linus yet; she didn't think she could handle any more loss—she wasn't handling any of it to begin with.

They all held their breath, waiting for Cook's footsteps to recede down the hallway. Then Meera crept upward once more. Kennick, Shael, and Linus followed close behind her, letting her take the lead. Before she opened the door, she sensed into the hallway. Two guards stood on either end, and she shaped the air away from the lamps burning all down the hall, extinguishing their fires all at once and leaving the hallway dark. The guards exclaimed in confusion, unable to see.

Meera and the others crept quietly around the door, and she grabbed Linus's hand to lead him in case he couldn't see with his human eyes. She still couldn't believe he had agreed to go with them, and yet, she trusted him and didn't think he would raise an alarm. The old Linus might have, but Meera supposed she had never shown him enough trust to find out. Maybe he wouldn't have stopped her from freeing Shael. Maybe he would have helped, even.

She continued to extinguish lamps as they moved through the palace, and they didn't have any trouble getting outside to the back gardens. Fresh air hit her like new life, and she gulped it in greedily. Then she looked to Kennick and Shael to direct them to where the raeken would land. Kennick pointed toward the canal, and they all ran through the winding garden paths and down the trail to the canal's beach. Meera glanced at Linus as they ran; how many times had they taken this path together? She had never thought they would do it again.

As they approached the beach, Cerun and Endu dove down from above, their glossy feathers shining in the moonlight. Linus balked at the sight and took a drink from his flask. Meera scowled at him but figured his flask would soon run dry anyway. Shael pushed Linus forward, apparently willing to take him on Cerun, and Meera went with Kennick to mount Endu. Together, they all rose into the air.

They were safe, and they were free! And yet, even with the soft breeze tickling her skin and the world stretched out before her, Meera still felt caged—she still felt locked in a dungeon with her past and her pain. Kennick wrapped his arms around her and held her tightly in an enclosure both warm and welcoming. Leaning into him, she rested her head against his chest. With a raek beneath her and Kennick at her back, Meera wished this could be her life's sentence; she wished she had never pledged herself to a greater cause or thought to stand beside another ruler. She wished that from the moment she had met Kennick, she had not wasted her time doing anything but loving him ... But she had.

She had made pledges and mistakes and had backed herself into a cell of her own making with no notion of how to fight her way out: she didn't know how to make amends for the bodies in her past, she didn't know how to end the war, and she didn't know how to move forward with Kennick after burning the remnants of their unborn child. It was all too much ... Meera gazed at the sky reaching out around her, and for once, looking down on the world didn't distance her from her problems—for once, feeling small wasn't a relief. She wished she were bigger than it all—big enough to break free of the mess she had made.

THE MIDDLE OF THE END

BOOK 5 OF THE RAEK RIDERS SERIES IS AVAILABLE NOW!

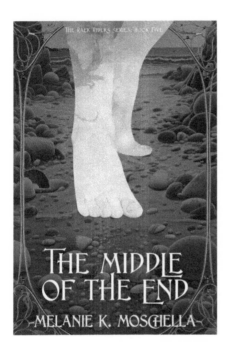

Read on for a preview...

CHAPTER 1
MEERA

MEERA LAY as still as she could, waiting impatiently for the sun to rise. The raek fires she kept burning illuminated her immediate surroundings but not the tree canopy overhead. Kennick, Shael, and Linus were visible—motionless on the pine needle forest floor—but beyond their cozy sphere of light was a realm of menacing shadows. The dark shapes of branches and leaves rustled on the periphery of Meera's shifting firelight, and she stared at them, wide-eyed and incapable of sleep.

She was too agitated—not because of the possibility of what lurked in the dark beyond her fires—but because of what paced and twitched within her; she was thrumming with the need to act, desperate to jump at her spirit's call for atonement. She had left her dungeon cell to start making amends for her mistakes, and the pull to start right away pounded in her head and buzzed in her blood. It was an itch creeping all over her skin that she needed to scratch. Sleep wasn't an option for her—only torturous stillness and seemingly endless waiting.

Ever so slowly, the leaves above her lightened from deepest black to greys and blues. Then, as her heart ticked by the unhurried minutes, they warmed to the yellows and reds of fall. The sun was finally rising. Birds chirped their good mornings and fluttered from their nests. The whole world seemed to awaken around her —ready for the new day—and she could only blink and hope that she was also ready.

Meera had long-since squirmed away from Kennick to avoid disturbing his sleep. Now she wriggled against the ground, trying to get comfortable and resisting the urge to spring from the forest floor and pace until she could actually do something—something meaningful, something good. Rolling onto her left side, she found Linus facing her, his eyes also open. For a moment, they just stared at one another. Then Meera grinned; she still couldn't believe Linus had come with them.

Like a log, she rolled several more times across the ground until she and Linus were face-to-face, collecting pine needles on her already grimy clothes. "Did you sleep okay?" she asked quietly, aware that Kennick and Shael were still breathing in deep, even rhythms.

Linus shrugged the shoulder he wasn't lying on. "To think I could have slept in an actual bed last night and woken up to Cook's breakfast," he replied.

"Yes, but you're free now!" she said, searching his eyes and hoping he didn't regret his decision. "I'm glad you're here," she added, reaching out and poking him in the stomach.

Linus grinned at her. "Do you remember the day we met?" he asked.

Propping her head in her hand, Meera nodded. Of course, she remembered—every detail of that day had been etched into her mind by fear; she had been so scared approaching Cerun to feed him for the first time. She remembered the Captain's anxiety and how he had all but run down the grassy hill to the canal. She remembered the smell of the bodies and the flies buzzing around her. She remembered Linus crying, staring at his dead brother. She didn't know why he wanted to reminisce about that day now.

"You went back in for the bodies even though no one told you to—no one expected you to," he murmured. Meera shrugged. "I thought you were some sort of angel, you know," he added, huffing a quiet laugh. She chuckled with him, still unsure of why he was saying all of this but glad of a reason to laugh, nonetheless. "But you weren't. You were just a person—a braver, better person than the rest of us," Linus concluded.

"No," Meera argued. "I was stupid and impulsive."

"Maybe at first, but you went back for the bodies when you didn't have to—Why?" he asked quietly.

She shrugged again. "You looked upset. I figured one of them was important to you, and I figured I was the only person who could get them," she answered dismissively.

"Yeah, but you didn't even know me. You just did it because it was the right thing to do. Most people ... most people wouldn't have done that—I wouldn't have done that," Linus said. "I guess I —I guess what I'm trying to say is that I want to be the kind of person who does the right thing even when it sucks."

"Even when you have to sleep on the ground?" she asked, smiling and raising her eyebrows at him.

"Even when I have to ride on a feathered monster," he replied, grimacing.

"Rough flight?" Meera asked with another little laugh. It was light enough now that she could see the strain around Linus's eyes and how rumpled his hair was. She supposed flying for the first time in the dark of night would be terrifying, and it hadn't been a short flight.

"I'm out of rum," he replied humorlessly.

"Good," she said unsympathetically. Rolling onto her back, she gazed at the colorful leaves overhead and wondered how much longer she would have to wait until she could actually do something. Then, on a whim, she asked, "Linus, what ever happened to the captain of the guard—the one I knew? Does he still work at the palace?"

Linus didn't answer at first, and Meera rolled back to look at him, stomach lurching. When she saw his face, she knew. "No!" she cried, forgetting to be quiet. "No! No!" Leaping from the ground, she tangled her hands in her filthy hair. Him too? The captain too? How many people had died because of her?

Linus scrambled up after her and put his hand placatingly on her arm. "Meera, he's fine. He's fine," he kept saying.

She didn't believe him. "He hanged. Didn't he?" she asked, her voice oddly high and strained. She couldn't seem to draw in a full breath, and the sound of her short, ragged inhales grated in her ears like nails on slate. The raek fires around them suddenly bulged and went out. Then Kennick was in front of her, putting his hands on her shoulders and trying to move her away. She didn't budge; she was busy searching Linus's face for answers.

"No, Meera. The captain is fine—he retired is all. I haven't seen him in a while, but I'm sure he's fine," Linus insisted.

Meera didn't believe him. "The guards? The guards that were there that day—did they hang too?" Kennick put his hand lightly on her cheek and tried to turn her to face him, but she ignored him; she only had eyes for Linus. She needed to know—she needed to know how many lives she was responsible for ruining.

Linus shook his head in answer, but Meera knew he was lying. Brushing Kennick aside, she took several steps away, just trying to breathe. Shael stood nearby staring at her—they all were—and she hated how concerned and scared they all looked. Shutting her eyes, she breathed, counting her inhales and exhales until her heart rate steadied. After one last deep breath, she opened her eyes and announced, "We're all up, so it's time to find Duchess Harrington!"

The three men standing before her were all silent and wide-eyed for a moment. Meera might have found it comical if she wasn't trying so hard not to fall apart. "Meera, slow down. We do not have any food or supplies. We need to collect ourselves and make a plan first," Kennick said. His dark eyes were so full of love and sympathy that she had to look away from them. She couldn't stand to think of their shared loss; she just wanted to start doing something—something good, something to make up for her mistakes.

"I—I need—" she tried to say, voice trembling.

"You need a bath, Meera! You stink! Your knell men might be too polite to say it, but really, you can't go anywhere or talk to anyone until you wash yourself," Linus interrupted, making a face.

Meera choked out a laugh from her tight chest. She felt like she was teetering at the precipice of her sanity, capable of laughing or melting down at any slight sway of conversation. After she laughed, she nodded; she knew Linus was trying to distract her, but he was also right—she really was filthy.

"Okay, so we need food, soap, and rum. Who has money? I'll go into town!" Linus declared.

Kennick and Shael both glared at him, not nearly as amused by Linus as Meera was. "We're not buying rum," she told her friend. She assumed Kennick had money, although he and Shael hadn't brought any supplies with them; they had thought they would be returning to the border right away. Meera cringed inwardly, hoping they weren't too upset by their change in plans.

"I will go into town and get us supplies," Kennick offered.

Linus barked a laugh. "You can't go into a Terratellen town," he replied, looking Kennick up and down pointedly.

Meera agreed, but she and Linus—the humans in the group—both had recognizable scars. "It'll have to be Shael," she said. "He's the least conspicuous looking."

"Let me go! I'll just hide my stump," Linus argued.

Meera opened her mouth to answer, but Kennick beat her to it: "You are not going anywhere. I do not trust you." Shutting her mouth, she glared at him. "Meera, for all I know, he came with us to try to get you recaptured. I do not know him, and I do not trust him—not with you. Shael will go into town, and the three of us will stay here," Kennick added, seeing her face.

"That's fine, but we can trust Linus," Meera replied, rubbing her eyes and wishing she had gotten a little sleep. She had thought she would start looking for the duchess right away, but instead she was doomed to more waiting.

Linus proceeded to recline on the ground, apparently unconcerned by Kennick's mistrust. Meera, Shael, and Kennick devised a list of supplies, and Shael put his riding jacket over his knell-style shirt to look more human for his foray into town. Before he left, he reached into the pouch he wore around his waist and handed Meera a bar of soap. "You need this more than I do," he said, wrinkling his nose in jest.

Meera took the soap and rolled her eyes at him before watching him walk away into the trees. "Going to go take a bath," she announced to Kennick and Linus, and without looking at either of them, she turned and walked into the woods in the opposite direction of Shael.

She had only made it ten feet into the trees, however, when Linus trotted up next to her. "I'll join you," he said.

She smirked, knowing he didn't want to be left alone with Kennick. "I don't remember inviting you to join me, but okay," she agreed, continuing to meander through the unfamiliar woods.

"Where are you going? Isn't the ocean that way?" he asked, pointing.

"I don't need the ocean. I'll just make a bath wherever I feel like it," she replied.

"Okay ..." he said, not asking her what she meant by that.

A few minutes later, Meera stopped. "Here looks good," she announced, proceeding to shape a large rectangular hole into the ground and fill it with water. She heated the water with her raek fire, and bending down to untie her boot laces, she glanced up to find Linus looking shocked and a little alarmed. His expression made her titter another small laugh. "I can shape raek fire, air, rock, water, and metal," she told him.

"How?" he asked, swallowing.

"A wild raek gave me the powers—Shaya, my raek," Meera explained. "Don't worry, they aren't contagious," she added, noting Linus's furrowed brow. Then she hopped down into her bath fully clothed, seeing as she didn't have privacy. It didn't matter; she needed to wash her clothes as well, anyway.

After a moment, Linus seemed to recover from his shock. "That looks nice," he remarked, peering into the steamy bath. "Mind if I join you?" He didn't wait for her to answer, however, before kicking off his boots and splashing into the warm water. Sighing, he leaned back against the lip of the makeshift tub.

Meera might have argued, but she was glad not to be left alone with her thoughts. She merely scrubbed her clothes and body with Shael's soap. Linus had the decency to avert his eyes when she reached under her shirt and into her pants. Meera spent a long time scouring her scalp, and after she rinsed the suds from her filthy hair, she shaped the water out of the tub and refilled it. She felt so dirty; she wanted to keep scrubbing and scrubbing, but she passed the soap to Linus instead and watched him half-heartedly clean himself.

He eyed her across the water, tossing the soap onto the ground between them when he was done. His usually honey-brown hair hung dark and wet on either side of his face. Meera was still getting used to how much older and more grizzled he looked now. "What's the deal with your husband?" he asked, scratching at his beard.

"We never actually managed to get married," Meera admitted, avoiding the question.

Linus raised his eyebrows at her, and she knew what he was thinking even if he didn't say it. "Yes, I got pregnant without being married," she said in irritation. She didn't want to think about the pregnancy. "Do you need a lesson on the finer points of conception, or has your mother covered that for you?" she asked snarkily.

Linus laughed. "Don't worry about me. I don't attract many ladies these days."

"Is it the general's uniform that scares them away or the drinking?" Meera asked, feigning obtuseness.

"Must be the uniform," he replied, casually lifting his left arm out of the water and pushing back his wet sleeve to reveal his stump. Waving it around, he added, "This is a big draw for the ladies. It's only good for one thing, you know."

Meera gaped at him a moment before throwing back her head and laughing—really laughing. It felt so good to laugh, too; for those few seconds, she forgot everything. The creeping figures at the edge of her mind disappeared, and there was only Linus's grinning face and the sunshine filtering through the leaves above. Then she wiped the tears of mirth from her eyes, and reality settled back over her.

CHAPTER 2
LINUS

LINUS REGRETTED HIS COMMENT at first—he was used to being around men and the kind of bawdy humor they digressed into to avoid talking about their real lives—but when Meera laughed, he smiled and relaxed. He supposed woman or not, she also needed distraction from the cruelties of life, and he was happy to provide some for her. Although, after her loud burst of laughter, his concern about her knell man rose to the surface again. "Seriously, Meera. If your fiancé finds me taking a bath with you, is he going to kill me?" he asked. He hadn't liked the look the red-haired man had given him earlier.

"Kennick won't hurt you," Meera replied unconcernedly. "Besides, I handle the killing just fine on my own," she added, and suddenly, her face changed; she was no longer smiling, and she was no longer looking at him. Picking up the bar of soap that he had tossed onto the ground, she began scrubbing her hands, arms, and neck all over again.

"Meera?" Linus asked, watching her movements turn more and more frantic. She didn't look at him. She kept rubbing and scratching at her skin, her big eyes round and panicky on her face. "Meera!" he cried, moving through the chest-deep water toward her. He caught one of her wrists in his hand and tried to use his stump to block her other arm, but just when he touched her, Kennick appeared at the edge of the bath. Linus immediately raised his arms and stepped away.

Meera seemed to come back to herself then. "I'm okay, I'm okay!" she said, looking between Linus and Kennick. She put the soap down with a shaking hand and disappeared under the water's surface. For several seconds, little bubbles trailed up from her, then nothing.

Linus stared at the reflective surface of the water and waited, holding his own breath. He watched and waited until his lungs forced him to suck in air. He took a step toward Meera, but he hesitated, glancing at Kennick uncertainly. He wanted to get her, but he didn't know what her knell man would do. Kennick was also staring at the water with a look of strain on his bizarrely angular face. Finally, Meera emerged, wiping water and hair from her eyes. She didn't even gasp for air; she just gripped the edge of the bath and hopped adeptly from the water.

Linus followed her out much less gracefully, and as soon as the cool air hit him, he regretted getting in the bath to begin with; his skin prickled with goosebumps all over. The next thing he knew, the bath was gone. The ground where it had been looked freshly churned but otherwise level with its surroundings. Suddenly, warm air buffeted him from all directions. He jumped and made a strangled noise, but then he realized that Meera was doing it to both of them—drying them. Supposing it was better than dripping dry and freezing, Linus stood stoically and tolerated the strange magic.

Kennick hovered near Meera, and when she stopped drying them both and reached up to touch her long—clearly matted— hair, he stepped forward. "Let me," he said, pulling off one of his bracelets and turning it into a comb. Linus stared wide-eyed at the comb for a second, but then he blinked and looked away, trying not to draw the man's attention. He considered retreating into the woods, but he didn't want to leave Meera alone with Kennick—

engaged or not, Linus wasn't sure what he thought of the knell man.

While Meera sat and Kennick started the tedious process of working his comb through her snarled hair, Linus plopped onto the ground and very slowly began pulling on his boots and gathering his hair behind his head. He always left his boots tied loosely to slip on and off, but he struggled with his hair; tying it back was one of the few things he often needed help with. He considered asking Meera for help but was too proud to do so in front of Kennick, so instead, Linus did the best he could, looping his pre-tied leather thong around his hair several times. He was sure it didn't look great, but it would do.

Meanwhile, he watched Meera as Kennick worked through the many knots in her hair. It looked to Linus like he was being exceedingly gentle, and yet, her face was slowly fracturing, her eyes filling with tears. Helplessly, he watched as her breathing became rapid and shallow. He tried to catch her eye, but she was staring at the ground before her like her life depended on it. Finally, her face shattered. "Enough!" she shouted, reaching her hands back and grabbing her hair. Linus saw a flash of light, and the next thing he knew, Meera was holding a large clump of hair in front of her, looking startled. "Oops!" she said quietly before whipping her head back to face Kennick. "I didn't burn you, did I?"

"No," the man said softly. He looked like he was in pain, but he stayed very still. Linus couldn't blame him—he wasn't sure he would risk touching Meera if she was burning things and saying *oops*.

"I—" Meera started to say, staring at the hair in her fist.

"I will fix it," Kennick told her.

Meera nodded and incinerated the hair she was holding. Kennick proceeded to detangle the remainder of her snarls. Linus wasn't quite sure what was happening. He thought maybe he should leave, but he hated the look on Meera's face. "Bartro made the captain retire after you freed the raek. The captain wasn't happy about it, but they had a ceremony for him and everything. I was still recovering and couldn't go," he told her. He was lying: Bartro had hanged the captain and the two guards who had failed to prevent the prisoners from escaping.

Meera's eyes slowly traveled up to his face and focused on him. "Really?" she asked, sounding small and vulnerable.

"Oh yeah! I heard Bartro even made a whole speech about the captain's service. He had a way about him, didn't he? Bartro? He could really make a person feel special," Linus replied. He didn't know what he was saying; he was just trying to talk—to distract Meera from whatever was going on in her mind.

"Did he make your stump tingle?" she asked, a fresh light gleaming in her eyes.

Linus laughed. "He certainly tried. He gave me a ring—said if I was only going to have one hand, I might as well make it as impressive as possible ... I lost it in a game of cards. Did he give you anything?" he asked. He hoped he wasn't stumbling into upsetting territory.

"He gave me a pen—a nice carved wooden one," Meera admitted. "It's at the bottom of a lake."

Linus nodded. He wondered vaguely whether Meera and Bartro had had a physical relationship, but he didn't ask. "He knew how to manipulate people, that man," he remarked. "It was all him, you know, Meera. The duke, the three boys—it was all him. He knew what he was doing."

"It doesn't matter. I played my part," she replied, still calm.

Linus's eyes shifted to Kennick, who had just finished detangling Meera's hair and formed a pair of scissors out of more metal from his body. Linus watched as the knell man proceeded to cut and even out Meera's mangled hair across her shoulder blades. Then he looked back at her face. "So, what exactly is the plan here?" he asked.

"I just want to talk to Duchess Harrington—to offer her my assistance with anything she might need. I just want to help her if I can," she said quietly.

"What if she demands that you do something ridiculous? What if she insists you should die for what you did?" Linus asked. He thought this was an incredibly stupid plan, and his mood was turning; he was growing hungry, and his head throbbed as the rum from the night before drained out of him.

Meera sighed. "I'm not going to blindly do whatever she tells me to do. I haven't lost my senses," she said defensively.

Linus wasn't so sure about that, but he didn't say so. "Then what?" he asked. He was starting to wonder what the hell he was doing there. He had wanted to do something good—something Meera would do—but he was a one-handed eighteen-year-old without magical ability and had no idea how he was supposed to do anything at all.

Meera shrugged. Kennick finished cutting her hair and began braiding it down the back of her head. "Then I'll go back to Levisade and do whatever I can to help Darreal end the war," she said. "You can come, or I can help you get settled somewhere else," she added, eyeing him.

Kennick finished Meera's short braid and tucked it under, fastening it into a nub at the base of her neck. Linus didn't bother answering her; he didn't know exactly what he was doing there or what he would do next. Instead, he stood and averted his eyes when Kennick tenderly kissed the side of Meera's face. He supposed the knell man didn't seem all that bad.

Together, they made their way back to the clearing where they had slept and waited for Shael to return with food and supplies.

Meera paced the small area, and Linus and Kennick sat down and watched her. Linus wanted to keep talking—to distract his friend from her thoughts—but he couldn't think of anything else to say. His own situation was gradually settling over him as his sober brain realized that the life he'd known was behind him. It was both a comforting and unsettling thought.

When Shael returned, they all ate and deliberated their next move. He told them that the Harrington's house was unmistakable and nearby, and Kennick had to prevent Meera from immediately leaving to find the duchess. Then the red-haired knell man persistently coaxed her to eat until she had finished her small portion of food. Linus ate quickly and reclined on the bare ground, fiddling with the pine needles under his hand.

While the others argued about who should go to the house and when, he tried not to listen. He didn't much care what they did in Harringbay. He thought being there at all was a mistake; Meera couldn't possibly get anything out of talking to the family of the man whose death she had caused. Linus suspected the other men felt the same way, and yet, they were all going along with it, hoping Meera wouldn't lose her shit again.

Drinking some of the water Meera had magicked into his flask for him, Linus wished it were rum. He didn't think this plan would go well, and he didn't look forward to witnessing any of it. A part of him wondered if he should just leave—set off on his own to start a new life—but he didn't. He stayed. Meera was the only friend he had at the moment, and he would stick out this foolish plan with her ... Then he would help her knell men pick up the pieces when it was a disaster, he thought with a sigh.

Eventually, he heard them decide that they would all go to the estate together the next morning, prepared to flee if need be. Kennick was going to spend the rest of the day scoping out the area, and Shael was—apparently—going to babysit Linus and

Meera. Linus lay back and shut his eyes, ready to doze through the rest of the day. He hadn't gotten many days off as a general and was going to consider this a vacation. He was at the beach, after all, he thought with a wry smile.

He had never seen the ocean, but he didn't bother rousing himself to go look at it. There wasn't much in the world he was especially interested in seeing. There wasn't much he hoped to do with his life at all—though he supposed he wouldn't mind sleeping with a woman before he died. He hadn't been joking earlier when he had told Meera that women weren't interested in him and his stump. There had always been prostitutes hanging around the war camps, of course, but Linus had found them too sad to touch. He would rather be with a woman who actually wanted to be with him—not that he held out much hope for that. He had loved Meera once, and she hadn't loved him back. Now he was crippled and unsightly. Besides, not everyone was Meera—most people were horrible.

Meera called his name, but Linus kept his eyes shut, feigning sleep. He was one of those horrible people, after all. He was under no illusion that he was a good person; he knew who and what he was. He may have impulsively—and drunkenly—followed Meera out there to do something good for once, but unlike Meera, he had no false hope that he could make up for his past actions with a few good deeds. He kept his eyes shut and pretended to sleep, doubting he would actually get any sleep without alcohol in his stomach. At the next opportunity, he was going to find rum.

THE COMPLETED
RAEK RIDERS SERIES

Milton Keynes UK
Ingram Content Group UK Ltd.
UKHW042224180324
439698UK00005B/448

9 798989 198665